The Lover of
The Opera

S.M. HARLOW

To my amazing husband, you are my one and only.
To my darling son, you are my heart.
And to my supportive friends and family,
thank you for always being there.

Prologue

London,
The Earl of Hillsdale's Estate
March 1858

"Once upon a time..."

"What is this? A fairy tale?!" exclaimed one of the young ladies gathered at the table. The four other women giggled to themselves, knowing full well the kind of story to come. They were bright in their light-colored day dresses, all rather beautiful, but dull in the eyes. Still wet behind the ears, in Miss Lucinda Kenyon's opinion.

"Will you be silent? Let her tell her tale." Miss Isabel Crane, daughter to the Earl of Hillsdale sighed impatiently. They all sat in plush sky-blue armchairs, at a polished wooden table in a bright yellow lavish morning room. The wallpaper held flying illustrations of birds and running foxes in a meadow. The fireplace was of great marble. A shimmering chandelier reflected the morning light around the room. Morning tea and plates of scones, creams, and pastries adorned the table where they sat.

It was an exquisite living area, only the best to prove their noble status, according to Miss Crane's mother, Lady Hillsdale. A woman of great means, who sought out her wealth and title through deceit and wit against other young ladies at the time. The very same teachings she taught both her daughter and Miss Kenyon from a young age. However, while it was important to the Lady Hillsdale that they stay far away from scandal, it was tirelessly a bore to Lucinda. That was when she decided to take up on other scandalous reputations. Tales where she could combine the truth and her own spin of the story. Such as her favorite subjects; The Six Rakes of Springfield.

She grinned, "The Lover of the Opera, is not just any tale. It is the life of a delicious and mysterious man. A Lord from a faraway land, shunned by decency, drenched in debauchery. Condemned to remain in his theater, where all acts of pleasure are sought to the unknowing women he consumes."

The ladies eased in, even the one who questioned her tale. "Who is he?"

Miss Kenyon motioned for silence when the others curiously whispered. "For many years, the Lover had been enslaved in the exotic deserts of the Mediterranean. He had to learn and excel in the acts of erotic pleasures. The only way he was ever to be released, was to perform and ravish all of the king's harem, until they were fully sated. But once he was free and had returned, the very presence of him was debilitating to any woman who set their eyes on him. They had no control over themselves, only for the hunger of his exquisite touch. So, for their safety, high class society shunned the Lover to his Opera house, where he now resides. Famished for women's flesh."

"Oh pish!" said one of the ladies. "That is absurd. There is no such person."

Miss Kenyon raised her brow as she casually glanced to the nonbeliever. "Oh no? Why don't you see for yourself? If you are brave enough, that is." She and Miss Crane smirked together.

Another lady spouted out, "Do you mean, that you and Miss Crane have actually seen this Lover of the Opera?"

Miss Crane blushed mildly, careful to conceal her heated thoughts. She glanced over to her friend, worried that she would reveal too much. However, Lucinda had no qualms about what she was about to say. She proudly grinned, "We were there not too long ago. At the L'Opera Magenta. It was there where we saw him, sitting alone in his theater box."

Suddenly, all at once, the ladies asked their thrilled questions. Few were surprised to hear Miss Crane being there, especially against her mother's wishes. Isabel couldn't help but giggle despite how flushed she felt. "Oh yes, he was dashing. I believe he even looked at us and smiled." They all sighed together.

"But really, who is he?!" The one who had questioned previously demanded.

Lucinda considered her answer but smiled wide, nonetheless. "His name is Bram Williams, the Earl of Kenwood."

A sort of stunned silence filled the room, not that it alarmed Lucinda, who rather expected it. She knew that each lady in attendance was familiar with Lord Kenwood's reputation. The very same title was warned to them by their mothers, by every party they attended, and through every foul word expressed by gentlemen in their circle. They knew that Bram Williams was one of their own, but because of his reputation, was shunned away from proper society. A pity, Lucinda thought, for such a handsome and wealthy man did not deserve to be rejected. But rather, pursued for what he has. His expertise in pleasure only being a plus.

A keen thought occurred to her then, and it made her grin. However, that soon passed when Lady Hillsdale stepped into the morning room. All the ladies stood and bowed. Many years of strict etiquette had taught the Countess the art of facial propriety. She entered with a deceptive yet graceful grin, a smile that Lucinda and Isabel knew far too well. She inspected her daughter, who straightened her posture and gown, then she turned her gaze to the other young ladies. The Countess nodded approvingly just before she sat and carried on another boorish conversation about the start of a new season. And what was to be expected of them. Lucinda sighed carefully. That was the end of the Lover of the Opera's tale. But that didn't mean it wasn't the beginning, she thought pleasingly, to her newfound agenda.

Chapter 1

London,
L'Opéra Magenta
April 1858

He pounded his hips into her, and she widened her thighs to meet his every stroke. He watched as she arched her back, urging him to grab her small breasts. Her nipples hardened against his palms and he bent down to graze his lips across one of them. She gave a high cry and grabbed his hair as she arched ever more. He scowled. He took hold of her hands and pulled them away from his head, then lifted them above her own and held them there. She moaned.

"More. I beg you, give me more!" The little ballerina whined as she hooked her ankles around his hips. She had a distinct French accent with a hardly noticeable lisp.

Bram Williams, the Earl of Kenwood, looked down upon this chit and thought to himself *what a bother*. She was naked beneath him; her little white ballet costume sprawled on the floor next to his foot. He was fully clothed with only his trousers opened for his grown shaft.

He raised her thigh higher, so her foot could touch the desk beneath her and pressed his cock even deeper into her willing flesh. She sucked in a breath and squeezed her eyes shut. Bram thrusted, rolling his hips slightly in a rhythmic circle. The little ballerina started to shiver and quake till she let out a piercing scream that he knew reached the halls outside his office. He felt the tight, warm, wet aftermath of her orgasm.

Bram continued to thrust and closed his eyes; his imagination forming an image long since envisioned. Warm caring eyes staring back at him. Delicate lips lovingly encasing a small shy smile. His cock began to pulse. He pushed further and faster. His own orgasm began to stir in his loins as he then took one big gulp of breath.

"Just like a Lord, you're insatiable and yet in control. Everything they said about you is true," the little ballerina said with a sly pout and a lisp then clasped her arms around his neck.

Bram opened his eyes and saw the little ballerina staring at him with hunger and a mischievous look in her eyes. He immediately lost his passion. He withdrew from the little vixen, pushed her legs aside, and began buttoning his pants. She looked bewildered as she sat there naked.

"Get dressed and go back down to the stage," he said sternly as he grabbed her costume dress and gave it to her. She clutched it close with a look that said puzzlement then it instantly turned to one of enticement.

She rose from the desk and rubbed herself against Bram. "Shall I? You have not cum yet my Lord. Allow me to finish you. Others have told me how needful you are, and I would love nothing more than to sate that delicious cock of yours." She dropped to her knees attempting to undue his buttons. Bram growled low and clutched her wrists to raise her. Her eyes widened as she stood on her feet.

"Get. Out." He looked at her with a severe frown and turned her towards the door. The little wench looked appalled but began to walk out the door still clutching the dress to her body.

Bram sat down at his desk. His cravat was in disarray to the side and his shirt was pulled out from his bottoms. A glass of cognac was still sitting on the corner of the desk. He grabbed it now and drank back the last remains. He leaned back in his chair and rested his hand on his mouth. Bram could smell the ballerina's musky sweetness on his fingertips.

The little ballerina's words circulated in his mind and he was consumed with the feeling of bitterness. The little strumpet was like all the others, the gossip bringing women like her to his door, trapping him within his Opera house. He began to think of his world and title. Aristocracy, the plague within society: he was tired of it all. The Lords within it were poppy cocks always addicted to seeking higher power, and the Ladies were just tainted to their core. They were the true reason Bram was trapped in his Opera house. He could not venture any further than the close circles that he had, unless willingly being subjected to the disgust of the Ton. He would rather be left in a desert to die.

His thoughts angered him. His cock infuriated him, for it was still partially hard. Bram had enough of this room and his thoughts. He stood up and tucked in his white shirt, then adjusted his black cravat. Passing the coat rack, he reached and grabbed his own then made his way out of his office.

The halls were halfway lit by small flames in Moroccan lantern lamps hanging on the side walls. The light hardly illuminated the dark magenta color of velvet. The air smelled of exotic perfumes and cigars. He could hear far off noises of chatter from the audience below. He approached a side staircase adjoined to the hall that led back to his office; a hall that was only for him. Heading down the staircase, he passed multiple frames of paintings of Moroccan scenery.

Bram reached the grand foyer and made his way to the front entry. His carriage was stationed at the corner outside his opera; his footman saw him approaching and he readied the horses. "Jefferson."

"Good evening, my Lord," Jefferson said as he opened the carriage door and Bram entered inside.

"Take me to Springfield, Jefferson."

"Yes, my Lord," Jefferson answered and flicked the reins.

Bram entered the grand doors of Springfield club. The smell of cigars hit him harsher here than in his opera. There were many sorts of men here, most nobleman, and businessman. There were sounds of discussions, laughter, glasses clinking, and the sounds of cards shuffling. Bram passed the many different chambers that were filled with men, gambling tables, armchairs, and liquor; he made his way towards a room reserved only for one particular group. He opened the doors and entered.

The room was dimly lit and had a fire burning in the hearth. There was one grand window which was now closed off by a large golden curtain. Six costly armchairs were arranged close together in the room and numerous paintings of landscapes and naked courtesans were hanged around the olive-green walls. Two men sat in armchairs pulled close together with a table between them. They were deep into a game of chess. Bram fell into one of the chairs and allowed himself to slump into it. He looked at the two men close to the fire.

Richard Lake, the Earl of Springfield, was leaning in the seat with his hands raised and clasped together, his elbows on the armrest. A glass of gin and tonic water sat on the corner of the table. He was giving his usual unreadable stare at his opponent; most likely reading the next chess move with ease, judging how his contender was flushing next to an empty glass at his side. Richard was the owner and creator of the very club Bram was in. The owner of five other clubs spread out through England.

Long ago, Richard had not always been as successful as he was today. It had been chance that he was here now. He had only shared one piece of memory with Bram, and that was to say; if it were not for the death of his father and older brother, he would have died in the gutter. When Bram had tried to question further of Richard's past, Richard just simply rubbed his scarred knuckles and mumbled under his breath, "Well, that time has passed. No use bringing it up now." He was known as the cold unmoving Lord. The Lord with no heart, the one who saw through deception. Everyone knew that no one crossed Richard Lake.

Richard and Bram met when he had arrived back to London five years ago. Before that time, Bram spent most of his early twenties in Morocco. He came to London when he was twenty-five; angered to have returned to this hell hole. His father had died, and the title was then passed on to him, his father's title and his scandal. When Bram found out about this club it became his only solace from the Ton's viscous gossiping. It was then he met Richard, and Richard showed him a world to escape to.

"Are you willing to make that move yet, Sterling?" Richard said to his opponent, his expression unchanging.

Sterling looked up at Richard with a mannerism that clearly said he was irritable, and then made his move.

Richard moved his queen. "Check mate." Sterling made a grumbling noise and rose from his seat. "Guff." He grabbed the empty glass and made his way to the decanter of scotch and served himself a generous portion.

Sterling McBrian, the Marquess of Grinsten Way, was in better words an unrestrained man. Bram was introduced to the man at the same time he met Richard. Though, back when they first met, Sterling was more intemperate than how he was now. Sterling had come here from Scotland with a grievous past that most could clearly see was rooted to his core.

Bram had found out what the seed of his torment was one night in Huntington's brothel. Much drinking had been done when Sterling confessed how he had lost his wife and child. Their death so tarnished his mind and heart that he saw no point to it all anymore. Bram looked at him now swig back the full glass of scotch. A dark satisfaction consumed the man's dark circled eyes before returning to the armchair across from Richard. "Anither gam, Richard?" Sterling said with a smirk.

"I wouldn't mind another win. Set it up," Richard answered before setting his eyes on Bram and noticing his demeanor. "Well, you look bothered. Over thinking again, are we?" Richard pulled out a cigar from a walnut wood box that sat next to the chess board.

"I didn't get my fill with a wench I had back in the opera house," Bram said with a scoff. He refused the cigar Richard offered to him.

"In that case, serve your blue balls a glass of liquor," Richard said with a crooked grin.

"Serve me a bevvy too, please," Sterling said quickly

after.

Bram smirked, raised himself from the armchair and walked over to the numerous sorts of decanters of liquor. He grabbed two glasses, filled one with a desirably strong vintage cognac, the other with scotch, and then delivered the full glass to Sterling. Bram returned to his own seat.

Richard made the first chess move and leaned back in his chair. "So, what did this 'wench' do to leave you so unfulfilled?" Richard sparked a match against the side of the wooden table and lit his cigar.

Bram swallowed half of the remains of cognac and let the flavor satisfy on his tongue before answering. "She conversed."

"A hen always ruins a guid feckin' wi' 'er talkin'," Sterling slurred while making his chess move.

Bram grinned, shaking his head. There was a time before when it was difficult to ever understand what Sterling was ever saying while intoxicated; now that years had passed it became easier. Bram watched Richard take out Sterling's knight. "Check," Richard said after removing the piece. Sterling cursed under his breath and swallowed the last of his scotch.

The doors to the chamber flew open then and a tall athletic fellow stood in the entrance of them with a wide grin chiseled on his face. He took a light step inside and closed the doors behind him.

"Good. Evening. Gentlemen." The man emphasized each word. He looked at the men sitting around in silence. "Christ, it is lifeless in here. Better take off my coat and bring some sort of thrill to this dismal place." He slipped off his black tailcoat and hung it on the coat rack next to the doors and made his way to the brandy. He poured himself a glass.

"Please, help yourself Philip," Richard said with composed sarcasm and brought his cigar to his lips. Philip filled his glass to the top with brandy and turned to face the gentlemen.

"Many thanks Richard. Now, cheers to this glorious night." Philip raised his glass in a high toast then drank back a portion. He let out a quite noticeable breath and then looked around. "Come now, what is the matter with the three of you? It's a grand night for drinking and women." Philip paused and leaned back against the table. "Which reminds me, where is Mark?"

"He met two Belgium scientists and went for a drink with them," Richard answered as he took out one of Sterling's rooks. Sterling cursed silently.

"Damn. I brought two wicked little ladies who are just dying to meet two fellow rakes of Springfield and here he is running off," Philip said and then finished the rest of his brandy.

"You know Mark, science is his first love," Bram answered after a while. Bram still felt bothered with all the thoughts that were still swirling in his head. Having Philip there was not helping things either. Bram enjoyed the man's company most of the time, but for this moment all he did was remind Bram how the women in their company were always dimwitted or wanting to obtain something more from their pockets. Or even worse, wanting to claim one of the notorious Rakes of Springfield that Philip loved to proudly call them teasingly.

Philip J. Wilson III, the Earl of Huntington, was a blue-blooded rake of London. He inherited his experience and character from many Earls down his bloodline. Before he died, the late Earl of Huntington was known so much for his taste of debauchery that a brothel was named after him. Once the title passed down to Philip, it had seemed that Philip was chasing for the lead to surpass his father. He became the king of wild parties and art soirees.

Bram had never seen him settle or even keep any woman more than a week, and that was only if Philip liked her. Bram had often wondered if that were because of the pressure of beating his father's reputation or if it was just because Philip couldn't find any woman that could keep up with his high spirit. Despite it all, Bram knew Philip as a man who was always in good moods and never stopped talking about women.

"So, what do you think, Bram? Shall you and I go and ravish these loose beauties?" Philip gave a sly smile as he moved over to Bram's side and leaned against his armchair.

"I'd rather not," Bram grumbled and swallowed the last of his cognac. Philip raised an eyebrow.

"You are in a sour mood tonight, again I may add," Philip said with a chuckle. He grabbed Bram's empty glass and went back towards the decanters. "You need another glass or else the ladies will think you a scrooge."

"I don't want to deal with any of these jezebels you brought, Philip. You join them in your own orgy," Bram answered back, his tone agitated. This time both Philip's eyebrows raised, and the corner of his mouth rose slightly.

"Bram just had an ill fortunate experience with a 'wench' back in his opera house," Richard answered for Bram. His face showed small signs of humor and grew when he removed Sterling's bishop from the game board. A loud sigh escaped from Bram and Sterling. "Sterling, you should know the scotch is your enemy and my ally," Richard added towards Sterling, he took a sip from his own glass.

"Well that certainly explains this outburst. It is in fact almost like what happened a fortnight ago with that Mademoiselle Violet," Philip said to Bram, completely ignoring the game in front of him. A fortnight ago almost the same situation had happened but with an actress from the same performance. Bram was beginning to be fed up with women who came clinging at his feet. They all seem to always want something.

"Bram, what you need is a good wild party with many sorts of scrumptious strumpets running about," Philip said while returning to the brandy and loaded his and Bram's glass. He gave him the filled cup before speaking again. "Stage beauties are always little nags anyhow."

Bram considered what Philip said. In truth, it had been a while since he felt satisfied. Too long since he enjoyed a woman's honest company. They never lasted longer than a simple tumble because they all sought something from him. His title, or money, they targeted Bram because he was worth something to their means. The other Rakes had no clue, but it pained Bram. For once he wanted someone who looked at him without knowing his wealth, reputation, or title. Bram was silent for a moment before commenting.

"What I need is for once, a woman who doesn't know who the hell I am." Bram looked up at Philip then and saw him smiling before he let out a whooping laugh.

"That will never happen!"

"Alright Richard, beat 'at," Sterling said after moving his queen. He had a smug look on his face as he leaned back in his chair. Richard slant forward and observed the chess board. He brought the cigar to his lips and smoked it for a moment. He moved his bishop.

"Check mate."

∞ ∞ ∞

Anita cringed as the carriage hit another pothole. Her bottom was sore from the long journey her family was close to concluding. The carriage ride was the final element and then she would be home.

Home...

Anita had not been back to London since she was fourteen. Returning now made her feel ever more alienated compared to how she felt when she first saw America. Arriving to a foreign land then gave her a sense of freedom and adventure. Coming back to London now gave her the oddest feeling of imprisonment. She contained a sigh. The reasons for coming back to London were not of her choice, but a necessity for another.

The sudden whine from her mother brought Anita back to her surroundings.

"Good God in heaven, my poor bottom cannot take any more of this!" Eloise S. Henderson, the Viscountess of Hemmingway, complained as she stretched out her bottom and rubbed it gently above her golden high-necked dress. Her light brown bonnet was pushed to the side as she leaned against her husband.

Her husband, Stephan J. Henderson, the Viscount of

Hemmingway, simply lowered the paper he was reading and glanced at her. "We shall be there shortly, my dear."

Anita's mother looked at her husband and blew a raspberry at him. Her father simply smiled at his wife. Anita smiled softly as she observed her parents. A memory of always seeing her father give his wife that simple smile whenever she complained arose within Anita's mind. She knew how that smile always warmed her mother. Her mother would just simply blush and continue to protest. Her father would naturally listen and let his wife rant.

Eloise was in pleasant words a caring mother, a bit on the eccentric side, but nevertheless a warm woman. Many years in America had given her the freedom away from traditional moral values that London society held so dear. Society in Pennsylvania was not obliged to follow the same standards and sophistication like in England. Families could be close with one another and allowed to grow together without any nannies and governesses. Therefore, Eloise felt deep down inside more love for her daughters than any other Lady she had known.

Stephan's gaze had gone back to the article he was reading. He raised his hand to his cravat to loosen it slightly and cleared his throat. Anita's eyes softened. She knew how much her father hated cravats. The tie had always been too tight around her father's thick neck. Stephan was not a bulky man; he was seen more as homely. That was how Anita always saw him. The years living in America had made the Lord of Hemmingway a hearty and patient man with tanned skin, a large mustache, and if one were to look closely, slight calluses across his palms.

The land he had in America was well cared for, not only by his land stewards but by him as well. Stephan had always taken upon himself to be included during the time of harvest. He would stay long hours outdoors with the farmers till all the duties were finished. When all responsibilities were said and done, he would then settle peacefully with his wife as he would listen to her cheerful bickering.

"That is what you said an hour and a half ago, Stephan! Children, is that not what he said?" Her mother looked at Anita and her sister with a miserable expression as she continued to rub her bottom.

Her sister, Annabelle C. Henderson, sat and giggled at her mother. Anita glanced at her dear sister's slight sun kissed face. Her heart warmed as she heard Belle's light-hearted chuckle. Her sweet sister looked like a dove in Anita's mind; she had lovely round hazel eyes, light golden-brown hair, and thin pink lips. Since a young age, Belle had always been the most cheerful between them both, whereas Anita was always the quiet and patient one.

Belle always loved to joke with her about how much they were like their parents. Belle, who loved to chat and bicker cheerfully, and Anita, who liked to quietly sit and listen.

"Oh mama, you don't need to worry. We must be much closer to our home now." Belle smiled sweetly at her mother as she slightly adjusted her peach colored dress on the wooden seat.

Her mother made a half smile half pout as she delicately patted Belle's knee from across the carriage. "Sweet dear, how can you be sure we're close. It has been ages; surely you cannot remember where exactly our town home is." Eloise began to fan herself, then cast a sideway glance to her husband. "Oh, Stephan! I informed you that we should have told Ninny and August to have our carriage sent for us at the docks. Now we must endure in this hardwood bucket of a cart," Eloise complained again.

"Mother, we are but ten minutes away from our town home. See? There is the bakery that I used to go with Ninny to collect the flour and pastries." Anita finally spoke for the first time since she and her family docked.

Anita stared outside the carriage window. Though her childhood bakery still had survived, many things had changed since she left. Trees were taller, and more shops had been built. Her family's town home was located not too far from Hyde Park. It was a little past five o'clock, but the streets were still buzzing with people. Most were walkers; lower class mixed with higher, others were on horseback finding their way towards the parks. Carriages rode past them, one after another.

Anita looked up into the sky; it was dreary. The dense fog mingled with the dark soot tossed out by the numerous chimneys. She had to take in short breaths for the smell of the great city had turned much harsher since the years she had been gone. She brought her head back into the carriage and closed her eyes.

She missed her home back in Pennsylvania. The green acres always plump with new harvest of wheat or corn. The usual clear skies, the occasional rain, and the humidity. The fruitful apple tree that grew alongside their large cottage, which always made their home smell of ripe apples whenever the wind blew the windows open.

Anita drew in a great sigh as she envisioned her family's beautiful warm cottage. It was built with brick and strong oak wood, white windows, and red shutters to match the bricks. The wood would creak with each step, always as if the home were speaking. She could see the large welcoming dark oak door opening to escort her in.

"Oh, thank the Lord up in Heaven! We are here!" Her mother almost shrieked as she lifted slightly off her seat to look out the carriage window at the Henderson estate. "Goodness, let's hope none of the neighbors see us returning in such a drab cabbie. What would they say?!"

Anita opened her eyes.

Anita opened her eyes. Her new maid had come in to open the rose-colored curtains and arranged her day clothing. The morning light illuminated the bedchamber which made Anita squint. She turned onto her back and sighed. Her dreams had been so vivid.

She had been on her garden bench, sitting and reading a book of grand adventures. The sun was warm as it caressed her skin, the sky blue. The sound of the breeze as it blew across the apple tree's leaves, the birds chirping, and the faint shouts of farmers in the distant fields. But just then, Anita was no longer in America, her bench was floating above a continent of sand and ocean, as was in her story books. The sight made her heart soar. That is, until she began to hear voices of gossiping women. The sky turned dark, and the rushing winds blew away her book, bench, and her adventures. It had felt real, yet now the memory was fading as Anita was slowly gaining consciousness of her surroundings.

Her bed sheets matched the rose-colored curtains as she raised and observed her old room. The walls were peach colored with soft silver rose inlays on the surface. A beautiful golden lamp sat next to the bed on a nightstand. The maid came back into the chamber with a basin and a jug of fresh water and placed it on her wooden vanity table.

"Shall I wait to help you dress, Miss Henderson?" the maid asked after setting a clean towel next to the basin.

"No, it's alright Claire. I can get ready on my own. Belle will probably need the help though." Anita smiled at Claire as she crossed over to the basin. She was a young pretty woman, perhaps only eighteen, but Anita immediately noticed her sharp eyes upon first meeting. Claire had wit and intellect beyond her pale freckled green-eyed face, and Anita liked that about her.

"Miss Henderson has already risen and dressed. She is downstairs now with Lady Hemmingway. Your morning meal is set and ready for you as well, Miss," Claire answered fittingly as she arranged the bed sheets.

Anita sat at her vanity table and considered what Claire said. Her sister was already awake at quite an unusual early hour. Their mother must have summoned her to discuss the plans for Belle in London. Anita dipped her hands in the cool water and splashed her face lightly. She took hold of the towel and sighed. Her sweet sister, Belle, was of age to be married now. In America, it took many tries for her mother to convince her father to return to London for this new season. It was only when rumors began to crucially rise about the ideas of war between the States was when her father finally decided to agree. Her mother happily began planning on how to show Belle off to the new Ton.

Anita's mother was so hopeful of this season, in a new place, with grander possibilities of marriage proposals. Her family was a mystery after living in America for nearly a decade. Anita never understood her mother's endless pursuit to have them married. But it was Anita, however, who disappointed her mother of that dream for them in America. She sighed again while dabbing at her eyes.

A small noise came from behind Anita. Claire had cleared her throat and took an unsure step towards the door. "Miss Henderson, are you certain you do not need any assistance with your corset?"

Anita had not realized that Claire had been waiting on her. She was still becoming accustomed to having a maid again. In America, there was hardly any need for many servants since their cottage was small and homey. Her family only had one butler, Mr. James; a cook who was Mr. James's wife, Helen; and a cleaning maid, Jane. Of course, there were the farmers for the fields as well. But since living in Pennsylvania, Anita did not require help for getting ready. She faintly recalled Helen's jolly laughter that always came up from the kitchen. She remembered Jane and Belle's love for gossiping about all the young lads in the town. Her heart felt light when she thought of Mr. James. He was always like a grandfather to her and Belle.

Again, she had not realized that she was simply staring at Claire in silence. She could see the dear maid was beginning to fidget. Anita offered her a calm smile and placed the now damp towel on her table. "I'm sorry Claire; sometimes I doze off with my thoughts and simply not notice what is going on around me. But no, I do not need any help, I assure you."

Anita rose from her table and walked over to where her corset and dress laid. Claire smiled very softly at her and moved a strand of red hair that slipped from her face. "Well then Miss, feel free to summon me whenever you need anything."

Claire curtsied and was just about to walk away when Anita stopped her. "Claire, would you please consider not calling me 'Miss Henderson' anymore? It sounds too impersonal. I insist you simply call me Anita."

Claire's eyes widened as a slight blush caressed her freckled face. She quickly looked down and back up again. "Very well, Miss...Anita." Claire curtsied.

Anita offered her a small smile. "Well, that's good enough I suppose."

Claire made a small breathy sound, as if the girl wanted to laugh but held it back. She curtsied once again and exited the room. Anita shook her head softly. The girl was witty yet somewhat shy. It would take some time for the both to get close. Thankfully, Anita was patient.

As soon as Anita had gotten ready and coiled her hair up, she made her way down the stairs to the morning room. Her family's old townhouse was much different compared to their cottage home. It had three floors: three bedchambers, one morning room, a sitting room, a study, and a library. It included a kitchen and a servant quarter. Despite it being a big home, Anita felt trapped within it.

The hall was dark as Anita reached the first floor; she did not hear one sound from any maids or from their butler, August. She turned to make her way down to the morning room, the floors creaking beneath her. Before reaching the door, Anita heard her mother's distinct loud voice burst out abruptly.

"YOU ARE GOING TO BE THE BELL OF THE BALL, MY DEAR! I can see it now!" Her mother giggled. Anita could hear Belle's faint laughter being muffled by her mothers'.

Anita turned the knob and entered inside. The morning light pierced through the wide glassed windows and Anita needed to squint to adjust to the sudden shine of the whole room. The morning room was bright blue with gold inlay. The first noticeable sight Anita was able to see was the large painting of her family hung over the fireplace. The painting was done of them when Anita was ten.

There were few other paintings hung around the room of flowers and small animals. A large beautiful designed carpet covered the wooden floor. Two cushioned couches sat close to the fireplace with a table stand and an armchair between them. Belle and her mother sat on one together.

Belle and her mother quickly looked up as she entered, and Belle gasped.

"Oh Annie, come sit! Wait till you hear what mama has planned for this season. I'm so thrilled I could just burst." Her sister's smile was as bright as the room.

Their mother patted Belle's knee before quickly adding with her own excitement. "Now dear, you mustn't burst just yet. We have much to do to set these plans into motion."

Another set of identical laughter came from Belle and her mother. Anita simply smiled and made her way to the medium sized table set up with food behind them while she continued to hear them giggle to each other.

The table was clustered with plates of eggs and sausage, bacon, and different sorts of cheeses, and lastly fruit tarts and tea. Certainly, their American appetite had not lessened a wink. Silently Anita blessed Ninny, their old cook, for having that knowledge in mind. Anita reached for a plate and filled it with a little bit of everything.

After pouring a cup of tea for herself, Anita went with her plate to sit on the opposite couch from her mother and sister. Almost immediately Belle burst out with chatter. "We are going to have a ball here! Can you believe it Annie, our first London ball?!"

Belle beamed, while Anita's fruit tart stopped midway to her mouth. Surprised, Anita looked to her mother. "We're having a ball here, mother?"

"Of course, why ever not? We have just returned from America, late in the season, we NEED to come out with a bang to get the attention of everyone," her mother answered simply with a grin just before reaching for her own cup of tea.

Belle clasped her hands together in excitement, while Anita looked at her mother with a small frown. "But where will everyone fit? We don't have a ballroom."

Eloise blew Anita a raspberry. "Oh, you're just like your father. No imagination! We will simply move all the furniture out from this room and the sitting room. There should be enough space for about fifty people."

Eloise looked proud of her answer, Belle squealed happily, and Anita gawked. Fifty people! She looked around, observing the space of the room. Though the townhouse was big, she was certain not big enough for fifty overly dressed people.

"Have you told father about this yet, mother?" Anita

asked.

Her mother looked away sheepishly. "Well... no. But he will gladly do anything for the happiness of his daughter. Besides... the invitations have already been sent out." Eloise coughed out the last words before sipping from her tea-cup. Anita sighed softly and closed her eyes. Sometimes her mother did the craziest things to get what she wanted.

The subject quickly changed to that of ball gowns, and which color would best suit Belle's eyes and hair color. Mid way through their conversation, Anita's father came in looking as blinded as she did when first entering.

"Good morning family," he said to them all as he made his way to the table with the food. He grabbed a plate and filled it. He grumbled something as he spotted the pot of tea. "Remind me to mention to Ninny to have at least a little pot of coffee for myself."

Belle giggled softly, and Anita smiled. Her father hated tea. Long hours in the field required strong coffee.

Stephan came around to sit in the armchair and rested his plate on his knee. He was completely oblivious to all the eyes staring at him. He took hold of one fruit tart and raised it. Eloise cleared her throat.

"Stephan, we are going to have a ball for your daughter within a fortnight. The invitations have already been sent out, and all other plans are in order so there is no need for you to fret. I have everything under control." Eloise took a long-satisfied breath.

Stephan's fruit tart stopped midway to his mouth as he looked at his wife in surprise. He looked around the room then back at her.

"We're having a ball here, Eloise?"

Chapter 2

Bram sat in an armchair in the main room at Springfield club. He had come here yet again after visiting his theater. He was deep into the seat with one hand resting on his mouth and the other holding onto a cigar. Springfield was now the only place he could run away to for sanctuary. The room was dark, save for several candles that were lit all around the room. His black coat was off and was hung on the side of the armchair. His cravat was loose around his neck. The faint smell of perfume still infused in the collar of his shirt.

When he had first arrived at L'Opéra Magenta there was quite a surprise waiting for him in his office. He had wanted to look over blueprints for a new theater construction in Morocco. Something he had long planned since he built L'Opéra Magenta. Instead, he found a naked little ballerina from two weeks before. Arranged on his desk, she had crooked her finger to beckon him to her with a sultry little smirk. He had sighed and thought to himself how he needed to buy a more enforced lock to his office.

"What are you doing here?" Bram had said while slowly approaching the naked ballerina. What was her name, he faintly thought?

She smiled coolly as she stood before him and leaned her hands back against the desk. Her small breasts had jutted out towards him; the cold air cooled them. "I simply couldn't

21

rest since the last we parted. I needed to see you again, milord. We need to finish what we started."

She had then moved up against his stiff body and rubbed her hands up his tailored jacket over his shoulders. She pressed herself against him. The faint smell of musk and something sweet he could not pinpoint wafted into his nose. He felt his cock twitch, and though his very masculine core poked at him to take everything she offered, he knew deep down in his mind that she only was seeking something to gain. Not him.

Bram caught her hands just when she began moving them lower to his groin and brought them between them both. She fidgeted, perhaps because of the uncertain energy she could not read from him. He wanted to ravish her, but the truth just could not allow him to let her touch him.

"You must go back from whence you came. It cannot work between us. You need to go seek out some other rich Lord, not I." Bram spoke to her as calmly as he could. But nothing prepared him for the sudden outburst that came from this nameless ballerina.

"No, MY LORD, you listen to me. You took my maidenhead and now I am spoiled! For all I know I could be with child now! With YOUR child! If you leave me here with no support, I will spread word to all of society that Lord Kenwood sired a bastard son!" Her words were so shocking and mispronounced that Bram was almost unable to believe what she meant by everything she had just said.

She was certainly no virgin when they first met, and Bram had not finished himself within her. The little wench was blackmailing him. Immediately he had no worry. The Ton had so many rumors on him; a bastard child was a cliché to his reputation. Nevertheless, that was the last of his patience.

He grabbed her shoulders, looked at her sharply and spoke slowly. "If you can honestly believe that anyone would give a bleeding fuck about a child you birthed and by whom, then I seriously hope for your life when every door and shelter refuses you entrance, and you die on the streets..." He paused, trying not to wince at his own words. "Because no one will want a lying whore at their door."

The deceiving ballerina looked shocked by his words and ripped herself away from his grasp. She grabbed her dress from behind his desk and pulled it over herself. Heading towards the door, she turned and cast him a venomous glare. She lisped, "I will get you for this, my lord."

Bram sighed and waved her off. "Yes, yes. Now be gone." He heard the door slam from behind him.

Sitting in the armchair at Springfield Club, Bram pinched the center of his brow. He now needed to end the production short and have a new performance playing by next week.

He heard a click at the door and glanced over to see Mark entering. He was dressed in a pleasant dark red coat with a black vest and white shirt, a matching dark red cravat at his neck and black breeches. Mark saw him from across the room and smiled calmly as he approached Bram.

"I thought you would be here," Mark said lightly with a smile.

"You're dressed to impress," Bram answered simply with a grin.

"Why thank you. I came to fetch you for Philip's soiree tonight," Mark said, looking proud as he grabbed his coat lapels.

Bram stared for a moment at Mark Ford, the Viscount of Trent. Mark was just a few years younger than he, yet he had already faced the negative forces of malicious talk from half of high society. He was but twenty-one when he became victim to the most classical treachery any man could face. Elizabeth Le Frey, a courtesan Mark was so devoted to... he almost gave away all his riches for her. He married the courtesan and that had been his downfall from the Ton. She soon left him only five months into their marriage for a Duke.

"You are coming tonight, aren't you?" Mark asked. His words cleared Bram's thoughts for a moment.

"Must I? It's always the same thing in Philip's soirees," Bram answered with a shrug. There were always women falling at their feet when they arrived.

"Apparently tonight will be different. It's to be a mask party," Mark said with a grin of his own. It looked odd on the man; he had barely any facial hair, making him still look incredibly young. Mark was twenty-nine, yet he still looked eighteen. Bram had met the man soon after the scandal broke out. He found Mark gambling at Springfield's, spending the last amounts of money he had after his father, the Earl of Cadogan disowned him. Mark's whole demeanor was that of a sullen, defeated man. Bram felt sympathy for the young lad, no man should face a betrayal by the hands of a first love. He began to speak with him, offering him a chance to join the debates between Richard, Sterling, and Sebastian. Soon enough, the man began to build himself back up again.

Bram grimaced, suddenly remembering the topic at hand. He hated masquerades. "I don't wish to wear a mask."

"No need to worry. Only the women wear the masks," Mark answered back with a wink.

Mark was a science man. He was a Lord who mostly spent his time in scientific debates and lectures. Perhaps it was a way to escape from the Ton's social events. In any which way, all the rakes in Springfield had to occupy themselves with some sort of distraction, and it had worked for the young man. Mark learned to build himself up by investing in studies and inventions.

Bram was silent as he considered many masked women for the taking. There would be loose women, adventurous, teasing, and perhaps even innocent. Bram faintly pushed away the last thought of innocent women. Knowing Philip, he would never invite such a rare type.

"Oh, come on, Bram. You have been such a grouch lately. Just come and scan the horizon. You never know what may lurk within the trenches," Mark spoke calmly with a hint of light humor.

Bram's lips cracked into a small smile. Mark had always been a good man, loyal and honorable, and overall a good friend. He somehow always helped Bram come out of his moods with his own lightheartedness.

"Very well, Mark," Bram said. He stood up and rested his now unlit cigar on an ashtray. He then swung his jacket around from the chair and placed it on. Bram pulled his coat lapels close together and buttoned them as he looked at Mark with a smirk. "If we run ourselves into a ditch of crazy mad-women, then I'm leaving you behind, be sure you know that."

Bram began walking towards the door. Mark followed, closing each stride to get next to him. "Haven't you always left me behind?" Mark answered with a laugh.

The doors closed behind them.

∞∞∞

The sound of violins tuning arose in the chamber. A low roar of chatter filled the morning and sitting rooms. Lit candles hung all around the rooms, slightly illuminating all the faces of different aristocrats. Many colors of dresses and formal coats flowed in and out of the chambers. The smells of wine, perfumes, melted wax, and hints of food hung in the air.

Anita looked on at all the many women and men squeezed in to prepare themselves for the upcoming dances. The crowd overflowed into the halls. Even though the over-all surroundings were tight, Anita was impressed that her mother succeeded in creating Belle's first debutante ball. The rooms were beautiful, decorated with fresh vases of pink roses, and ribbons with flowers hung from different lamps and the chandelier. All the furniture was moved to storage to make way for more space for dancing in the sitting room. A large dining table was set up with many different sorts of food and refreshments in the morning room. Chambers upstairs were used for the ladies to rest in, and for coats and shawls.

Anita could not have believed it before, but every plan her mother decided on turned out successful. She searched for her mother now. Eloise was scurrying from one room to another, being sure to interact with each guest. Anita could see her chattering with enthusiasm and then swiftly take leave for another patron. Anita could not help but smile and slowly shake her head. Her mother was as excited as Belle was.

Anita looked for her sister. She was across the room with some other young ladies. They were all dressed in their best, long flowing dresses of different spring colors. But to Anita, her dear sister stuck out the most. Her mellow pink dress matched the roses set up all around the rooms. The dress was set low on her shoulders but was full and modest with white lace at the edges of her bodice and sleeves. Belle's hair was coiled beautifully at the back, and two curled strands of hair fell close to her temples. She had a jeweled studded pendant in the shape of a rose pinned in her hair. She was radiant in Anita's eyes. Judging by the reactions of all the other suitors, they thought so as well.

Anita sighed wearily; her dear sister surely would find a husband soon enough. A small pain shot through her of the faint memory of her mother's trial during Anita's opening season. The thought faded away as two low voices grew louder as it got closer.

"You would think to consider an assembly hall for a debutante ball. I mean honestly, it is so constricted here," one voice said.

"Indeed! How can we possibly dance in such a confined place?" a second voice answered in return.

Anita noticed the two young ladies had stopped only a few feet from where she stood. She casted a glance over and found two brightly and overly adorned dressed ladies. They were younger than Anita, perhaps around the same age as Belle. Their dress hoops were larger than any Anita had ever seen. It is no wonder they felt confined, she faintly thought with a small scowl.

"And that dinner, IF you can call it that. It was so very American," the one who first spoke said. Anita could now see it was the one dressed in a bright sky blue with matching peacock feathers in her hair.

"Well, they did just arrive from America. So of course, they still have that sort of food in mind." The other was dressed in a yellow color with white lace that covered most of the dress. She was wearing white pearls tight around her neck.

"Did they honestly think that we would eat what

they served? That chicken fried steak and that sort of pasta? What was that dessert they had?"

"I believe it was called a peach cobbler and a cream pie."

Anita slightly huffed. Of course, she knew that it was a bit eccentric of her mother to place some American food on the menu, but Eloise found it clever to introduce a few of their new cultural traditions to the old. Most of the guests agreed during their discussions at dinner. These ladies were beginning to poke at Anita. Usually she did not mind the rudeness of others, but knowing how hard her mother and sister applied themselves to making this ball possible in such a short time, she could not take any more of these ladies' crudeness.

"So, what do you think of our little miss debutante?" the lady in yellow asked. Anita grew tense. Now they were to talk about her sweet sister?

"Well, she is pretty. A bit tanned, perhaps because of the American sun. But the poor dear, she needs the most help with her fashion." The one in blue giggled quietly.

That was the last draw. Anita's sister adored her dress, and her mother paid a pretty penny just for Belle's coming out ball. No one was going to ruin it for Belle. Anita turned towards the ladies and cleared her throat noticeably. The ladies casted Anita a disgusted look, but that only made her lift her chin at them. Before she could speak, a young woman approached the ladies from behind.

"Do you not think it tiresome to be talking about your sweet hostess behind her back? Or is it fun to reach things from out of your rear?" the young woman said with a mischievous smile. The two ladies and Anita looked shocked at the beautiful young woman.

She was dressed in a lovely maroon colored dress that slipped down the shoulders. Red ribbons played across the bodice and sleeves. She wore a simple red crystal necklace, and her brown hair had curls that framed her face while a braid was pinned at the back.

The lady in blue looked at the young woman hotly

before answering. "Miss Godfrey, how is it any of your business what we say in private?"

"Oh, Miss Lucinda Kenyon, I will hardly say it was private. A fox can hear you snickering from afar, both you and Miss Isabel Crane," Miss Godfrey answered with now a half smile. "Which reminds me, Miss Crane, Lord Venclaire is looking for you. I believe he said you owe him the next dance. You wouldn't want to miss that, as I'm sure your mother, Lady Hillsdale, will surely be upset with you for missing such a rich catch."

Miss Crane grimaced ever so slightly; it was almost unnoticeable if not looking directly at her. Anita almost grimaced with her, almost. She had been watching Lord Venclaire with other ladies on the dance floor and noticed how the lord would always step on his dance partner's feet.

Sure enough, Lord Venclaire came into eyesight as he slipped his way towards them. He stumbled a bit as he squeezed past some guests but made it in front of Miss Crane. Lord Venclaire was a tall gangly man, much older than the young Miss Crane. He was pale with crooked teeth and had orangey hair that was slightly thinning on top. He mumbled at first, but then cleared his throat nervously.

"Miss Crane, the quadrille is about to start. I will be happy to assist you onto the dance floor," Lord Venclaire said with an awkward smile that he cast to each of the ladies as he extended his hand to Miss Crane.

Miss Crane smiled awkwardly back, as society dictated that she must act accordingly and with manners. She grasped his hand and was practically pulled out towards the dance floor. Miss Kenyon shook her head slightly as she then looked at Miss Godfrey with a glare. She huffed and left them standing there staring after her.

After a moment, Miss Godfrey's body was beginning to shake, she suddenly burst out laughing. It startled Anita at first, but she soon joined in with the young woman. The whole event worked out so perfectly, Anita couldn't help but think that this Miss Godfrey planned it all.

"Oh, that was the most fun! I would do it again just to see that look on Miss Kenyon's face." There was a wicked gleam in Miss Godfrey's eyes. Anita smiled and giggled softly. Strangely there was a sense of familiarity about the young woman in front of her. Her green round eyes with that sparkle, her curly light brown hair, but most of all, that sly smile.

"Have we met before, Miss Godfrey?" Anita asked after all their laughter had subsided. Miss Godfrey half smiled at her.

"It is good to see you again, Annie." Her half smile slowly grew into a whole one.

Realization struck as a memory came crashing into her mind. It was a faint memory of Anita and a little girl running into a big kitchen to steal a whole dish of trifles, and a big cook screaming at them to shoo away. The young girl had the same sparkling green eyes, light brown curly hair, and especially that clever grin.

"Christina?" Anita asked slowly, her eyes slightly widening in recognition.

Christina Godfrey, the daughter to the Earl of Silverton, gasped out loud and took hold of Anita into a tight hug. Anita could tell Christina held in a squeal to avoid any attention their way. Of course, they were already having curious eyes wondering to them because of their sudden embrace.

"I cannot believe how long it has been. You have changed so much, Annie!" Christina said into Anita's ear. Anita smiled softly and hugged the young woman tighter. She had not seen Christina since she left for America. The two little girls cried in each other's arms when Anita's family was leaving, holding one another tightly just like this moment.

"I have changed? Look at you Christina; you have grown so beautiful." And it was true, no more innocent grin resided in her now wicked smile. She still had that curious spark in her eyes, but it had evolved to an adventure seeking lure. The young Christina was now a woman.

The two ladies squeezed one last moment before releasing one another. Christina seemed very aware of all the onlookers curious of their friendship, so she then winked and held on to Anita's hand.

"Let's go up to one of the resting rooms, so we may

have a more private conversation." Anita had no time to agree, she was already being whisked away up the stairs. Anita chuckled softly. Christina's excitement had never faltered, and that gave Anita a feeling of relief. Not everything had changed completely.

They both rushed past two matrons coming down the hallway. The older ladies were startled by the abruptness and stopped with a squawk.

"Oh, excuse us, Mrs. Flanders and Lady Blanche," Christina shouted back at them with a giggle. Anita could not help herself; she looked back at them with a smile and waved. The two matrons shook their heads in a disapproving manner and continued down the stairs, jabbering to each other.

Anita noticed that they came around to her own bedchambers. The halls up on the third floor were not as lit as the floor beneath them, for no one expected anyone coming up here. Something inside Anita told her that was what Christina had planned. They reached the end of the hall to where her door was and entered inside. There was a small fire burning in the fireplace; Claire must have started it an hour before to have the room warm for when she returned. Anita would thank her for that when she next saw her.

Christina made her way to the nightstand and lit the candle there. After some light had formed around the corner of the room, Christina sat on the bed and padded the cushion next to her with a wide smile. Anita smiled back with a small shake of her head and sat down beside her.

"Oh Annie, remember when we used to hide up here, while our parents had their own small gatherings downstairs?" Christina said. The candlelight made her features look soft and weightless.

"I remember. Now we're hiding from an enormous ball downstairs," Anita said with a small chuckle.

"At least little Belle looks so beautiful; she has truly blossomed from that little chick that used to want to follow us around everywhere." Christina laughed wholeheartedly and then after a moment, sighed.

"How much I wish that I could've been there for your debutante ball, Annie." Christina looked displeased. Anita had thought the very same thing when she was at her own seasoned ball. A faint feeling of dread at the memory crossed her chest. Anita had never felt so out of place than her own coming out season. She did not know much of anyone who had attended, and neither did the guests know of her. Meeting anyone that night was trial and error, for when she was younger, Anita could not help but be awkward.

Anita smiled softly and patted her friend's hand. "It is all right Christina. You probably would not have liked it. It really was quite a bore."

Christina looked cynical at that and even pouted her lips slightly. Anita could not help but look away from her old friend's direct stare.

"You did not meet a man?" Christina asked suddenly.

Anita's eyes widened and whirled back to Christina. Her friend strangely looked serious. Anita felt her heart pound against her chest as her worst memory came to mind.

"No," Anita answered simply. Christina's eyes still pierced through her, unwavering.

"There wasn't any man who was interested... in marriage. Nobody courted me." Anita slowly released a held breath. Anita could not get any farther into this conversation. Not without evoking the past. Her friend still did not speak a word, just simply stared at her silently, and that was the worst when it came to Christina.

"Come now, tell me, how was your debutante ball?" Anita tried to reverse the conversation. Christina just raised a brow.

"The same as yours, it was quite a bore. There were no intelligent men, and all the women were merely speaking of fashion or about others. I was considered dense and ill-mannered to be courted. But that was no bother to me; I had other plans in mind." Christina's brows rose even higher as a wicked smile formed on her lips.

Anita's own brows furrowed. Before she could question more about her friend's ball, Christina stood and dashed to her closet. She looked through the different dresses and colors. She looked as if in deep thought at each fabric before discarding it and picking up another. Anita stood up and crossed over to her.

"What are you doing, Christina?" Anita asked as she stood out of the way from flying dresses.

"I'm searching for a dress that will best match the masks that I have."

"Masks?" Anita asked, baffled.

Christina turned to her while holding a dark magenta colored dress. She smirked and looked her over. "Yes, my dear, masks. We are going to go to a masquerade ball. And you aren't saying no. I planned this when I first heard your family was returning."

Anita was now completely bewildered as she faintly accepted the magenta dress.

"What of Belle's ball? I cannot leave her there." Anita fumbled with her words.

"Belle won't even notice you're gone. You did not catch all the gentlemen suitors suckling her feet? Your mother is in a daze by all the people who have shown. And your father disappeared in his office with a plate of food," Christina answered swiftly as she placed herself behind Anita and began undoing the buttons of her dress.

"How do you know all this?! And Christina, thank you but I can undo my own dress!" Anita said quickly as she turned towards her friend with half of an uncertain smile. She walked around behind a wooden screen and undid her gown.

"Like I said Annie, I planned all this," she answered simply. Anita stepped into the gown that Christina had given her. Leave it to Christina to plan a grand fiasco if it turned out to be. Anita stepped out around the screen and her friend gasped with a wide smile. The gown had always been nice in color, Anita never thought it went well with her skin tone, but she did love how the material wrapped around low on her shoulders.

"Perfect. We are ready for the grand ball now," Christina said with delight. She grabbed a shawl from the closet and wrapped it around Anita. "We must go out from the servant's entrance. My carriage is waiting there."

Before long, they had both quietly and unnoticeably

sneaked through the servant's entrance and into the awaiting carriage. Sure enough, there were two decorative dazzling masks sitting next to Christina. She gave one to Anita and placed the other on herself. The color of the mask matched perfectly with Anita's gown.

They were riding for a while before the sounds from outside began to uplift the air. Anita peaked outside the carriage curtain and gasped as she looked on at all the extravagantly dressed women and men. Many were walking and standing in front of a large private land that was very grand. The carriage was riding down the long drive, grass surrounding the whole front yard and trees leveled up the lane. Red lit lanterns were tangled around each tree.

"Christina... are we at the right place?"

Christina moved so that she was able to peak outside the carriage window. She grinned at the crowd and sat back comfortably.

"Not to worry, Annie, we are right where we need to be."

Anita looked back at her friend, sensing that she knew very well the property that they were approaching.

"How did you come about hearing of this ball?"

"Let's just say, years after my coming out season; I finally met the sort of people I was able to be myself with." Christina held a warm yet small smile. It looked as though she was harboring a memory.

Christina glanced back to Anita and caught her curious stare. She smiled and tilted her head slightly. "Anita, you will have a good time here. It will profoundly change your life."

Strangely, Anita felt a nervous thrill wash over her. In that moment, she could not understand what it was, but it felt like something was going to happen within this event.

The carriage had stopped in front of the grand mansion. The door opened and both she and Christina helped themselves out. As the carriage was rolled away, the light from the open front door illuminated the large front porch. The sound of an orchestra was faintly audible from the outside. There was no host awaiting them, neither a butler, the guests could just walk in. That slightly surprised Anita, but hardly, for who knew what sort of party Christina was taking her to.

Christina and Anita glanced at each other for one last moment. Anita took a noticeable deep breath. Christina's smile grew even larger.

"Well, this is it," Christina said. And they entered inside.

Anita hid herself inside a dark moonlit library. There was no fireplace, only a small candle she had found and lit next to a dark wooden desk. The library was massive, ever larger than the library in her home. Whereas her family's library was a small one wall filled of books, this library had three aisles of filled shelves. She was astonished by the home she was in.

When Anita and Christina entered the home, she had gasped at the sight before her when they made their way to the grand ballroom. There were candles scattered all about, bright red lanterns filled every corner with trails of vines lining across each wall. The whole scene was played out as if every room were outdoors. It was as if everyone was in a midsummer night's dream.

Women and men all dressed in their finest fabrics, however, they closely resembled theatrical garments. All the women were adorned with glitters of jewels and masks. Males dressed as gentlemen. Servants were dressed in loincloths to really give the feel of a wild soiree. Anita was shocked at everything she had seen.

Many of the guests were intensely intoxicated. There were not any known dances that Anita was familiar with; in fact, all the guests had their own movements among each other. To her amazement, couples danced together in the most improper way by holding each other close and caressing one another. At that point, Anita had lost Christina within the fray. She searched endlessly for her, but to no end Anita could not pinpoint her.

Anita wanted desperately to rip off the mask and

search more carefully, but with all the guests dancing about it was becoming monotonous. Anita kept colliding with people too drunken; she would almost lose her footing on several occasions. She felt like a lost dove hidden in a cave filled with bats. By the sixth time her dress was trampled on, Anita finally decided to search for refuge. She sighed with relief when she found her salvation, the library. She had decided that it was the perfect place to wait in peace till she was ready to search for Christina again.

Taking off the mask, Anita moved through the aisles scanning the titles of books, not needing the candle to see. The room was touched with silvery light from the open window, the moon shining through with brilliant glory. Anita smiled as she stumbled upon the title *A Midsummer Night's Dream*. She pulled the book out of its shelf and flipped through the pages. She stopped at the point where Oberon, the fairy king, instructs his servant, Puck, to fetch a magical flower to rub over the eyes of his fairy queen, Titania, and to a human named Demetrius. The magical flower had juices that once rubbed on the eyelids of a sleeping person; would awaken and fall deeply in love with the first thing they see.

Anita had always appreciated the love within the tale. Though, it may have all been a mistaken dream, each character knew who they genuinely loved in the end. Anita briefly sighed, then noticed she still had her dance card from the ball bound around her wrist; she removed it and placed it in the page of the book then closed it. As she was about to return to the desk to sit and read, a flash of blue light caught her eye. She stopped and turned slowly to look out of the window to her right.

Up within the sky, the full moon blazed its silver light. Much to Anita's surprise, the silver light seemingly shimmered to blue. The faint blue aura began to consume the silver rays till it dominated the whole moon. Anita felt held within a trance, as she stared in awe at the brilliant blue moon before her. The dark clouds finally parted, melted away from the moon's striking rays. The moon was so beautiful, like a dream. For a moment, Anita wondered what it would be like to have a love that would consume all of her.

Suddenly, like a caress, chills ran across Anita's neck. A loud crashing sound of a door opening and then slamming happened at that moment. A faint giggle and a low grumbling sound signaled to Anita that it was a woman and man together. She darted back in the last aisle and leaned against the shelves. She quietly banged her head against the books.

"Drat…" Anita silently whispered. This could not have been worse, she annoyingly thought.

A noticeably loud moan escaped through the lips of the woman and then a gasp of breath. The man sounded a grunt. Anita held her own breath. Was this couple going to fornicate in this large library, with Anita here? The sounds became more urgent, and that caught Anita's curiosity. Why would a woman make so much noise? Her curiosity wrenched her forward. Anita moved slowly and quietly down the far aisle. She peeked around the edge of the shelf and caught sight of the woman and man. Anita held in a gasp.

The couple was frantically kissing one another beside the door. The woman was dressed in a scarlet red gown; it had no sleeves over the shoulders or covered at her neck, instead the corset hung at her breasts tightly. She wore a matching simple mask, tied neatly under her hair. The man was dressed in a fine black coat, and pantalets. A white cravat hugged around his neck. Their bodies pressed tightly together; the woman panted every second in the man's arms. The woman's stockinged leg wrapped around the man's thigh, and he caught it, raising it closer to his hip. Anita noticed the man's hips beginning to move in a thrusting motion, and that made a chill run down her spine to a now sensitive area. She could not help but notice herself shaking.

The man now broke the kiss, and slowly moved his lips down the woman's neck. Each languishing kiss ended with a small lick of his tongue, and Anita grew hot as she saw the way he expertly moved his mouth lower to the woman's bosom. He cupped the woman's covered breast and nipped it slightly. The woman and Anita both gasped; the woman gasping with pleasure, whereas Anita gasped in surprise. She looked down and to her amazement found herself clutching the book. Anita closed her eyes and ridiculously thought that perhaps this was all a dream that she had created, a feverish erotic illusion.

She took a deep breath and opened her eyes to glance again at her created fantasy. Anita instantly lost her breath. The man was staring directly at her from the woman's cleavage. For a moment, they both stared at each other, silently. She could not very well see his features, but his eyes were an intense black. He pierced her with his gaze, and she fell lost within the blackness. A thrill caressed across her body, and she instantly felt the warmth build between her legs.

"Don't stop now, my Lord. We still need to unsheathe your mighty sword." The woman moaned faintly.

Anita's eyes widened slightly as she saw that the woman cupped his groin. Hearing the woman's voice brought her back from her trance. She moved from the aisle's edge and hid behind the shelves. Anita could not believe that she was caught staring. Her cheeks instantly flushed as he probably thought her mad for watching.

Before she could act out the idea of running past the couple and straight through the party to the streets, she heard the man grunt something to the woman. She heard the door open and his low dark voice commandingly telling the woman to leave. Anita could hear the woman protest, but something must have forced her to exit, for she heard nothing more from her. The door closed. Anita knew she was now alone with just herself and the man.

She stood there, staring at him. Her eyes were round in surprise as she watched Bram thrusting into the unknown woman against him. He would have never noticed she was there if she had not made a sound. But she had gasped, and

Bram turned to find a young unmasked woman watching him intensely. For a moment, he was frozen, unable to understand that someone else was in the room with them. She was barely visible, hidden in the dark, nothing but the light of the moon framing her body. But he could see her innocent eyes; the glow from the candle showed them looking at him now, unwavering. Suddenly, Bram felt chills caress his nape as a sharp sense of familiarity washed over him.

"Don't stop now, my Lord. We still need to unsheathe your mighty sword." The woman moaned faintly.

Bram felt the woman grab his groin and he groaned slightly. His cock was hard, but the woman's touch tainted his lust. It tampered even more as he saw the unmasked woman's eyes widen even larger and she hid herself beyond the shelves. *No, do not go.* Bram turned his attention back to the woman in red and grabbed her wrist lightly.

"I believe you should go," he said sternly.

The woman looked at him in surprise and confusion. She opened her mouth to speak but Bram opened the door beside them. He began to pull her calmly towards the exit.

"Now wait a moment, my Lord. I thought..." The woman abruptly stopped as she looked at Bram's expression. She shut her mouth, forced her arm away from his grip, then adjusted her mask and left. Bram closed the door.

He stood next to the door silently. The room was deathly quiet, save for his breaths. A small creak came from the floor aisles, and his ears perked at the sound. Bram took one slow step towards the first aisle of shelves. He just could not explain it, he felt this need. It was an instinct that forced him forward. It told him to capture and devour. It was an overwhelming desire. A curiosity that consumed him.

Bram's eyes adjusted to the dark as he slowly walked down the first aisle. Another creak signaled to him that the woman was in the third aisle away from him. He could feel his heart begin to pound with adrenaline and that caused him to take quicker steps. He passed the second aisle, peaked around the edge and paused. He saw the woman's back to him; her posture was stiff which told him she was alarmed.

Bram approached her slowly. The thought of capturing this woman surprisingly thrilled him. Not wanting to startle her to the point of running, he stopped just halfway down the aisle.

"Do you think it exciting to secretly watch a couple embracing?" Bram said.

The woman whirled around and faced him. Her eyes were large and wide with surprise and for a moment Bram did not breathe. That sense of familiarity overwhelmed him. He waited for a response, but she did not say a word. Not even a sound. She just stood there, breathing deeply, her bodice rising and falling, capturing his gaze. Her gown was a beautiful color of magenta that melted lovingly against her skin. His gaze trailed up to her neck where small tendrils of hair glazed across her flesh. His sight reached her gaze and a chill ran down his neck. She stared directly into him.

"Do you often hide in places where you know couples will run away to fuck?" Bram said each word slowly as he took one step at a time.

With each step he made, she made one behind her. He followed her, till they both passed the open window. The moon caught his eye, and for an instant he glanced away from the woman. The moon was a force that encouraged this need, lured him to take her. Out of his mind, he continued to move towards her until she banged against the desk with the lit candle. A book had fallen from her grasp, but her gaze never faltered from his.

The candle now lightened her face. Bram could faintly make out a shy blush across her cheeks, and that sight lured him ever closer. He took one last step; he was now only inches away from her body. Her mouth opened slightly, and he thought she was going to speak. But she did not, instead she licked her lips slowly.

He could not understand the emotions he was feeling, but they were raw. So wild that he had enough of thinking, but of action. Bram filled the inches between them and pressed himself against her. She gasped as he wrapped one arm around her waist. He raised his other hand and caressed it across the fallen hair at her neck. Her eyes faltered slightly into a daze. Bram leaned his face closer to hers.

"Do you ever wish to do what the couples you watch are doing?" Bram knew he probably sounded ridiculous, but he paid no attention to his thoughts. He needed to taste her without knowing why.

She half moaned an answer. At least he thought she tried. He could not know for he already set his lips upon her. The contact set his cock on fire. His whole flesh came alive as he felt her body respond to his kiss. She gasped, and it took his breath.

He lost all control then. His hands moved all over her, feeling the lush curves and dips of her body. She felt warm and welcoming. She smelled of sweet roses mixed in honey. It was such a foreign aroma he had never experienced before; it made his head spin in delight. His mouth watered.

Bram leaned her back against the desk and expertly placed himself between her legs. Her gown constricted around her thighs, separating him from her. Bram impulsively growled, his body needed to touch hers. He heard her faintly whimper. He believed she held in so much pent passion, for she was quivering all over.

That knowledge nearly broke him. All thoughts envisioned raising her gown over her thighs and shoving himself into her warm flesh to sate her. Breaking the kiss, he trailed his lips softly down her neck. She sighed and opened herself to him. Bram reached her breasts and nuzzled them with his cheek. Felt her soft skin.

At that point, his need took over. Bram moved his hand to her calf and began working his way up her leg. He felt the gooseflesh build on her skin as he found his way up her thigh and under her gown. He reached her undergarments and found the opening between her legs. Her curls welcomed him, and his hand felt the warm wetness of her womanhood. Bram groaned at the response her body had for him.

He lifted his head and found her staring at him again with the most honest of expressions. Her eyes were soft and unclouded as she watched him. That image set Bram's cock inflamed and it painfully pressed against his trousers. He slowly curled his fingers over her swollen nub; she sharply inhaled a deep breath and raised her hand. Bram thought for a moment that she was to caress his face, and the strangest feeling of longing came to him as he closed his eyes.

Instead of the delicate stroke he was expecting, a stinging sensation seared across his cheek. The woman had slapped him. Bram's eyes sprang open to see the woman breathing heavily, staring at him still with soft eyes but now slightly uncertain. She licked her lips as she closed her legs. Bram took a step back, and she stood from the desk.

They were silent as they stared at each other, both breathing deeply. Laughter and music began to steep through the walls of the room, ending the dream. The candle flickered. Time seemed frozen to Bram.

"Thank you..." The woman finally spoke. And without further word, she stumbled away from him and quickly swept open the door and ran out.

Puzzled, Bram stared at the wide-open door. He could not move. All thoughts were on the unknown woman who had run from him. Her voice, like her eyes, was soft and quiet. And despite the odd event that just happened, the memory of those small words made his cock pulse. He soothed the mound against his trousers and took a step to the side.

Something shuffled at his feet and Bram looked down. He picked up the book he had pushed aside. He read the title and found it was *A Midsummer Night's Dream*. This was the book the woman had dropped in her surprise. An interesting choice, he thought. Bram noticed an indent in one of the pages and opened it. He found a dance card placed inside, and his brow rose.

Little by little this woman was fascinating him. He did not know her, but he knew deep in the hollows of his soul that he must. He just needed to find her first...

Chapter 3

Anita blushed as she crossed her legs once more beneath her golden-brown day dress. She was thinking of that man again. Every day, after that evening, she kept rekindling the memory of how his fingers had felt between her thighs. His sure caresses of what he wanted. Anita bit her lip; she had been so close to letting him consume her. Her belly still quivered at the thought of what more he would have done.

Her half eaten raspberry tart lay crumbled on her plate, the lemon tea now cold on the table stand. She still remembered his kiss. It was hot, demanding, and almost possessive, yet, familiar. She faintly thought in the moment of their embrace, that he wanted her to take all of him, his desires, his sorrows, and happiness.

Anita stared out through the morning windows. The sun was out and bright against a few pale clouds. The way his dark eyes had looked through hers, silently commanding her to stay and be there with him. Anita had felt needed by him. But she had fled, with her lips bruised and still warm from their searing kiss. She had felt that longing and ache in her chest that moment between them, and that reminded her of the past she wished to keep buried. A mistake, she determinedly thought over, that should never happen again.

Anita sighed, and then looked back down at her half-eaten tart. She placed the plate onto the table stand in front of her then raised her cold cup of tea. The faint smell of lemon arose to her nose. The man smelled of cigars and spice. The most exotic smell she had ever inhaled on a man and she remembered how she could not stop breathing his scent into her body.

Anita grumbled. This man just could not escape her thoughts, and it was continuing to frustrate her. Not only had this stranger ignited something within Anita, but her curiosity was like a consuming plague. She desperately wanted to know who this man was, and if she would ever see him once more. Would her lips ever touch his again…? Why on Earth did she thank him as well?!

Right before she was to berate herself once more, a door click interrupted her thoughts. Anita blushed softly when she saw her mother and sister enter the room. She should not be thinking such things, even when Anita knew she would never see that man again.

"Oh, my dear, you are up early. Have you eaten already?" Eloise asked. Her mother and sister seemed to match today. They both were wearing their own version of blue. Belle had on a lovely sky-blue day dress that framed across her shoulders with long sleeves. Her mother wore a high neck navy dress with white lace on the collar.

Anita smiled and nodded to her mother. "Yes, I have, mama. The food is still warm; you and Belle should help yourselves before it becomes cold."

In truth, Anita had not eaten much of anything since the night with the man. Her mind was not certain of the reasoning, just that her stomach had been ridden with knots. Looking at the half-eaten tart, Anita was surprised she was able to even get that much down. Her mother and sister crossed the room to serve themselves some eggs, bacon, and fruit.

They returned to the couch across from Anita and sat. Eloise ate a big spoonful of eggs and smiled peacefully. She made a soft moaning sound then popped a bacon strip into her mouth.

"Oh my, nothing is better than a warm breakfast, isn't that right my dears?" Eloise said happily.

Belle answered with a moan of her own as she nibbled the food on her plate. Anita simply nodded and stared down at her teacup. Eloise's brow rose as she studied her daughter across from her. Anita was much more detached today than any other.

"Anita, are you alright, child? You seem out of sorts this morning. In fact, you seem flushed. I dearly hope you are not coming down with something."

Anita looked up at her mother and did a mental shake. She needed to snap out of her thoughts or else they would betray her. She told herself at that moment to not think of that man any longer, and that is final. Anita gave a nod, more to herself than to her mother.

"I assure you, mama, I'm well. Just had too much tea, I suppose," Anita said with a small smile. Eloise inspected her daughter with a tilt of her head. Belle simply stared at them both with wide eyes and a spoon of eggs reaching her mouth.

Eloise opened her mouth, seeming to speak, when August the butler came into the room with a gentle tap to the door. "Good morning, ladies," he said with a small tilt of a smile.

They all turned their heads to him and addressed him with a good morning as well. Anita held in a giggle as she watched August step forward. August had been her family's butler since before Anita was born. And since she was young, August had never changed personality or even wardrobe. That included the silly worn out powdered wig he seemed to have always hung on to. The silly thing always, without fail, tilted to the left side of his head.

August approached Belle just as she was about to sip her tea. With a smile, he brought the hand behind his back around to show a stack full of envelopes. "Invitations, Miss Belle."

Belle's eyes widened just as she made a squealing noise before snatching the invitations from a chuckling August. Eloise crooned her voice to a high pitch just as she seized half of the envelopes from her daughter. Scanning through the addresses, Eloise sang even louder.

"Oh my, there are so many! Dear Belle, there are about

six invitations to balls and other letters to meet matrons for tea!" Eloise and Belle snuggled closer to each other to share the letters.

"Look mama, there is even one for an outing in the country! Oh, how much I have wanted to go to Kent." Belle practically glowed as Anita watched her sister across from her. Anita smiled at her as she glanced up from her letters with a wide grin. Though Anita was happy for her sister, she had a heavy heart. She hoped with all her soul that her sister did not suffer the same fate Anita had experienced. She looked at her sister now and hoped that she would find a man that would treat her with all the love in the world.

"Now, we must prepare for all these gatherings. We need to go to the dressmaker at once and order in some new dresses. Oh, and shoes! August, can you please be a dear and be sure our carriage gets ready for our departure." Eloise practically sang out her happiness. August tilted his head in a slight bow that only made his wig fall ever more to the side. He smiled slightly and flustered when he righted his wig, then he made his way out of the room.

"New dresses, mama?" Belle said cheerily, clasping the letters to her bosom.

"Of course, child! You must look your best in new company, and for these balls," Eloise answered as she patted her daughter's knee. She glanced over to Anita just as she picked up her cold cup of tea. "You will need some new dresses as well, Anita."

Anita nearly choked on her tea. She looked up at her mother. "Mama, surely I do not need any dresses. Belle will be attending these balls more than I."

"Nonsense, it is sure that you will be attending most of these balls. How else may you meet a suitable bachelor?" Her mother spoke matter-of-factly.

Anita sighed, unsure how to respond to her mother's promising response. It is not as though Anita did not want to marry; it was simply the idea of marrying a man she did not truly know scared her.

Already once had she been misled by the charming smile of a so-called gentleman...

Before her thoughts could invade her, August once again entered the room. His lips were drawn into a thin line.

"Miss Christina Godfrey, ladies." August's announcement sounded as if he had a cramp in his throat. He stood aside at the door entrance to allow Christina to enter.

Christina entered with a covered smirk. As she passed August, she patted his arm.

"Straighten up, old chap." She gestured a point towards the top of her head with a wink. August stifled a cough as he quickly corrected the drooping wig. He bowed slightly with a shy smirk before silently taking his leave.

Christina could not help but giggle slightly before turning fully back towards the room. "Sir August will never stop being a darling." Her eyes twinkled. Christina was dressed in a handsome gray day dress with black lace caressing the modestly low collar and long sleeves. Her hair was a brush of golden-brown silk combed up and pinned in a side curl.

Eloise perked up in her seat once she realized who the young Christina was. Immediately she rushed over to embrace Christina like a mother hen. "My word! This could not possibly be little Tina Godfrey! Oh, how you have grown, child. And so fetching as well. I bet the eligible bachelors are just crooning over you!" Eloise ended with a giggle.

Christina could not help but smile widely. She brushed a silk strand back over her ear as she answered. "Oh, I wouldn't say crooning. More like hiding, my Lady Hemmingway."

Eloise gasped dramatically, gently patted Christina's arm as she walked her back to the couch. "Dear me, I hope you aren't purposely frightening the boys away child." She sat her down between herself and Belle.

Belle faced Christina upon the seat as she reached forward to embrace her as well. "Christy! I'm so happy to see you again!"

Christina's eyes warmed as she embraced the little Belle she once braided hair with. "And I you, my darling Belle. You've blossomed into a stunning flower." She curled a strand of Belle's hair with her finger and smiled.

Belle blushed modestly before looking back over at Anita with a smile. Anita returned it as she sighed inwardly with relief. She was thankful to see Christina well. After the party, she had not heard a word from her friend since. Anita had felt guilty for leaving Christina behind as she scouted for a cabby that night.

"So, tell me dear, how is your father? Oh, would you care for some tea or breakfast?" Eloise asked cheerfully, already rising to pour a cup.

"Oh, please don't fret yourself, my Lady Hemmingway. I'm quite alri-" Christina didn't get the chance to finish her sentence before a cup of tea was already served in front of her. She smiled, holding in a breath and accepted the warm cup.

Eloise chuckled softly as she sat back down beside Christina. "So now, your father, how is he?"

Christina took a sip from her tea before answering nonchalantly. "He's doing reasonably well for an older fellow with a few gambling debts and a new mistress who is nearly the same age as I..." She sipped at her tea once more.

The room was silent, save for the noise from the streets now streaming through the morning windows. Suddenly Christina broke out in laughter and that same mischievous gleam in her eyes.

"Oh, dear me, did I say too much?! Please, let me re-phrase. My father is living happily in Kent now. He has found a new hobby in raising horses. Has been for the past five years now." Christina set down her cup of tea between the plates of half eaten food.

"Oh my... still spirited as ever, little Tina!" Eloise chuckled nervously as she pinched at her high collar. She lovingly patted Christina's hand before saying, "Well, sounds to me as though your father is still trying to fill that hole your dear mother had left behind. God rest her soul."

Anita noticed Christina's eyes had glazed over at the mention of her mother. She recalled the period when they were young, and she was told of what happened to the late Lady Silverton. When Christina was born, her mother's health had weakened after the stress of labor. She was able to pull through, but only to continue having health problems as Christina grew. It was till she was ten that Lady Silverton had succumbed to a fever and passed. Both Christina and her father had never been the family they once were.

In fact, while Christina's mother was still alive, Lord Silverton must have been worried with phobias for both his wife and daughter. After the birth of Christina, he had kept both under seclusion. Only after the death of his wife, it seemed like he died with her. Christina was left to do whatever she pleased; it never made any difference to her distant father.

"So, you now are taking care of his townhouse? Does it ever get lonesome there, child?" Eloise asked as she reached for her plate of eggs and bacon. She offered a spoonful of eggs to Christina.

Christina giggled before shaking her head at the eggs. "The townhouse is now mine to run. Father thought it as a good way to learn how to run my own household for whenever I get married. It is unbearably quiet and such a bore, but now that you all have arrived, it feels like old times again."

Christina glanced at Anita with a warm smile. She gifted Christina with one of her own. Indeed, when they were young, it was as though Anita's parents made Christina one of their own daughters. It was the least they can do after how much happiness the two girls brought each other.

"Like old times indeed! Except now, you girls are all grown up. And dear me, I'm getting old!" Eloise feigned a swooning gesture that caused all the ladies to giggle.

At that moment, August knocked gently before entering the room. He clicked his heels before announcing, "The carriage is ready, my Lady."

At that, Eloise perked up excitedly. "Oh, thank you August. Tell Smith we'll be there shortly."

August nodded and made his way out the room. Eloise glanced over to Anita and Christina. "Would you girls like to come with Belle and I to the dressmakers? We have many events approaching that we must prepare for." Eloise practically beamed.

Anita smiled but shook her head. "No, mama. Christina and I are going to stay and chat. The both of you are sure to have fun."

Eloise blew a raspberry at her eldest daughter. "Old times indeed! Even as a child, Anita, you never liked going dress shopping! Come along Belle! We'll be sure to look for dresses for your sister as well!" Eloise stood and adjusted her dress just as Belle rose.

"Be sure to continue visiting Christy! I wouldn't want you to miss any important events we'll be attending!" Belle said happily as she leaned down to embrace Christina in a hug.

"I'll be sure to, darling. Good luck!" Christina smiled as she squeezed Belle close.

The two ladies practically danced out of the room and out to the carriage. The room was quiet; a faint sound of ticking from the clock mantle in the hall absorbed the silence, the sounds from the streets chiming into the tune. Anita observed Christina's demeanor as she relaxed into the couch and took in a breath.

"Your mama has not changed after all these years. Still sweet and energetic as ever." Christina chuckled into her hand. "I believe Belle is forming into her image splendidly."

"In her own way, yes. But with the patience of father." Anita smiled lovingly of her sister.

Christina stretched her position on the couch so that one leg was set comfortably beneath her bottom. She leaned against the armrest as she took in a deep breath, signaling her satisfaction of the position.

Anita chuckled, observing the almost child-like position. "You look like a young girl like that."

"It is a finer and more comfortable way to sit in these blasted corsets." Christina laughed as she winked at Anita.

Anita smiled and shook her head slightly. She was glad to see her friend had never lost her free spirit. Christina always had an aura of wild charm, unbreakable wit, and endless beauty. Anita could not understand the haughtiness of others when it came to them being introduced to Christina.

A thought came to Anita as to the reasoning why Christina had chosen such a wild soiree to attend. Was she tempted to the life of scandal, or had she just merely wanted a moment to escape the tight chains of the Ton?

The thought of the soiree sent a chill caressing across Anita's nape. Without fail, her   mind quickly wandered to the dark library, with its silver glow, and the scent of cigars and spice.

"...are you listening, Annie?" Christina interrupted her thoughts.

Anita mentally shook her head and timidly smiled up at her friend. She could see her friend's curious gaze as she studied her.

"I'm sorry Christina, what did you say?" Anita asked.

"I asked you, where did you go?"

"Go...?" Anita asked, brows furrowing.

Christina's brows lifted then she sighed with a chuckle. "My, you were truly in a daze just now. I asked, the night of the party, where did you wander off to? I couldn't find you until I realized that you had gone."

Anita's eyes widened slightly before darting down to her fingers on her lap. She tried to tamper down the flustered feelings that began to form in the pit of her stomach. She was not certain if she should dare tell Christina of the encounter she had.

When Anita looked up at her friend, she could see the concerned expression on her face.

"Were you all right, Annie? Did something happen?"

"Everything was well... I ended up in the library until I realized it had become too late. So, then I left," Anita decided to say. She could not take any more of her friend's pointed stare, so she stood and walked over to the tea pot by the food and refilled her cup.

"What about you, Christina? The moment we walked through the doors you had disappeared." Anita turned from the table and did her best covered smile.

Christina opened her mouth slightly, and then closed it. She turned her gaze away from Anita, shielding her face. Anita quickly grew concerned for her friend, but as she made her way to Christina's side, she could see the faint red blush caressing across her cheeks.

"Christina...?"

Christina closed her eyes as her fingers gently touched across her lips. "I suppose I have a confession to make..."

Anita was fairly confused for a moment until she saw the serene smile caress Christina's face.

"I went to that party for a purpose. Please, Annie, don't think wrong of me when I speak this."

Anita smiled and nodded reassuringly.

"This is not my first soiree, Annie. In fact, I've been to perhaps more than my fair share of invited tea brunches." Christina chuckled to herself.

"I've grown to love these parties and have met a great deal of wonderful people. One of which has stuck out more than all the rest." Christina took a pause. She had wandered into her own daze for a moment.

Anita took this moment to study her friend's face. Christina had a look of awe on her as she thought of this one soul she spoke of. She still had admiration in her eyes when she said,

"I've grown to care for someone, very much so. He is the reason why I continue to go to these parties." With that being said, Christina looked up at Anita. The look she gave asked for Anita to be the confidante of her secret.

Anita smiled and took Christina's hand into her own. "Who is he?"

"I cannot say. At least not now... we are keeping it under seclusion." Christina half smiled.

Though Anita felt that she should be surprised, perhaps even shocked, she was not. This answered what she had wondered before. Christina was free and judging how no one seemed to notice her actions, cunning as well. Anita could not help admiring Christina's bravery to take control of her own life... even envied it a little.

She thought that if she had the same courage to do what she most desired, would she have come back to London? Would she have stayed at that party? Would have been able to let that man continue...?

Thinking of that night, Anita had to ask, "Why did

you take me to that party, Christina?"

"I honestly had to consider it, Annie. I was not certain at first to do so, but when I saw you at Belle's ball, I knew. You looked trapped. Silently begging to be free from there. It was a sign to me to take you." Christina's grip tightened around her hand.

Anita's eyes widened slightly but slanted away from Christina's gaze. She took in a deep breath. It was true, she had felt caged in. The truth was, being back in London was a prison.

She glanced down at their joined hands and patted her friend's hand. "Thank you... You always knew how I truly felt, Christy."

Christina let go of her hand to raise Anita's chin to catch her gaze. "I also know when you are hiding something, Annie. What truly happened at the soiree?"

Anita had to swallow; her throat suddenly grew dry. Her first response was uncertainty as to whether to confess to her friend what had happened that night. But looking deep into her friend's eyes, she knew Christina was still the trusted girl that Anita had confided everything to when they were children.

After a moment Anita took in a deep breath before speaking. "The library was a peaceful place to hide from that eccentric company. I had thought that would be a wonderful place to be alone, but I was wrong. A man came in. He was with a woman at first, but he soon dismissed her as soon as he discovered I was there."

Anita glanced at her friend and found the worried look in her eyes. She quickly responded, "Nothing terrible happened Christina, I assure you. I was safe from beginning to end."

Christina took in a comforting breath, then relaxed. "Then what happened...?"

Anita recalled the moment once more; the memory took her in almost as in a daze. "What happened next, I wish I can say it as though it made sense, but it really didn't. Nothing felt like it made any sense. He came toward me, and even when I would step away from him, it was as though we were linked. He came closer and closer, until we were practically in each other's embrace. The next thing I knew, he began to kiss me..."

Christina coughed quietly, and that drew Anita out of her trance. She looked to her friend and found the playful glint in her eye. "Did you two...?" Her brow rose.

Anita flushed. "No! We just kissed..." Anita was too flustered now to even dare bring up what the man did with his hands...

Christina blew a raspberry, "Well, then, what ended up happening between you two?"

Anita glanced away a bit embarrassed to say the next part but sighed anyway. "I ended up slapping him and... thanking him, then took off."

Anita did not look to her friend until the sudden roar of Christina's laughter filled the room.

"You slapped him, and then thanked him?!" Christina's laughter did not falter.

Anita's shoulders slumped as she made a face to her friend. "Yes...it's not that funny, Christina!"

"Yes, yes, it is!" Christina continued to chuckle. "Why did you thank him?" She wiped a tear from her eye.

Anita covered her face and grumbled, "I have no idea!" Then she slumped down into the couch.

That only caused Christina to laugh more. She covered her side complaining how it ached. Seeing that made Anita smile, until she could not hold it in anymore and she chuckled herself.

Christina began to calm and relax her side with only a few light chuckles escaping her lips. She continued to smile at Anita.

"Well then... did you at least enjoy it?" Christina asked.

Anita hesitated, unsure. Though it all happened at once, she could not lie to herself. She did enjoy it all, even the shock of allowing that man to touch her. The realization struck her, and she blushed. Anita looked up at Christina, bit her lip and nodded.

Christina gasped and with a clever glint in her eye

jokingly said, "Oh my Anita, you've tasted the wildlife, and enjoyed it!" She began to laugh.

Anita shook her head and smiled. She touched her brow and laughed. "I suppose I did... for that moment."

Once Christina settled, she rested her hand on her cheek and took a long sigh. "Describe to me how he looked."

"Why?" Anita wandered.

"Just for humour's sake. I would like to try to imagine this charming dream of yours. "She paused after seeing Anita's look. "I'm joking Annie, I'm not that off my wagon. But really, just to see if perhaps I may recognize him."

Anita took the moment to consider, and figured why not? She had admitted more than she thought she would, why not continue.

"He was tall, if I were to guess, perhaps about six feet. Dark hair, a bit long on all sides. It was hard to tell since the room was dark, but his skin looked warm, like desert sand. Nothing like the usual men around London. Rather exotic. He smelled of cigar and spices. But it was his eyes that captured me, Christina. They were black as onyx, and his stare was transfixed on me. So intent, and yet yearning." Anita paused, she realized that night would forever be engraved in her dreams.

Christina looked at her friend with a small smile, she saw in her friend's eyes the same look she had for her gentleman. Christina recalled the details of the man Anita described.

"So, we have a fellow who is sun kissed, rugged, smells of cigars and spices, and lastly has black colored eyes. Hmm." Christina thought for a moment.

"Did he look like a regular man? A merchant perhaps?" Christina asked.

"I don't suppose so. His garments were very well tailored, like a gentleman would wear. He moved and spoke in such a way that was intellectual, blunt, and heated." Anita blushed after saying, "He was certainly very comfortable in taking charge."

Christina quickly looked at her friend, even as Anita stood up to walk towards the curtain opening of the windows. Christina gasped silently at an idea of a possible person. It could not be, but if it was, perhaps...? She steadied her thoughts. There was no way of knowing, unless...

Christina rose and stood with her friend next to the window. They both looked out at the street and watched carriages ride by. The sun beamed true as Christina faced her friend.

"If you had the chance to meet him again, Annie, would you?"

Anita looked at her friend and caught the awareness in her voice. If given the opportunity to meet this man again, even for once more, would she?

Anita let out a breath that she did not realize she held.

∞∞∞

Bram scanned through the list of names of actors for the upcoming production. He wrote out contracts for each one. He knew now how it was proper business to formulate boundaries with the performers, and to better deal with dilemmas if they arise.

Bram picked up a glass of cognac that was sitting beside his left arm and let out a hefty exhale. His gaze flew to the note crumbled on the floor by the furnace. About a week ago he cancelled the last ballet spectacle, and immediately began making plans for a new showing. He had felt instantly inspired at the time. A muse had set him on his path.

He would smile at the thought whenever it occurred as he prepared. The memory of that woman had turned into a flaming curiosity. A burning need to the possibility of seeing her again. The funny thing he had thought was how he could not forget her eyes, soft voice, and the biting slap she had surprisingly delivered.

He thought that this play may bring her to him. If he promoted exactly right, it may inspire her to come to his opera and watch, and from that wishful chance he could have the opportunity to devour her. If she let him...

Another grin sprang from his lips. Bram never experienced a woman refusing him, or at least teasing him in such a way and then running away from his advances. It appeared to him afterwards as a challenge, one he felt no objection to. He was astounded, however. He never felt such desire and confusion before over a woman.

Bram's gaze fell back to the crumpled note on the floor. His grin instantly died. Bram's chamberlain for the theater, Troy, delivered the message this morning. The man looked reluctant to give it to Bram, and that was when he felt uneasy. It now made sense why. When Bram opened the note, he was astounded by its contents. One of his brows had quirked when he read it.

Lord Kenwood,

What you had done to me was unforgivable! You made me believe that there was more between us than a fuck! You used me! You used your charms and title to woo me into your bed, and then tossed me aside as if I was nothing. I swear to you, that if you do not make haste, and call on me, I will show you what it means to be used.
I shall wait on you,
B.

It took Bram a moment to realize who had written the letter. It was the ballerina from the last performance. She had the nerve to write to him, even attempted to intimidate him. He scoffed at the note. Charmed her with his title? The little chit came pouncing on him the moment she learned who Bram was. He had barely said a word before SHE pulled him towards one of the dressing rooms.

Slightly amused by her attempted threat, Bram crumbled the note and tossed it. He had grander things to mull over. Bram needed to immediately begin production. The actors were in order, the contracts were written, the stage crew and costume makers were informed, he found a director to lead the play, and now he just needed the music.

As if on cue, a knock sounded at the door. Bram gulped the remainder of his drink and sat up in his chair. "Come in."

Sebastian came through the door and gave Bram a smug look. He approached the desk with his hands behind his back. "Hard at work?"

"Kent, just the man I wanted to see. I do hope that's sheet music behind your back and not a pistol," Bram answered with a grin.

Sebastian laughed lightly. His turquoise eyes were glinting as he brought the written music around his back. "If it was a pistol, you would have no way of knowing until it was purposely brought to your attention."

Bram chuckled, knowing full well the truth behind that statement. One of the Rakes of Springfield, Sebastian Kent, the Earl of Rockfield was one of the most popular scoundrel women fawned over. Not that he would notice anymore. Compared to the time they first met, Sebastian was much more resigned than he was. Being shipped to London as a youth, Sebastian arrived crossed and betrayed, eventually forgotten until one day, in his mid-twenties his departed father surprisingly left him the late title.

Bram had asked why it was so surprising one night, and Sebastian looked to him swallowing back a bottle of strong aged wine and a faraway expression of bitterness. "My father was the one who betrayed me."

It had taken Bram a moment to realize, but he did remember the first time the two of them met. Bram had stumbled upon Sebastian, drunk, and looking for him to duel. Bram suspected the duel would not last long considering how drunk Sebastian looked, but the man was polished when it came to boxing. Bram had ended up throwing insults in hopes of distracting the man, but once he slandered the late Duke of Rockfield, Sebastian had become relentless with the fists and a monstrous glint in his eye. Given the fact Bram had no notion on why this man was seeking him to duel, once they separated Bram called out to him.

"Who do you think you are?! I have no quarrel with you," Bram huffed.

"Not with me, friend. And my name is Kent. Remember it," exclaimed Sebastian.

"You're drunk, FRIEND. Clearly we do not know each other." Bram circled the man. He tried to be furious, but he could not help noticing the man's passive expression. Beneath his red gaze, was raw ache.

"How do you know me?" asked Bram.

Sebastian dropped his fists, stood his ground, and bore into Bram. He drew in a ragged breath.

"Your father agreed to advocate for me in London. He played a part in ruining my life." Sebastian took a step towards Bram.

Bram did not move, allowed Sebastian to reach two feet away from him before speaking. "My father is dead."

"I know. Tis a shame I had not come sooner. But alas, I have you to slay the blame on." Sebastian shoved at Bram and approached him. When he had reached close enough to meet his gaze, Sebastian pulled out a monogrammed silver pistol.

Bram did not flinch, just simply regarded the man.

"You dare not draw back?" Sebastian asked.

Bram shook his head slowly. "Clearly, you have been wronged. And since my blamed father cannot be here to attest, might as well be I."

Sebastian paused, contemplating Bram. After a moment, he drew back, and turned his back on him. Bram could see the man's hand clenched in a fist. In what seemed like a long wait, Sebastian finally began to walk away. Bram collected himself and watched the man and his shadow walk down the dirt path and away from sight.

It took Bram less than a month to locate Sebastian Kent. He was shacked up in a bordello, high on opium, and pleasing every woman in sight. Bram picked him up and insisted he come with him to Springfield's. After some convincing, and a few strong cups of coffee, Sebastian finally agreed. It was there he was introduced to Richard and Sterling. Since then, Bram learned of Sebastian's history with his father. He had also come to find Sebastian's love for music.

Bram had decided to ask Sebastian to write the occasional sheet music for plays. As time progressed, Bram now saw the passive Earl for who he was. Loyal, talented, and brave. However, Bram could still see the raw ache left in the man's eyes and hear it in the longing music he wrote.

"Your letter was quite a surprise to me. I had thought the ballet was going well. The reviews gave it mention." Sebastian's words broke Bram's thoughts.

"Yes, well, I decided it would be best to end short. Allow the production to move on to other cities. Besides, I have a good feeling about this play." Bram smiled, more to himself than to Sebastian.

Sebastian's brow rose as he observed Bram. "Or more like your cock fell into the wrong hen house."

Bram grinned. Sebastian had traits Bram always favored, and one was his ability to be straightforward and blunt with his words. He chuckled before answering.

"Perhaps. But more to the point, I am eager to start this showing. I hope your music is ready?"

Sebastian placed the sheet music in front of Bram on the desk. The pages were crisp with precise inked scales of tunes.

"I did my best, but with only a week's notice, I reluctantly wish to say that this is a rough draft. By when were you thinking of beginning the show?"

Bram scanned through the pages. "I wish it at the beginning of next month."

Sebastian scoffed. Taking a seat in the wooden velvet chair in front of the desk. The man's coat almost nearly matched. It was clear he was in deep thought until the moment his gaze fell upon Bram's empty glass.

"Would you care for a drink?" Bram asked.

"Do you have any wine?" Sebastian asked dryly.

Bram shook his head. "I haven't had time to purchase more since the last you came, my apologies."

Sebastian waved it off. Bram admired the man's control. He had not had a strong glass of liquor since the times at the bordello. Being in good company and music to focus on helped Sebastian slowly walk away from his demons. Not before the rumors of his debauchery spread, however. The ladies at the bordello praised his name, nicknaming him the Insatiable Kent.

"Why on earth are you rushing this? It's not like you," Sebastian stated. He focused in on the ink stains on his fingers, no doubt from the music sheets he hurriedly wrote. "Besides, didn't you have that theater house you wanted to start building?"

"'Tis a challenge I was given, and in no way will I fail in this," Bram answered solidly. "And I've already informed the builders to expect my blueprints by mid-May."

Sebastian looked up and examined his friend. Never had he witnessed such determination in the man's eyes. Perhaps like the night Bram fetched him from that cathouse, but now different. Sebastian was not certain of what. But he paid it no mind. He knew Bram would explain in a matter of time, after he pulled himself out of this focused state.

"Are you coming to my début showing?" Sebastian decided to change the subject. Bram was still reading the music sheets when he answered.

"When is it?" he asked.

"A week from now." Sebastian tried to lick off the ink spots.

Bram sighed, "Why is it that you and Philip always have parties near the same time? It gets in the way of a man's business."

Sebastian smirked. "Perhaps it's due to the fact we invite the same company, they are ever seeking our soirées. You will enjoy it, Bram. I discovered a violinist fresh from Spain. A woman. It was rare to hear one play with such passion, I just had to choose her for the début. Are you listening, Bram?" Sebastian then noticed the faraway look in his friend's eyes.

Bram had been struck with Sebastian's words. Philip's and Sebastian's parties did usually carry the same crowd of invitees. If that were the case, then maybe, there was a chance Bram would see that woman. A sudden doubt caressed his nape. He had never seen that woman in any party before Philip's soiree; what were the chances he would see her? Then again, Bram was guilty of never attending a function long enough to notice. He had taken up the habit of whisking off women who desired him.

Now, Bram thought, he would wait. He would wait until he spotted her. His chest heated at the thought, the chance of seeing her. The possibilities. A slow smile inched across his face.

"Bram?!"

Bram's gaze fell upon Sebastian. The man had on an annoyed look. "There's no need to shout, Kent."

"No, there wouldn't be, except for when a friend is clearly dozing out of a conversation. Damn man, did you hear anything I said?"

Bram gave him a pointed stare and smiled, "What time is the début?"

"Evening. As usual." Sebastian stood up, made his way to Bram's cigar box and helped himself to one. He clipped off the end and tasted the fresh tobacco's edge. He began to walk towards the door, stopping and looking back at Bram before saying. "You shall have your music by the end of the month, you crazed mutt."

Just before he stepped through the door, Bram called out, "I dare not doubt that, Le Insatiable Kent."

Sebastian smirked back at Bram and gave him a one finger salute then walked out of the office. Bram chuckled and focused down at the sheets on his desk. Suddenly Bram felt heat build in his neck; he reached for the collar and loosened it.

The possibilities were in sight. Bram could not ignore the hope building in his chest. What if he did see the woman at the debut? How would he react? Remembering how things had ended, clearly, he had to consider his approach. He could not simply advance on her and hope she would fall into his arms, or worse, refuse him. He would have to tread carefully.

Bram opened a drawer from his desk. He pulled out the dance card the woman had left behind. Knowing full well dance cards were passed among balls and gatherings of high society, Bram suspected the woman must have come directly from one. If that were the case, Bram felt the heat pass along his nape; that would mean this woman may be a part of the Ton. He drew in a sigh, unsure how to consider it.

It was hard for Bram to trust a society where he grew

up experiencing harsh judgment and intolerance towards change. He learned enough watching his father and mother outcast because of who they were. His father, a bastard Earl, and his mother, a Moroccan actress. The pair had been disowned by the Ton, leaving them alone. His mother had carried on, raising Bram with all the love in the world. His father's reputation, however, had suffered. Especially when it came to business.

Bram's grip tightened around the armrest. His father had been ignored by valued business Lords, leaving him to rely off the earnings of his lands. Numerous years had suffered because of bad crops. His father did his damnedest to scrape and preserve the properties. The hardship had left his father bitter, and eventually the stress had brought him fevers. He passed on, leaving Bram the title, and his estates in shambles.

After witnessing his father's downfall, Bram made an oath to never find himself scraping by. He would work hard, live the life he wanted, and stay the hell away from the Ton. He found other means to rise and become successful. The L'Opera Magenta was built, its exquisite architecture becoming popular amongst numerous classes of people. Bram had collected several construction investments that had earned more than enough to raise his title's name on the list of well to do Earls. He did all of this without the connections of the Ton.

Bram glanced back down at the dance card in his hand. The woman had seemed like everything Bram ever wanted. But what if it was just an illusion? Something that Bram had wanted to see? What if this woman was cruel in judgment? Hiding behind an angel's face?

Bram would rather be cast out than to be forced into a marriage against his will. Or worse, be fooled into one. If this was the case, he thought, then should he go to the debut? Should he approach her now knowing the likelihood that she was a lady of high society?

Bram set the dance card back into the drawer. He stood and walked to the decanters of liquor. He chose his favorite cognac and as he was about to pour, Bram paused. He remembered the woman's eyes. They were looking straight into him.

Chapter 4

London
One week later
The Earl of Rockfield's Estate

Anita could not believe she was in this household, with many guests passing through the art covered halls. Upon arrival, Christina exclaimed how the Earl of Rockfield's home was truly an inspiring sight. She had described it as another Louvre but smaller, and she was not jesting. The large estate housed various halls decorated with art from different regions. Anita was in awe as she passed one long hall adorned with Parisian art.

Towards the end of the hall, Anita noticed a handful of paintings that had a similar model. The last portrait held the same beautiful woman, sitting comfortably at a desk, a bookshelf in her background, and holding an artist's brush and palette. Above all, Anita noticed the woman's elegant hand resting at the edge of her cheek. A serene smile shined through the painting. The woman was happy when this portrait was done.

Suddenly Anita felt someone stopped beside her. Glancing over her right shoulder, she saw a man dressed in a velvet blue tailcoat and black trousers. His eyes were highlighted from the coat color. The man's dirty blond hair waved across his head, lengthening at the nape. He had a passive faraway look in his eyes, and Anita could not help but wonder what he was thinking.

Anita glanced back to the portrait. She cast a look down the hallway, checking to see if Christina was near. But she was not. Anita hoped she had not lost Christina again. Especially after her friend promised to not leave her side, but she told her she was to fetch the host of the début and introduce them.

"Do you care for the painting?" the man to her right suddenly asked. His tone was calm.

Anita cast a widened look towards him, surprised that he spoke without introduction. But once she saw his small smile, Anita felt unusually comfortable in his presence. She looked back at the painting before answering.

"She is undoubtedly the most elegant woman I have ever seen. I could see why she was painted several other times."

The man chuckled, "You have an eye for art. How did you know it was the same woman, when among all the others, she is depicted differently?"

"It's the smile, and the shape of the eyes. They are similar."

The man nodded, understanding, and yet surprised at Anita's observations.

Anita looked at the man and noticed his features. "If I may, you and this woman have fairly similar traits."

The man smiled, "Well I would hope so. She is my mother."

Anita was stunned for a moment, remembering that at least two of the other paintings were a touch inappropriate. But as she observed the man's passive eyes, she could tell he was waiting for her to react. She smiled softly at him, "She is exceptionally beautiful. Was she in Paris when she modeled?"

The man had paused before answering, scanning Anita's face. "She was born there. At only sixteen, she became the apprentice to Louis-Léopold Boilly. She was proud to be a painter, and that pride grew when her paintings began to get notice."

"That's quite an accomplishment for a woman of her time. What happened to her next?"

The man's features changed. His lips grew tight, and the light in his eyes faded ever so slightly. "She married.

Whisked off to another country. She tried to continue painting, but not being in the city, her art went unnoticed. She became a possession, and a lot less of the free spirit she was."

Anita observed the man's face. Saw the cold memories cross his gaze. She gently touched his sleeve and offered a warm smile. "And then she had you, her greatest masterpiece, I'm sure."

The man's features softened as his gaze fell upon hers. He nodded and smiled up at his mother's portrait. Before Anita could say another word, she heard Christina's call for her down the hallway.

She was quickly approaching as she said, "There you are?! I've been looking everywhere for you, darling!"

"I'm right where you left me. I thought I lost you again," Anita answered.

Christina giggled and grinned at her friend, "Not you, Annie. I was talking to Sebastian, here."

Anita was confused for a moment, until she turned and saw who she now knew as Sebastian grin back at Christina before doing a half bow.

"If I knew that the great Godfrey Rose wanted to see me, I would have hurried my way to her side," Sebastian answered with a glint in his eye.

Christina laughed, embracing Anita's arm around her own. "Oh, I'm sure you would, you charmer. Well, the reason I wanted to find you was to introduce you to my dear friend. But it seems you two have already become acquainted."

"I suppose you could say that. She and I were exchanging opinions about the artwork. In no way however was I given the pleasure of knowing her name." Sebastian took a step forward to capture Anita's hand and brought it to his lips.

Anita was reeling over the sudden outward conversation. And when Sebastian grasped her hand gently, she could not stop the soft heat forming across her cheeks. She smiled but before speaking, Christina answered.

"Allow me then to appease you. Sebastian, this is Annie." Anita cast a quick side glance to her friend. "Annie, this is Sebastian Kent, our host."

Bowing, Sebastian kissed Anita's hand. As he rose, he gifted the two ladies the most charming smile Anita had ever seen on a man. However, something in the way that grin did not reach his eyes gave her pause.

"Annie, it is an honor to have you in my home. Please, become acquainted with the art. And I do hope you will stay for the début. I have welcomed quite a gem to come play for us tonight."

"Is it anything like the last musician you showcased? What was his name? Anton…?" Christina asked.

"Rubinstein. He is doing quite well for himself, now that he released his piano concerto. But no, this musician is nothing like Mr. Rubinstein. In fact, she is a violinist fresh from Spain." Sebastian grinned in satisfaction. Clearly, he was pleased at finding such a musician.

Both Christina and Anita smiled in wonder. Anita finally spoke, asking, "Who is she?"

"Her name is Mariela Donizetti. The daughter of Giovanni Donizetti, the violinist. I met her father last year when I was finishing my tour across Spain. He insisted I hear her play, and believe me ladies, you are in for a treat. Her music invokes a sense of awe and longing the likes I have not heard from another in a long while," Sebastian had answered finally with a faraway look in his eyes.

Anita had a sense that Sebastian was harboring a lot of memories. Whether they were good or bad, she was not certain, just that she could tell he often got lost in them. At that moment, Sebastian brought his full attention back on them. He grinned before saying, "Be sure to make it down to the art gala at eight o'clock to get good seats. I'm certain it will fill up quickly."

"I believe they will if she is anything like her father. I have read about Giovanni Donizetti. He is an exquisite violinist. Growing up with him as a mentor, I do not doubt her talents. We'll be sure to make it for good seating, just as soon as we meet with Miriam," Christina remarked.

Sebastian nodded, placing his hand over his chest, he commented, "I shall look forward to witnessing the two of your responses. As for Miriam, I last saw her in the garden by the west wing. Forgive me if I do not accompany you, I must check on other arrangements before the showing."

Christina looked pleased before swinging Anita's arm around her own. She began to half turn away before replying, "Not to worry. We shall escort ourselves to the garden. Good tidings, Kent!"

With that, Christina pulled Anita to follow. They reached the end of the hall when Anita finally spoke again. "Christina, who is this Godfrey Rose? And that was terribly informal of you to introduce us with just my nickname."

They passed a few halls adorned with medieval art and guests before Christina turned left down a longer hall embellished with Greek statues. Anita almost felt unnerved over how well Christina knew where she was going, and the feeling tipped further when Anita began noticing the exposed anatomies of the Greek art pieces.

"If you have not noticed my dear, our company isn't exactly formal. In fact, none of them introduce themselves with their title. They don't care about that." Christina noticed Anita casting glances at the statues and pushed her gently closer with a giggle.

Anita scowled with a laugh at her friend before pushing her back. Once they reached the end of the hall, they turned the corner and approached two long doors that opened to the gardens. Anita's eyes widened to the beauty of it.

The gardens were largely encased in four wide circles: a fountain connecting them all at its center. Within them, different shades of colors of foreign and domestic flowers the likes Anita had never seen paired together. The sun was setting in the distance, descending an enchanting awe across the yards. Anita was immediately captivated, so engrossed that she did not notice the feminine presence approaching them until she heard Christina speak.

"Miriam! So good to see you!"

"And I you, darling. I feared for the worst when I couldn't find anyone to my liking," Miriam exclaimed.

Anita smiled as she observed the woman. She was beautiful beyond compare. She wore a deep purple dress that hung low across her shoulders. Her lush dark brown hair was curled and pinned with a diamond headpiece to the side, cascading down her shoulder. She also wore a lovely diamond choker to match. As Anita listened to the two ladies talking, she could not help but admire the woman's almond shaped eyes and the lightly dusted freckles across her nose. The woman spoke with purpose and clearly Anita could tell she had an inner wisdom beyond her years. When the woman cast a glance over to Anita, she laid her full attention on her.

"Where are my manners? Good evening, my name is Miriam. And you are?" Miriam reached out to grasp Anita's hand and shook it.

Anita smiled pleasantly and shook it back before answering. "How do you do? My name is Anita Henderson, daughter of – "

"Oh, there's no need for that, my dear. We are all equals here. In fact, if I were you, I would keep that on the low. You wouldn't want anyone to know a lady was here in this company." Miriam spoke matter-of-factly.

Christina laughed before answering, "What of you Miriam? Everyone knows you're Lady Barnsdale."

Miriam smirked, "Well that's different, I'm a widow. And American. No one cares about that."

Anita's ears perked at that. "You're American?"

Miriam nodded as she grinned. "As are you?"

Anita smiled wide and nodded. "How did you know?"

"Your accent. From where have you sailed?"

"Pennsylvania. And you?"

"My late husband found me in New York. And he just had to ship me back to London to show off. Unfortunately, the passage back did not suit his health. He passed leaving me here to fend for myself. Luckily, London has been good to me. Shall we walk the gardens?"

Both ladies agreed, and they walked down the steps and onto the dirt path around the garden circles. As Miriam and Christina chatted, Anita thought over what Miriam had said about titles and the company they were amongst. They stopped to admire a statue of a satyr chasing two nymphs in mid transformation. It had live English roses cascading down the length of their bodies. Anita gently touched Christina's arm. "Is the Godfrey Rose your nickname here?"

Christina hid a wicked grin before laughing out loud. Miriam smirked, whereas Anita looked on in confusion.

"I suppose I have another confession to make to you, Annie. A few years back, I grew so tired of the normal day to day life. I was most certainly not popular among my own. I was caged up in my home practically wilting away." Christina paused, considering what she was saying. "I made the decision to break out. I went to theaters and art galas. That is when I met Miriam, and she advised me on how to live the life I wanted, safely. I was able to get involved with play productions, and that is where I created my name. Most everyone just calls me Rose."

"After your mother?" Anita asked gently.

Christina's eyes softened, and she smiled at her friend. "Yes. In her honor."

Anita nodded. She had suspected that was the reasoning behind Christina's latest actions. She knew her friend was too spirited to be kept behind dead walls. Again, she admired Christina and her lust for life. Being around her again sparked something deep inside Anita that she did not even notice was missing. Anita yearned for a life of her own as well. To live without the worry of consequences from her family and the Ton. She missed the wilds of America, where it had felt like an adventure every day. Perhaps, there was a way she could have that here in London.

"You're certainly not wilting away now that Richard is in your life," Miriam said nonchalantly.

Anita turned to her friend as soon as she noticed Christina blushing harshly. To her surprise, Christina did not deny it. Her friend looked at her with a bashful smile and nodded. "I guess the truth is out. Well sort of, Anita has not yet met Richard."

"Oh, I'm certain she soon will. He is coming tonight, is he not? And he will be pursuing you without a doubt," Miriam declared.

"You never know; he may have business to attend to." Christina's voice sounded breathy.

"Business with whom, your underskirts?" Miriam laughed into her fan.

Both Anita and Christina gasped. Christina nudged Miriam's arm before adding, "Don't speak that way in front of Anita. You'll shock her!"

"Oh, come now, Anita was thinking the same way." Miriam grinned.

Anita could not help the smirk that was spreading across her face. In truth, that was what she was thinking. But she still could not help asking, "Is he courting you?"

Now it was Miriam and Christina who gasped. Christina looked down at the walkway before answering, "It's complicated, I'm afraid. He and I are comfortable where we are."

"Or more like he only knows you as the Godfrey Rose, and not the Honorable Christina Godfrey, daughter to Lord Silverton," Miriam spoke silently.

Christina cast a look to Miriam that said for her to keep silent, but once Christina saw Anita looking at her to confirm the truth, she sighed. She nodded her head slowly. "I'm afraid that's true too. But like I said, tis complicated."

"Complicated enough that you cannot tell him who you are?" Anita asked quietly.

Christina took in a deep breath as she stopped to face both Miriam and Anita. "What is happening between Richard and I will remain private. All I ask from the two of you is to support my actions, and not to judge."

Anita touched Christina's arm and showed her concern. The last thing she wanted was for her friend to feel like she was being offended. "I am on your side, Christina. I just want you to be careful and happy."

Something in Christina's eyes was pleading before she spoke. "Believe me when I say that I am, Annie."

Anita nodded reassuringly. Miriam looked at the two of them and scoffed, tapping the edge of her fan against Christina's shoulder. "Darling, we are the last people here to ever judge you. Look at us, I'm with an imbecile with a perfect rump, and your friend here is looking for a man who she doesn't know yet."

Anita's face flushed hotly as she looked to Christina with an accusing frown. Christina shook her head as she raised both her hands up. Miriam's eyebrow rose as she examined both women.

"My dears, no proper lady comes to these parties looking to dance formally and have an escort. There's only a handful of reasons to come to these gatherings. And judging by your reactions, I was right to assume you are here to find a man."

Anita willed her flush to disappear as she considered confessing. She was hesitant but sensed that Miriam was certainly not the kind to judge like the rest of the women in the Ton. Perhaps, she may even know the man that Anita had encountered. Gaining her strength, Anita admittedly nodded, looking Miriam directly in the eyes.

Miriam smiled wide and drew Anita close until both their arms embraced. She walked them towards the end of the garden path and sat on the bench there.

"So, what sort of man are you looking for?" Miriam asked directly.

Anita was taken aback for a moment, suddenly envisioning the man that had played amok in her dreams for the past two weeks. How could she best describe such a man?

"She has already met him. But their meeting was brief, so she doesn't know who he is." Christina announced, and smiled apologetically as Anita cast her a look.

"Oh, well we can still try to work with that. Where did you meet him?" Miriam asked comfortably. Anita could sense how much Miriam wanted to help, with no judgment in her eyes.

"At the masquerade ball Christina took me to," Anita explained.

"At Philip's ball?" Miriam's eyebrows rose as she looked between Christina and Anita. At Christina's nod, Miriam chuckled. "What a gathering to be meeting a man. That night was just filled with all sorts of surprises."

Anita could not agree more. It was a strange night for her, where nothing had made sense.

"Perhaps it was all because of that blue moon, strange and magical things always happen on nights like those." Miriam inspected the edge of her fan.

"Do you believe in that sort of thing, Miriam?" Christina asked.

Miriam glanced up at the two ladies with a half smirk and then stood. "Perhaps, but I believe more of the likely chance that whomever Philip had invited, Sebastian had done the same. They are associated with the same crowd. The man you are looking for is probably in there right now."

Anita was struck by Miriam's words. If it was true, then the chances were likely that she would see him again. Anita had not fully thought out on how she would react if she encountered the man again. She knew what she was doing was scandalous, but Anita felt this need to break free. She was tired of missing her home in Pennsylvania, weary of the fact that she was confined in London. Anita was curious about where things may lead if she continued this. She was well past the age of courting, there was no worry about having suitors. Her mother would be too busy with Bella to notice. But then, Anita remembered her experience back in her old hometown, and the pain she caused her mother.

"Annie, are you coming?" Christina called.

Anita looked up seeing Christina and Miriam already half away from her. She stood and straightened her gown. She mentally shook her head and thought that in no way was this like what happened at home. She was making her own choices now. And knew that she was not going to get involved in any courting sham again. Besides, she ended up thinking, who knew what would happen?

By the time they made it to the art gala that was interestingly located a floor below the main hall, the room was half full of attendants. Most of the front rows were taken and the middle and back were quickly filling up. Sebastian was not jesting when he said to arrive early, Anita thought. She was about to suggest three seats located by the west wall when Anita noticed Christina and Miriam not beside her.

Miriam had wandered to a corner with a pair of men standing and having a conversation. Anita noticed one of the men, a tall dark-haired fellow with a clean-shaven face and a well-tailored roasted chestnut colored suit, smiled wide as she approached and embraced Miriam by the waist. Christina had been stopped near the entrance by a man Anita could not make out. He was standing with his back to her, so all Anita could see was the charming smile and happy glint in Christina's eyes. She saw the man stroke her friend's cheek before, to her dismay, grasping her hand and making their way out of the gala.

Anita sighed, happy for her friend, but still not looking forward to sitting by herself. When she turned to locate the seats she had spotted earlier, they were taken. Perturbed, she found a seat at the back of the audience. When all the attendees began to settle, Anita saw the host, Sebastian, step out onto a little stage in front. The guests began to clap as he greeted them with a half bow.

"I am pleased to have you all here to witness a star in the making. Allow me to introduce to you all, the splendid Miss Mariela Donizetti."

The audience clapped as a young woman stepped onto the stage. She was holding her violin against her and clutching the bow. Anita could make out she was dressed in a modest light cream-colored gown, her hair unbound, lusciously curled and long all around. She had her eyes closed. To Anita, she looked foreign and exquisite; and when she opened her eyes, there was determination firing through them.

The woman began to play, and immediately Anita was taken aback. Her eyes fell as she listened carefully to each tune played. There was a sense of yearning and inspiration behind the woman's music, and Anita allowed it to wash over her soul. She smiled, feeling herself come alive.

The music reminded her of a soft warm breeze passing through a large echo forest. Dancing leaves filling the air, and a cloudless sky, the sun warm against the skin. It reminded her of home. Of the long days of peace and quiet, with only a good book and a cup of tea to sooth the longing.

Her gaze slid open as she recalled the simple days, only to realize that they were miles away.

Before Anita could envision anymore, she thought she felt a soft shiver pass along her back. She glanced to her left and observed guests sitting down the row, enchanted by the music. Each one of them swaying softly with the melody, as she had. When she turned to glance to her right, she stared into two very dark black eyes.

Anita gasped silently, frozen in her seat. Her mind stopped all thought as her senses consumed control. For a fleeting moment, Anita almost wanted to close her eyes. The man's scent, cigars, and spice, made her heart race. The look in his eyes, determined and yet covetous, brought about the realization that he was real and staring daringly into her.

She had no certainty of what to do, nor say. She was lost, barely acknowledging that he was reaching out. When he grasped her hand, she felt chills run across her nape. His gaze tore from hers as he looked down at her fingers, almost examining them. She took the chance to study his features. The dark library did little justice for this man's appearance. He was beyond handsome, save for a slight scar above his left eyebrow. His hair was dark brown, reminding her of cherry wood. He had a barely visible shadow of facial hair that Anita had to refrain from the urge to caress.

When his eyes lifted, there was a look that Anita recognized. It was desire, and a knowing. He knew Anita wanted him. He could see it by the way she licked her lips, in which she could not hold back. He made her mouth dry, her blood race, and other private areas throb in ways she never felt before. When she thought he was going to speak, he stood, adjusted himself, causing her to blush, and walked out from the gala. Her gaze followed his shadow until he fell out of sight.

Anita drew in a much-needed breath. Her mind reeled over the reality of his presence. He was here. He was real. And he sought her out. She bit her lip as she held back a smile and looked down at her gloved hands. Her brows furrowed as she realized a small note was tucked into her palm. Her eyes widened as she glanced around. No one seemed to notice the encounter. The music continued playing. With that in mind, she opened the letter in her lap.

If you wish, meet me in the East wing. I'll be eagerly awaiting your arrival on the staircase.

Anita crumpled the note in both her hands, suddenly conflicted. He wanted to meet, and he was leaving it up to her to make the choice. She breathed in slowly, calming her racing heart. Anita had to remind herself that she was no fainting beauty, but a sensible wallflower. The situation had turned into what she had least expected. When she arrived at this gathering, she had not been fully convinced that she would see him again. But now that he was here, and had even approached her, she was stunned.

Several scenarios played across her mind. If she chose not to go, then she would rightfully keep her modesty intact. If she did not, however, she would always wonder what could have happened. She forced herself to carefully weigh her options. Gazing amongst the crowd, she thought of the chances that something like this would ever happen again, with a man who stole her senses and left her heart racing. The likelihood was grim, and becoming a spinster was a greater possibility. The idea was depressing.

No, if she was to grow old and alone, then she would rather have a beautiful memory to look back on. With a man she chose. And a secret she would longingly keep. Using the music to gain courage, Anita stood and adjusted her gown. She quietly made her way up to the exit and began walking down the hall to where she suspected was the East wing.

Bram tried not to pace across the first level of the staircase landing. He did not need to draw attention to himself or look a fool when the woman came to meet him. If she even decided to come, Bram thought prudently. He decided to make her choose. If she were really a high-class woman, she wouldn't make this choice lightly, perhaps would not even come at all.

The thought sent an unnerving, disappointing feeling through his gut. He had planned before the party to give her his note if she were to show. He even arrived earlier than usual. It had certainly surprised Sebastian who had thought he was not coming. But his friend dismissed it and had welcomed him to his private chambers for drinks. As the hours passed, the other rakes of Springfield arrived and were escorted in.

Everyone was dressed in their finest, but as they merrily chatted with each other, Bram grew more tense. He knew by now guests were roaming the estate, and he could not help wondering if one of them was the woman. He could not understand why he needed to see her; perhaps it was due to the recent deprived pleasure he had experienced. But after seeing her in the gala, he finally understood why.

When he had spotted her sitting alone, softly swaying to the violin's music, he could see the longing on her face. The same kind of look he knew he owned. And when he sat close to her, what he witnessed before, he saw again. She was waiting for him. Her eyes drew him in, and it took everything he had to not pull her out that gala.

Bram noticed he was pacing once more. He stopped and grasped the wood rail. She had not come yet. Bram was telling himself not much time had passed by, he was just being impatient. But the sudden thought of her not coming struck him once more. Even if she did, what should he say? The plan of conversation had not come to mind, and the realization unnerved him. He knew he could not simply have his way with her. He would have to converse.

The thought gave him pause, and a feeling of uneasiness swirled through his gut. Suddenly, a movement caught his eye, and he glanced down the upcoming stairway. His breath caught as he sighted a dark brown halo coming into view. A slim woman, with an easy grin walked past him. Her gaze stayed on him as she crossed, and her smile grew. Bram looked away, divulged in his thoughts. She had not come.

Gripping the rail, he decided it was more than enough time since he gave her the note.

Bram went down the stairs and walked towards the west wing hall. He wondered if it was wise to make his way back to the gala. The thought of seeing her unmoved and un-interested felt like it would bring to his attention the hurt ego he tried to ignore.

He decidedly turned right at the first corner he ap-proached. Bram found himself walking down a hall inspired by Egyptian myths. He crossed mini statues of Gods and crea-tures. Jewels, ornaments, and pottery lined the walls. When Bram turned the corner, he almost stumbled a step as he abruptly stopped.

The woman was standing in profile half down the hall. She seemed engrossed in the painting she stood in front of. Bram considered whether to approach her. He suddenly felt the effects of déjà vu shoot across his spine. And when he saw the woman lean gently to one side and suck on the soft bot-tom of her lip, the action pushed Bram closer.

As he drew near, he glanced at the oil painting the woman was engrossed in. It was a depiction of Cleopatra at the end of her life. The ancient queen was sprawled across silk furs in a gold encrusted canopy bed. Proudly wearing her golden jewels and crown, she was unabashed by her royal nudity. Her arms were coiled above her head, a noticeable bite wound branding the inner arm. Her two handmaidens curled on the floor as they wept for their Lady, a black snake trailing between them.

Bram glanced back and found the woman staring deeply in the face of pure pain and ecstasy. "She ended her life to keep from getting captured by her enemies." Bram spoke, waiting to see her react. To his surprise she did not flinch, nor move. She continued to stare into the canvas when she answered.

"She died for love."

Bram had to mentally slap himself. The sound of her voice was just as he remembered, both clear and soft. He had to stop his hand from reaching out and caressing her hair, but at that moment, she spoke once more.

"When Antony killed himself, she was heartbroken to the point that she had no wish to live anymore. The enemies coming for her was just a confirmation." She took a step back so that they were both standing aligned. Bram caught her scent as she moved, roses and honey. He smiled, easing closely to where they barely touched.

"That was a bit frivolous of her if you ask me. She was a queen, who needed to take care of her people. Besides, there is no certainty that they were really having an affair."

She smiled softly, glancing at him, and then quickly back at the painting. "Perhaps that's true. We would never know since it was only a tale. But if it was certain, then she was brave. Loving someone to the point of sacrificing yourself, it is both frightening and valiant."

"Are you brave?" Bram found himself asking.

Anita took a moment to consider her answer. She looked to the beautiful stricken face of Cleopatra and sighed softly. "I don't know."

Bram could not hold back the urge and reached for her hand. She grasped his willingly and turned ever so slightly to face him. Bram had to swallow back the craving to capture her lips. The torment only worsened when she licked them.

He appreciated her honesty, especially in her gaze. She was not afraid to reveal her uncertainty, and yet as she observed him, Bram could see her desire, and her intelligence. She wanted to know him.

"I do believe my note said the East wing staircase." Bram grinned, satisfying himself by gently touching the curl swaying at her temple.

Anita stood very still, sensing the warmth from his hand that was hovering above her cheek. She was caught in her thoughts once more. When she had the feeling that someone was again behind her, she had known it was not her host like before. Rather instead, she felt the energy of his run across her nape. Immediately she had known that the man had found her. Ever so softly, the man's fingertips slowly glided down her cheek, his gaze following. When they touched the corner of her lips, she drew in a breath.

"I found myself lost. This home is big, and I ended up here." Anita surprised herself by answering. She turned slightly so her lips grazed his thumb. She quickly detected the scent of cloves and cardamom. Once more, her head felt light.

Bram grinned. Bringing his hand back so it rested on his coat lapel. He brought his arm up in offering. "Shall I escort you to the East wing?"

Anita inhaled quick silent breaths as she considered his offer. She knew this was the moment, the choice had to be made. She formed up all the courage she could make and accepted his arm. But before taking a step she gently touched his hand. "Before we go, do you mind if I know your name?"

After a moment he answered, "My name is Bram. And you, my lady of mystery?"

Anita considered what name to give. She stood a bit straighter, unable to hinder the blush forming across her cheeks. Anita decided that this was going to be the one and only time to let go and be free. She was going to let this man show her a reality that she had thought would never happen. Only for this once, she determined. "My name is Annie."

Bram smiled and bowed his head ever so slightly. He tucked her arm closer to his as he led them down the hall and towards the East wing. He felt warm satisfaction spread in his chest, and a rush of arousal built in his groin. He glanced to the beautiful blushing woman beside him and thought how he could not wait to pleasure her. He knew he had to go slowly; she had clearly never experienced anything like the situation at hand.

Knowing this only excited Bram more. The possibility of being this woman's first should have deterred him, but it only made Bram more determined. As they climbed the staircase, Bram felt hopeful, and it only grew when he caught her smiling shyly at him.

Chapter 5

They entered a dark lit bedroom. Anita looked about, trying hard not to focus on the canopy bed. A few oil lamps were spread throughout the large guest room; Anita could make out the forest green colored drapes and matching design rug under the bed. A closed door located next to a cushioned loveseat made Anita suspect it was the lavatory. When the bed drew in her attention once more, Anita paused.

She felt a slow caress smooth down the center of her back. Her eyes fell as Bram closed in, resting his face to her nape. He breathed in her warm scent as he reached for the pin in her hair. The wavy locks dropped easily into his palm, the lush curls like satin to his skin. Bram moved himself in front of her, gliding his hand to her cheek.

He grinned as he watched the serene smile ease into her features. When she opened her eyes, the look struck him. Honest and trusting, she gazed at him like no woman before. Bram pulled her face gently closer until their lips hovered above one another. He bore into her, waiting to see if she would allow him. To his surprise, she leaned in an inch, the top of her lip grazing his chin. Her sweetness stirred him, and he leaned down until both their lips met. The sensation rocked him to his toes, as he heard her breathe in deeply.

Her lips were soft under his, relaxed, and molded perfectly. He drew her body in closer until their bodies melded together. She moaned quietly, and his head swam. When he tempted her lips open, he slowly teased his tongue with hers. She made a surprised sound which caused him to smile against her lips. He felt her grin as she eventually began to ease into the rhythm of their embrace.

As their kiss lasted, it took everything in Bram not to grind against her. His swollen shaft was pressing against his trousers painfully. Bram found himself reaching for the clasp to her bodice, but with that he noticed her immediate tension. "Do not be afraid to speak. I want this experience to be good for you too."

She hesitated for a moment. Bram became aware that he was eagerly waiting to hear what she may say. That thought gave him pause, but when he was considering whether to back away, she gently touched his coat lapel.

"I'm hoping that perhaps, if you do not mind, that you'd be the first to undress. Or if that may seem odd, we can undress one at a time?" Anita asked quietly. But she knew he heard her well, for he smiled wide.

"That's quite alright. I'll undress first," Bram answered with ease. He could not help finding her innocence fetching. It left him feeling comfortable.

Bram removed his coat and then his cravat. After he took off his vest and reached for his shirt, he took special care to watch her reaction. She was transfixed on his fingers. And when he finished with the buttons and removed it, he saw the heat and longing enter her gaze. Bram reached for her hand and brought it to lay on his chest. She bit the bottom of her lip as she boldly caressed her fingertips down to his navel. Chills shot through his body.

Anita watched her fingers glaze across the taunt ridges of his body. To her amazement, he was soft, even with the crisp hairs that led from his navel and lower. Her curiosity was ablaze when she followed the trail. To her satisfaction, Bram's stomach dipped as if tickled. He reached out and stilled her hand. When she glanced to him, Bram was watching her intently.

"Your skin…" Anita whispered in awe.

Bram grew tense. He had grown with society judging him for his skin tone. The thought of her commenting on how different he looked nearly tampered his mood. "What about it?"

"It reminds me of warm sand. So beautiful." She spoke softly, her eyes dipping back down to the hair around his navel.

Bram grinned, surprised by her answer. It unusually warmed him to know what she thought of him. But then, the way her eyes sparkled with curiosity when she noticed the bulge aching through his pants sent him back in uproar. He touched her cheek to bring her attention back on him. Bram knew he had to go about this carefully.

"Are you certain you want to continue this? I do not wish to be left here standing in the nude." Bram ended with a chuckle.

Anita blushed, she agreed with the sentiment. She did not want to ruin the moment they were creating. To her amazement, she felt comfortable within his arms, if not still a little shy. *But that shyness will soon end*, she thought. Anita nodded to him, she brushed her hair over the shoulder and turned so the clasps to her bodice showed. "Would you please... assist me?"

Bram was taken by her formality, and even amazed by her courage. As he slowly unhooked her bodice, long gone was their rushed first encounter. To his astonishment, he was enjoying the pace they had set. He was relishing the moment. However, when her creamy skin began to show through the bodice, Bram's mouth watered. She was not wearing a chemise or a corset cover. Her nape and upper back were now exposed to his gaze, and Bram knew he couldn't control his urge. He leaned in to brush his lips against her skin. She was warm and smelled of honey. Goosebumps rose across her shoulders. He helped her take off the bodice.

When Bram reached for the clasps to her skirt, he moved slowly, waiting to see if she would stop him. She did not, and Bram continued down. When the skirt dropped to the floor, she turned and stepped out from it. His excitement doubled over. She was without a hoop skirt, and from what Bram could tell, she was not wearing any drawers either. Anita was bravely standing there in only her corset and petticoat.

Anita did not know what to do as Bram studied her.

She tried to seem relaxed but as he ravished her with his gaze, she could not refrain from fidgeting slightly. Instead of picking at her fingers, she brought them behind her back. Bram's gaze darkened as he sucked in a breath. She looked down and found the reason. Bringing her shoulders back had slid down the edge of her corset. The top of her breasts flowed out to the point that almost all of her was exposed. She yelped slightly, bringing her arms back around so to lift her corset, but Bram stilled her.

Taking her hand and kissing it, Bram led her to the bed and laid her out. It was getting harder to not ravish her, especially with the way she was looking at him now. Her eyes held him, the small wrinkle between her brow gave him a smile. She was anxious to know what he intended to do, and he was eager to show her. The pleasures he had imagined were now possible. Bram could not wait for her to moan, to see her beaming with ecstasy.

With much control he did not believe he had, he reached for the first clasp to her corset. Her eyes widened slightly once she realized what he intended to do. He grinned and caressed her cheek before speaking.

"Breathe, my lovely." Bram leaned down to graze his lips across hers the moment she gasped. His grin widened, loving the sensation of her taking his breath.

He caressed his lips down to the hollow of her neck, inching them lower until he reached the first clasp once more. He unhooked it, and then the next one. She gulped and continued to breathe in deeply. When he reached the last one, Bram focused on her.

Anita felt the dark blush forming across her cheeks, but she had no objection to what was about to happen. She was about to show her body to this man that she had fantasized about since their first encounter. Instead of feeling shocked, the lower part of her stomach tickled. He was watching her intently just before he removed her corset. The moment seemed frozen; that is, until his gaze fell on her breasts.

Anita watched him lick his lips just before he

glided his fingertips down between her breasts to her navel. Anita gasped, taken aback by the sudden jolt of warmth pooling between her thighs. She never felt such a sensation, at least not since the time in the library. She found it hard to breathe. Especially when his gaze darkened, and he leaned forward. Before Anita guessed what he was about to do, his mouth found the sensitive peak at her breast.

Immediately Anita jumped and arched her back. She heard a moan and was surprised to find that it had escaped from her lips. Her body became hot and sensitive, and when he brought his hand to fondle the other taut peak, she nearly jolted off the bed. If it were not for his body over hers, she would have.

Anita faintly noticed his body falling closer to hers, but when his hips began to spread apart her thighs and she felt a hard rod-like bit grind against her, she pulled away. Bram rose above her, his eyes in a daze.

"What is the matter?" His voice was low.

Feeling uncertain whether to ask, Anita found herself embarrassed. Surely this man would think her a prude and would laugh at her. But when he lifted her chin to seek her answer, she could not deny the sincerity in his gaze.

"Is that... normal?" Anita pointed at the large bulge pressing against his trousers.

Bram looked down at his cock straining for release. For the life of him, he could not hold back his smile. His suspicion of her virginity was now answered, and though he felt like he should have been troubled by this realization, he was remarkably charmed. No other man had been where he was, so deliciously comfortable between her legs. And no other man had claimed what he soon would. To his surprise, he felt unusually possessive of this knowledge. Striving to look calm, and not the beast that was clamoring to claim her, he decided to show her what she needed to learn.

Bram rose from the bed and stood beside her. She sweetly covered her breasts with her palms. Watching her so modestly touching herself sent a rush of lust to his now aching ballocks. Reaching for the opening of his pants, he slowly unbuckled them. Her eyes were fixed on his groin and her lips slowly parted.

"Allow me to show you." Bram slid his trousers and drawers down to his feet and stepped out from them. He expected to see her shocked and looking away, but she did not. Rather instead, she gazed at his inflamed member curiously, with a tilt of her head.

"May I touch it?" she asked gently. And it nearly drove him to groan. The thought of her soft hands on him rocked him to his core.

Bram climbed onto the bed and laid out beside her. She scooted closer, her hair sprawling over his chest. He could not stop from admiring the curls against his tanned skin. As he appreciated the closeness, Anita reached down and slid her fingertips alongside his shaft. Bram jolted.

"Did I hurt you?" Anita asked in concern as she drew her hand away.

Bram huffed a chuckle. Holding her hand, he shook his head. "No, my sweet, you just caught me by surprise. You may continue if you would like."

Anita bit her lip, soothed that she had not hurt him. In fact, she realized she was excited over his reaction. Encouraged to explore, Anita reached for the strange shaft once more. Instead of grazing the side, Anita decided to grasp it along the underside. It was hot, and to her amazement pulsed against her palm. It was a bit longer than her palm, and when she closed her hand around the base, her fingertips barely touched.

Anita noticed a small bead of clear liquid seep out from the tip. Beyond curious now, she smeared the tear with her finger. Bram instantly quivered and took a hold of her hand.

"Easy, my lovely. You're making it hard to stay in control." Bram was slowly panting.

"I'm sorry. It is surprisingly soft. I never imagined something like this would be," Anita admitted.

Bram smirked, "It is called a male's member. A shaft. Or if you wish to be crude, a cock."

To his satisfaction, she once again began to blush. It did nothing, however, to deter her from reaching out to his cock once more. He stilled her and rose from the bed. He moved himself between her legs and rested his hands on her knees.

"We need to get you ready." Bram slowly drew down her petticoat.

Anita gasped, trying hard not to hold on to the last piece of fabric on her person. "Get ready for what?"

"For you to accept me into you." Leaning forward, Bram brushed his lips across her navel as he brought the petticoat down to her ankles.

Anita sighed loudly as her belly dipped and she felt herself start to quiver. "I don't quite understand."

Smiling against her skin, Bram looked up at her. "My shaft will be entering your body. I need to get you wet and needing for it to not hurt."

That gave Anita pause. She rose on her elbows before speaking. "Why would it hurt?"

"I don't intend for it to hurt, my sweet. But if you still have your maidenhead, then there may be some discomfort. It will only last for a moment, until your body relaxes, then it will become very pleasurable."

Anita took a moment to consider what he said. Despite her nerves, she looked to him and gave a small smile. "I trust in your confidence, Bram."

Now it was Bram who paused. He looked at this beautifully naked woman before him and felt something warm course through his bones. Thinking back, he never really had any of his lovers call him by his first name. The majority would call him Lord, or Kenwood, but never his name. The realization struck him.

Bram caressed his hands down and across her body. She was warm and soft, and the crisp hairs between her thighs glistened. He smiled, confident that she was clearly ready, but Bram wanted to enjoy this. Wanted her to never forget what he was about to gift to her.

Anita could not refrain from wiggling. Bram's touch was both exquisite and maddening. The sensation nearly drove her insane, especially with the way the ache between her legs throbbed. She hardly noticed when Bram slowly drew closer to her thighs, until she felt his hot breath caress across her curls. Anita drew in a breath before quickly closing her thighs around his head.

Bram grinned and gripped her legs to open a little. "Trust me, my lovely. This will be genuinely nice."

"But…" Anita could not finish what she was to say. Bram had already dipped between her thighs and licked over her aching bud.

Anita moaned and gripped the sheets beneath her. Quickly her head swam as every lavish lick sent chills across her body. She felt like she was on fire, and Anita briefly noticed a tightening beginning to ache in her core. Keeping his mouth on her, Bram brushed his hand up to her breast and began stroking and teasing the peak. Anita gave out a cry.

Her body tensed and began to shake. She shut her eyes as a strange euphoric sensation pulsed across her being. It erupted and for a moment, Anita thought she was to faint, but the pleasure alone jolted her awake. When it began to subside, Anita was left limp and panting. Bram lifted his head to gaze at her with a satisfied grin.

"That was… remarkable. What was that?" Anita breathed.

"A lover's kiss, to inspire what the French call la petite mort, 'the little death'. A woman's pleasure," Bram answered as he kissed his way up her thigh.

"I have never imagined… Such wonders."

"Tis not over yet." Bram gripped her thighs and brought them closer to his groin.

Anita's eyes widened as she observed him edge his tip close to her opening. Again, she held her breath, uncertain of what was to come.

"Breathe, my lovely. Remember to relax." Bram began to push his tip into her, and immediately he had to pause and adjust. Only an inch, and she was too tight for him to bear. Bram had to mentally remind himself to go slow and stay in control.

She was hot and wet, he thought, as he pushed

another inch forward. Bram noticed her eyes squeeze shut, and her body grew tense. When he reached her maidenhead, Bram paused. This was it. No turning back. He guided his hand down between them and began to stroke her nub, all the while leaning forward to suckle her breast. When he heard her begin to moan, he pushed forward and stilled. Liquid heat poured across his cock, and Bram had to grit his teeth from the pleasure of it.

"Are you all right?" He heard her faintly ask.

He half chuckled, gazing into her eyes. They were in a half daze. "I should be the one asking you that."

She gave him a small smile, and that nearly made him come. When she wiggled slightly, Bram let out a half groan. "I'm sorry, I just needed to adjust a little," she explained.

"That's alright. Does it feel painful?"

Anita shook her head. When she brought her legs higher around his hips, to her surprise she drove him into her a little deeper, which caused them both to moan in unison.

"I'm afraid I won't be able to hold off any longer. I need to move inside you." Bram groaned.

To his delight, she nodded and bit her lip. She held onto either side of his shoulders as he began to move. With each stroke Bram shook, the warm wet canal easing and welcoming him. Knowing he wouldn't last, he began to stroke her once more. She let out a cry, and he felt her inner walls grow tight around his shaft.

Bram's resolve nearly broke, but when he glanced to her and found her honestly looking into him with a slight smile hovering above her lips, his control was destroyed. Bram pulled back to rest on his knees, lifted her bottom, and began to drive into her. He stroked her nub with all the ferocity he felt and to his relief, her head fell back as she found her pleasure. Watching her find release drove him over the edge; Bram pumped into her, until the ache in his ballocks signaled his orgasm.

Bram pulled himself out just before releasing his seed, his orgasm shaking him to his core as wave after wave pooled on her navel. When Bram was finally spent, he collapsed next to her, panting. Eyes closed, he was stunned. It had been too long since he experienced a pleasure such as that.

When he opened his eyes, he saw her curiously dabbing at his seed. Unfamiliar emotions flowed through his chest as he rose from the bed. He tried to decipher them as he walked into the lavatory. When he returned, he placed a wet cloth over her navel and helped clean off the remains. He noticed the silent blush caressing her cheeks. He brushed his fingertips across her lips.

"You look as though you are in shock." Bram offered her a smile.

"Your seed is what creates a babe, is it not?" Anita asked quietly.

Bram observed her face, to his surprise he could not detect what she was thinking or feeling. "Yes, that is true. However, I did not spend my seed inside you. You will not be expecting one down the road."

Bram finally saw a hint of relief cross her features. He smiled and sat down beside her. Long gone was the shyness towards her nudity. Rather instead, she looked to be in deep thought. Surprisingly, Bram wanted to know what sort of musings she was concocting.

"Was it everything you had imagined?" Bram found himself asking.

"Yes and no. Some from what I have overheard by the maids gossiping, and the other, I had no idea. Did you know that I was... untouched?" Anita looked away, embarrassed, but quickly glancing back when she heard his chuckle.

"I had my suspicions. Not to mention you weren't exactly devouring me like a usual wanton woman would." Bram smiled more to himself than to Anita.

Anita watched as Bram's eyes glazed over in memory. Then she realized that this man had much experience in the acts of intimacy. The way he knew how to take care of her made her imagine that he had done it before with other young ladies. The thought notably distressed her. She suddenly remembered her days in Pennsylvania, to a time when she was courted. To a man she thought she knew, and then who had deceived her. Her stomach began to ache from the memory.

"Would you please bring me my clothing?" Anita asked softly.

Bram stood and walked to their clothing. He brought them back to the bed and offered her corset. Anita stood and slid on her petticoat, then her corset. As she straightened on her skirt, Bram was already dressed.

Bram could not ignore the sudden distance he felt in the room. The mood had changed in her, and it strangely baffled him. By the time she righted her bodice, Bram approached behind her to help with the clasps. She silently accepted the assistance. When he was finished, he turned her in his arms. She was no longer looking him in the eyes, just simply stared at the center of his chest. He lifted her chin until she met his gaze.

He leaned down to catch her lips, warm and sweet. He breathed her in. However, he could not miss the stiffness now in her kiss. Bram drew back with a curious scowl, but before he could ask, she spoke. "Would you please get me a glass of water?"

Mildly confused by her request, he nodded. He stepped into the lavatory to look for a glass.

Anita listened carefully to detect where Bram was in the other room. When she determined that he was distracted, she quietly stepped out from the bed chamber as quickly as she could. She rushed from the room towards the staircase and made her way down to the main halls.

She was absently trying to raise her hair back in order, her thoughts roaring in her mind. Anita knew what she was doing was absurd, but her emotions were uncontrollable. The memories, the events that just happened, and her feelings were all colliding together at once. In no way did she want to regret and ruin the moment she had with Bram, but if she had stayed there any longer, comparing him to her courtship in Pennsylvania, she knew it would have been soiled.

Anita was relieved to see the front entrance. She passed a few guests who looked at her with curiosity. She tried to ignore them, but when she realized that one was Christina who was waving at her from across the room, Anita quickened her steps. She apologetically waved at Christina and glanced behind towards the end of the hall. Hoping to not see Bram following her, she looked back to her friend and gave her a sad smile just before stepping out of the home and back into reality.

∞ ∞ ∞

Bram stood still as he studied the empty bedroom. Holding the glass full of water, he walked to the nearest dresser. Placing the cup down, Bram did a mental shake. She was gone, once again. The truth baffled him as he glanced over to the disarrayed bed, to the few drops of blood on the sheets.

Did he miss something? He could have sworn that he took care not to hurt her. In fact, he knew he gave her much pleasure. He told himself to think. What had he missed? Immediately, he felt he had done wrong. Frustrated with himself, Bram had crossed an innocent girl over the line.

Remembering how she seemed just before he left to get her water, she was distant. Was that her beginning to regret what they had done? And then there was her worry about conceiving a babe. No wonder she had panicked and undoubtedly ran off.

Bram ignored the resentment that slowly grew in his chest. He knew he should have expected her to feel vulnerable and confused. Strangely, he felt compelled to seek her out and comfort her. This feeling only baffled him more.

Instead of trying to make sense of his thoughts, Bram stepped out from the bedchamber. There was a chance she may still be in the home or that someone had seen her. He found his way down the East wing staircase. The performance must have ended; guests were coming out from the gala. Bram searched through the crowd, hoping to see long dark locks of hair.

Before he could reach another hall, Bram was stopped by Richard. "Slow down there, Kenwood," Richard said as he tasted an unlit cigar.

"Not now, Richard. I'm looking for someone. Did you see a woman with long dark hair in a blue dress wander in here?"

Richard's brow arched as he keenly observed his friend. He shook his head before saying, "Not in the least. Should I be curious or troubled by your spontaneous change of self?"

Bram gave Richard a pointed stare just as he raked his hand through his hair and looked about. It was true, no one ever saw Bram so bewildered. Especially Richard. Bram blew out a breath. "I had just met the woman my fantasies are made of, and she ran out on me...again."

Richard stared at Bram for a long moment before patting him on the shoulder. "Well, I guess it's going around. Good luck finding her, my friend. Perhaps at the next party." Richard placed the cigar back into his mouth and walked off.

Bram looked about in a daze. He knew she was gone. But even when the disappointment began to settle in his chest, Bram considered what Richard had said. There was a chance he could see her at the next gathering. Surely, she would attend. Hopefully, he thought.

Chapter 6

London
Conway Hall
June

B ram pulled at his cravat as he increased the speed to the newspaper he used as a fan. It was a warm day and being in a crowded discussion hall did not cool matters in the slightest. Nor did it help distract his running thoughts. He glanced over to Mark who sat next to him. His friend was completely engrossed in the topic of the present speaker.

"How much more of this, Mark?" Bram exhaled a breath.

Without taking his eyes off the speaker, Mark replied, "He is only just beginning to explain how mechanical, electrical, and heat energies are the same, and can be changed from one into another. If this man can prove his theory, then he has discovered how to conserve energy. Truly remarkable, I do not see why he was ridiculed a few years back."

"His name is James Joule, right? I have never heard of him, and probably neither has the scientific community. If they had not discovered it, they would shun any other who dare to."

Mark shook his head. No doubt he was thinking of the society they lived in. Just as they were shunned, so were others who were not known in bigger richer circles. "Ridiculous." Mark said under his breath.

Bram nodded, again lost in thought. The lives they had, though comfortable and adequate, were still strained by judgment from others. Even now as they sat, Bram noticed a few looks and sneers being cast in their direction. Yes, Bram thought, even amongst men of equal value can one feel exiled. Bram grinned at the others who were still looking and offered them a wink. The men scoffed and averted their gazes. Inwardly sighing, Bram thought, was there no place where he would feel welcomed?

He paused, knowing full well that answer. Remembering the only time when he did not feel ridiculed, judged, or used was when he was with her. Annie. Bram could not resist the urge to grind his teeth. He knew he shouldn't feel anger, but even when he understood her possible reasons for leaving him that night, it did nothing to alleviate the tension that grew every time he went to a gathering and found her not there. Nor did it calm his raging desire for her. More than once, Bram found himself feverishly grinding into his bed from unsated dreams of her.

A month had passed, and Bram still had not seen or been called on by her. Quite frankly, he was surprised, even intrigued, but at the same time he should have known this was to happen. She was a woman of means; no doubt she was simply seeking a moment of pleasure outside her usual high-class society. Before she was to be married off to a rich lord. Again, Bram ground his teeth. The thought did not appease his pride. However, thinking back, he reminded himself that she did not seem like the sort to use others for her own gain.

Bram scratched the back of his neck, his feelings causing him strife. His mind torn, he did not know what to think. But the truth remained, Bram still wanted to see her again. He just had no idea how. L'Opera Magenta opened with its new production a month ago, and within only a fortnight the show acquired rave reviews. Despite being there every night of the showings, Bram disappointingly did not see Annie. Soon after, Bram began to lose hope that he would ever feel that sense of comfort and arousal again.

Bram sighed, and that only drew in Mark's attention. "Very well, Bram, let's away." Mark began to gather the booklets he had been writing notes on.

"It's alright, Mark. We can stay," Bram said as he stopped Mark's arm just as he was rising.

"Are you certain?" Mark examined Bram's features when he settled back down on his seat. "What's the matter?"

Bram shook his head as he focused in on the new speaker at the podium. He realized just how much this woman had affected his thoughts. "I'll tell you later."

He needed to get his mind in order, focus on matters at hand. He had a theater to run. Investments to pursue. Gatherings to attend. And a new opera house just starting to be built. He could not waste his time on fantasies and searching for a woman he barely knew. Not to mention managing to handle a certain ballerina who was relentlessly trying to irritate him.

The ballerina had not ceased her letters of threat, in fact, her bluffs only heightened. She had begun to send a note once a week, informing him that if he did not act on her coming pregnancy then she would inform the appropriate authorities. Bram decided it best to save these mailings in case she made do on her word. Nevertheless, it irked him that she played as though she had him wrapped around her finger.

As Bram and Mark entered the carriage, Bram tapped the board above them. "To Springfield's, Jefferson."

The carriage lurched forward until a smooth rhythm began to sway. The sound of hooves grinding the ground echoed around them. The streets were packed with passing carriages and riders. Footsteps and conversations filled the air as wave after wave of people made way through the sidewalks. The warm sun was beating its rays of light on all who crossed its path, including Bram's carriage. The interior was heating as they rode, and once again Bram pulled at his cravat.

"Bloody hell, it's hot," Bram said with a gruff.

"Shouldn't you be accustomed to this weather?" Mark commented with a smirk.

Bram cast him an amused glare. "I haven't lived in Morocco in several years, Mark. I thought you were smarter than that."

Mark chuckled under his breath before pulling one of

his notepads onto his lap. As he scanned through the writings, he leaned back into the cushion. "So, are you going to tell me what the matter with you has been?"

Without answering, Bram pulled up the flap cover to the window and rolled it up so a warm breeze could enter. When he settled back into his seat, Bram found his friend giving him a pointed stare. With a shrug Bram searched outside the window, not particularly looking at anything, or for anyone. But that did not stop the image of Annie, sprawled on the bed in her nearly undone corset, from casting havoc in his mind's eye.

"Does this have something to do with that woman from Sebastian's party?"

Bram whipped his head to find Mark watching him intently. Again, he tried to shrug and looked away before answering. "What do you know about it, Mark?"

"Only from what Sebastian, Richard, AND Philip have said." Mark looked down at his notes.

"What? Sterling wasn't a part of this discussion?"

"Sterling is in Scotland," Mark said without taking his eyes away from the book.

That gave Bram pause. He glanced back at Mark. "When did he leave?"

Mark shrugged, "We don't know. Richard received word last week of his whereabouts. He's back at his estate."

That was strange of Sterling, Bram thought. In all the years of staying in London, Sterling had never indicated the desire to return to Scotland. Especially since the last time he was there was when he lost his wife. Something must have happened, but Bram had no clue.

"So? The woman? Have you found her yet?" Mark asked with a smirk as he glanced over his notebook.

"How did you–?" Bram sighed. "Am I really the center of gossip between you men?"

Mark chuckled, closing his notepad. He crossed his legs. "It is clear that you are obsessed with this woman. Something, I might add, we have never seen you do."

"I'm not obsessed. Only intrigued." Bram tried his best to hide the truth from his friend.

Mark scoffed, "Please. I know you Bram. Even now as you try to hide the truth from me, I can see that you are constantly lost in thought, thinking of her no doubt. And even when you are working, it is related to that woman."

Bram could not hold back his look of confusion. "What on earth are you talking about? My work?"

"A Midsummer's Night Dream? That is unlike any other showing you have done before."

Bram drew in a heavy breath. Clearly his obsession had become obvious. He shrugged, trying to seem nonchalant. "It doesn't matter now."

"Why is that?" Mark leaned back as he continued to study his friend. His hands came together across his knee and began twiddling his thumbs.

Whenever Mark leaned comfortably into that position, it indicated to Bram that he was ready to diagnose the situation. If it was not for the fact that he was a Lord, Bram could've suspected Mark to be a psychologist. It was a shame that ability had not grown stronger before Mark was tricked by his now late wife.

Bram sighed; crossing his legs, he leaned one arm against his knee and brought his hand to rest at the edge of his chin. He half shrugged and glanced out the window of the carriage. They had begun to reach the streets near Springfield. Coachmen passed, crates of food being pushed by vendors. People brushing pass one another to reach their destinations. Some with serious expressions, others with smiles on their face as they spoke to companions. Bram wished he felt that lighthearted with his friend now. However, he shamefully admitted to himself that he felt empty.

"Bram?" Mark brought him out of his thoughts.

Once again Bram sighed, "I do not know who she is, Mark. I've only ever met her twice, and on both occasions, there wasn't much talking involved."

Mark smirked and chuckled to himself. Shaking his head, he asked, "Well, do you have a name?"

"Not quite. Just a first name. But I'm certain London is filled with women by the name of Annie."

Nodding, Mark leaned his head back as though contemplating. For a moment they were silent, the horse hooves trailing the sound behind them. Suddenly Mark popped his head up to look at him. "Bram, other than the parties, is there anything else that could be connected to this woman? Anything she could have said?"

Bram gave Mark a pointed stare. "If there was something, I would have thought of it, man. I just have to face the fact that-" Suddenly Bram was reminded of the dance card he found the night they first met.

"What is it?" Mark looked at him curiously.

"Well... there was a dance card I found in her possession."

"Really? Well that may be helpful in some way. Do you remember what was on it?" Mark asked innocently.

Bram wavered, abruptly realizing to his chagrin that he currently had the dance card tucked away in his coat pocket. For a time, he had it so, not fully comprehending the reason, but to have it close. He pulled it out now, ignoring the fascinated lift of Mark's brows.

Scanning the crinkled card, it came to his attention that it was unfilled. Mildly scowling, he passed the card to Mark. "There is nothing there that could help us. Would seem that my mystery woman is a wallflower."

"Is that so bad? It's obvious that this wallflower enchanted you," Mark said with a grin as he scanned the paper.

Scoffing more to himself than to Mark, Bram once again was lost for words at his friend's comment. It was true, and it was hard for Bram to admit out loud.

"This is the crest of Lord Hemmingway," Mark declared.

Scowling, Bram took the card to examine it closely. "Who?"

"Stephan Henderson, the Viscount of Hemmingway. His lands have manufactured polished stocks of grain and corn."

"I have not heard of him," Bram remarked.

"It has been years since I've seen his crest. The Viscount had worked with my father when I was a child. Last I have heard of him was his move to America. I suppose he's returned and hosting parties."

Bram considered this new information. His new assumption was that, if Annie fell into these circles, then there was a solid chance he could find her at these gatherings as well. The look on Mark's face proclaimed to agree with Bram's theory.

"If you would like, Bram, I could seek out upcoming parties hosted by the Viscount," Mark offered with a helpful grin.

"You're not afraid to do that, Mark?" Bram asked with a lifted brow and a smirk.

Mark half laughed and shrugged, "The last year or so has been good. No proud mamas have sought or harassed me. The talks of scandal have subsided, thankfully. Besides, I now intend to speak with the Viscount. I remember him as being quite open minded to inventions. Perhaps I could interest him in an investment."

"That would be good then, Mark. I thank you for your help."

Mark nodded with a smile, then reached for his notebook and began writing with a small piece of charcoal shaved down to a point.

As the carriage rode on, Bram suddenly felt that small spark of hope within his gut again. He quickly quieted it down, however, not wanting to feel disappointed if he was to fail in finding Annie again. But there was no mistaking it, Bram felt closer than ever before. Soon Bram was going to see her, he just knew it somehow. And this time, Bram thought, he planned on not letting her run away again.

Anita stood against the wall as she observed the numerous feet before her, frolicking in sync with the others on the dance floor. Once again, she found herself attending another party she had no wish to be in. She was truly proud of her dear mama, however. Eloise had succeeded in preparing another extraordinary ball, one that she had rented a hall for. Hearing of these plans before the date, Anita had guessed that the gathering would be extravagant. Anita was stunned at the outcome.

More guests than she assumed had arrived. Clearly the older class remembered her mother and father. Even now, Anita watched them across the room, standing together, yet apart, conversing with acquaintances and friends. It was an event not meant just for her sister, but for the whole family. Her mother had intended to refresh them all into the new season. A dusting of the cobwebs, she had stated.

Belle was positively glowing. Not that it was a surprise. Anita's sister was a natural when it came to crowds and parties. She was meant for London society. At that moment, Belle turned her gaze to Anita from across the room. She smiled brightly and waved at her to join the group she was entertaining. Anita felt hesitant, the circle included gentlemen.

Instantly, Anita was reminded of Bram. She quickly stared back down to the feet of the dancers; afraid someone would notice the harsh blush now forming across her cheeks. This was the reason she hadn't wanted to socialize with anyone. For the past month and a half, Anita relentlessly thought of Bram. During the dawn's morning light, throughout the day, and up till late at night, when her dreams plagued her with sweet torture. She felt blissfully cursed by what had happened between them. And now, Anita would forever be reminded of the most exquisite experience she ever had.

However, that is where she was condemned. Since that night, Anita had felt awful with how she ended things. At the time, it seemed like the only choice, but now logically remembering all that happened, she should have at least said goodbye. Or a thank you...

Anita winced and grumbled to herself. A thank you? How idiotic was she? Twice, not once, she had run from him. And for what? Her fear? Remembering how he treated her, a small smile touched her lips. Bram was delicate, considerate of her inexperience, but most of all hungry to have her. That alone astounded Anita and weakened her breath. Her desire for him surmounted her guilt. Despite wanting to desperately see him again, Anita stopped herself every time Christina had invited her to a party.

It was not because she did not wish to see him. She wanted to, desperately, and that was why she reasoned with herself to not go and find him. Anita knew in her gut that if she were to meet Bram, there was the chance she would lose all control over herself. The promise of his dark gaze had made her realize this. Anita licked her lips and took in a deep wavering breath.

"Unlike the parties we have been to, wouldn't you agree?" Christina came and stood beside her.

Anita shook out of her daze to look up at her friend. She smiled and gently touched Christina's elbow. "I didn't think you were coming."

"I couldn't miss little Belle's invitation. I know how much it means to her." Christina leaned back against the wall, and chuckled.

"What is so funny?" Anita asked. A great relief coursed through her now that Christina was here.

"I truly don't remember how long it's been since I was a wallflower. Being here reminds me of those days." She scoffed. "I never want to go back to that."

Christina stared off into the crowd, her cool smile now diminished. Anita observed her friend. Christina was no longer a part of this world, and there was no mistaking it. Even now she stood out like a rare orchid amongst all the golden roses. Anita felt a pang strike her heart. As she looked on at all the attendees, she found herself not as one of them either. And perhaps had never been...

"Oh dear..." Christina said under her breath.

Glancing up, she noticed her sister approaching, and to Anita's dismay, the group she was with were following close behind. Surprisingly, she recognized two of the women behind her sister.

"Annie! You didn't come, so I came to you!" Belle smiled happily, taking Anita's hand in her own. "Christina, I am so happy to see you here as well!"

Anita smiled softly to her sister before turning a polite glare to the other ladies' present. Christina smirked and sent them a wink.

"Annie, Christina, this is- ".

"Miss Kenyon, and Miss Crane." Anita announced their names in a gruff whisper. She remembered the two ladies from Belle's debutante ball. They were the ones that had the audacity to speak rudely of her sister. The fact they were in conversation with them left Anita feeling displeased. They didn't seem all too cheerful either.

Miss Crane looked so flushed that it harshly contrasted against her daffodil colored gown. She was clearly trying to avoid eye contact with both Anita and Christina. Unlike her companion, Miss Kenyon, who freely directed her glower to them both.

"Ah? You all have already been introduced?" Belle looked wide eyed and curiously at them, unaffected by the clear negativity between the women.

Miss Crane did not answer and instead opened her fan, whereas Miss Kenyon simply made a small agreeing sound and began to look across the crowd, clearly dismissing the conversation. Anita stared at the two and tried her hardest not to shake her head. The way they acted was beyond her.

After a moment, one of the men in the group cleared his throat, which brought Belle's attention back on them. "Oh yes! I am sorry Lord Brunswick. Ladies, this is Lord Jonathan Barrel, and with him his brother George Barrel."

Lord Brunswick approached Anita to grasp her hand before she even offered it and took a bow. Anita quietly nodded, and half curtsied. His brother George simply leaned forward and offered a nod. Anita forced a smile and curtsied once more.

"My Lady, it is a pleasure. Allow me to introduce myself properly, in no offense to your sister. I am Lord Jonathan Richard Barrel the third. Earl of Brunswick." Lord Brunswick offered his most charming smile, and Anita could not help but notice the slight crook of his jaw. Once again, she nodded, uncertain of what to say. His brother George drew her attention when he had not so discreetly rolled his eyes.

"Ah yes, I should have introduced you more properly, Lord Brunswick. My apologies." Bella had nervously laughed.

Immediately Anita noticed the small frown that wrinkled her sister's brow and she stepped closer to stand with her. Anita could not bear to see her sister embarrassed even for something so trivial. Already Anita had her assumptions about this Lord Brunswick, a pompous cad. When the Earl turned to Christina, he noticeably turned red and his shoulders stiffened. Christina simply grinned.

"No need for introductions, Belle. I'm quite familiar with Lord Brunswick." Christina raised her eyebrow, as if daring him to speak.

Lord Brunswick simply cleared his throat and turned his attention to the other women. Anita was curious about the history between them, but as Christina met her gaze, she winked and mouthed *later*.

Now all of them standing in silence, Belle began to look worried. Seeking something to say, Anita looked to Lord Brunswick's brother, George. "Do you enjoy art, Mr. Barrel?"

George had sighed before rolling his gaze to meet hers. "Not really. I rather prefer the races."

"You mean the horses?"

"Of course, what else is there?" With that George turned his body away from the conversation.

Anita was repulsed by the behavior both brothers portrayed. Certainly, no charming gentlemen. Even Miss Kenyon and Miss Crane had turned away from them. Anita inwardly shook her head. Certainly, these persons had missed what it means to be in polite conversation. In fact, all the gatherings her sister and mother had taken her to, all seemed to be lacking. Something was amiss amongst all the attendees. Anita realized it then that they were missing their hearts.

At that moment, Belle tugged on her arm. Her sister looked up at her with a somber smile. "Let's dance, Annie?"

Anita's eyes softened, and she held her sister's hand. "Yes, let's have some fun."

With that, Belle's warm smile returned as they made

their way to the dance floor. Anita glanced back to Christina, who smiled and opened her fan. She gestured her fan to the dance floor and winked at her. Anita was thankful that the cotillion was beginning. It was the perfect dance to simply trail around the other dancers. She and her sister faced one another along the row. Belle was already laughing when the music began, and they danced down the line sideways. Anita could not hold back her own smiles; she laughed along with her sister.

Watching Belle, Anita felt alive once more. Dancing along beside her, she remembered a time of when they were young. Her dear sister had asked to teach her how to dance, and though it took a whole day's evening to lesson her and fail, together they had the most astonishing time. Even when their mother was chiding them for their poor sense of step, they each had bright smiles and could not stop their laughter.

By the end of the dance, Anita was smiling and flushed. She and Belle started to walk off the dance floor once the waltz began to tune in. Just as Anita was about to step off, her hand was suddenly grasped, and she was being pulled up against a warm hard body.

All breath left her once she focused on who had captured her. She blinked slowly, uncertain whether she could have collapsed during the cotillion, and was now seeing visions. It was not until the fresh scent of spice caught her attention that it made her certain that she was not dreaming. Bram had her within his arms, and he was devouring her every feature. His eyes were taking their time detailing every curve and flush.

Finally, he smiled, calm, and at ease. "This would be easier if you follow my lead, my sweet."

Chapter 7

Bram finally had her in his arms. He found her, and by God, he was not intending to let her go again. Even when she tried gently to tug her hand out from his, Bram all the more tightened his hold. Not taking his eyes off her, he led her to the edge of the dance floor and positioned her close within his embrace. Despite the hushed breaths from the close onlookers, Bram placed his hand low on the small of her back and interlaced his hand into hers in the most intimate way.

He found her blushing and looking down at their feet, seemingly afraid to face him. He felt surprisingly charmed by her shy grace. When the music began, his hand on her lower back drew her closer as he then led his first step. She perfectly followed suit and in the same instant took a noticeable gulp. The music grew and before long Bram had her once around the dance floor.

Bram was in awe at how graceful she felt, all the while she still stared at the floor. How much he longed to raise her chin to capture her lips. If it were not for the fact that they were in a Ton ball, Bram would have done so. Or even better, if they were both back into the comfortable surroundings of Bram's environment, in freedom, he could fully embrace her the way he wanted to now.

Longing to have her gaze upon him, Bram brushed against her as he twirled her past a couple. "Annie..." he whispered softly.

Surprised, her gaze shot to his. To his satisfaction, he caught the shiver that ran through her body. She took a deep breath and immediately glanced back down to the floor.

"Is the dance floor your partner, Annie?" Bram asked with a sly grin.

Anita glanced up but stared at the onlooking crowd. "How...?" she asked quietly.

"How what?" Bram twirled her once more around the corner of the dance floor.

"How... did you find me?" She hesitated but was able to finish her sentence. This time she looked at him, and Bram had to find his rhythm. It never failed to amaze him just how it threw him every time she cast her honest gaze at him.

Bram had to hide the gripping desire to pull her against him. He had to focus on his surroundings. He was not in his world anymore. He was in hers...

"Did you think I wouldn't find you?"

At that moment, the waltz ended, and as guests clapped, most of them observed the interaction between them. Bram silently cursed, as he took a quick glance around. Looking to her, he said, "This is not the time or place. Meet me outside in the gardens. If you do not show, I will come looking for you."

With that, Bram bowed, but before stepping away he laid a gentle lingering kiss to Anita's hand. As he walked away, all eyes were on him, and Bram could not shrug off the burning sensation at the back of his neck. He had almost forgotten where he was. Where he had taken himself to for the sake of Annie. Never had he imagined he would be attending a ball amongst all the riches of the Ton again.

∞∞∞

As Anita watched Bram step away out of sight, she noticed how everyone near her was gazing after him wide eyed rather than at her. She suddenly had a suspicion that they knew of him more than she did. When they began to whisper amongst themselves, Anita's guess was confirmed. She made her way off the dance floor. No one seemed to notice as she weaved through them. Anita rubbed on her arm; chills were still present from when he had kissed her hand.

Bram told her to meet him in the garden, and if not, he would come seek her out. Anita suddenly felt overwhelmed yet faint. She could not believe that he had found her. Her disbelief, however, turned to silent joy. He had searched for her. Where it had seemed impossible, he found a way. Anita looked all and around herself, feeling like a different woman. Like someone hiding a secret, and she could not help but smile.

Almost at once, Christina bumped into her. Anita had to stop short, as Christina held fast her shoulders. Her eyes wide, her voice astonished. "That was...?"

"Yes..." Anita answered, gathering a breath.

"Are you alright? What are you to do?" Christina cruised her past the dance floor towards one of the empty pillars that no one stood amongst.

"He asked me to meet out in the gardens." Anita leaned into the pillar, her hand brushing across her lips.

"He asked?"

Anita felt her cheeks heat, as she observed the new group on the dance floor. "Well, it was more like a statement, than a question. Really."

Christina raised her eyebrows, and half grinned. "My, it would seem like he missed you."

Anita looked down to hide her small smile. Indeed, it did seem that he had missed her. And deep within her chest, she was glad. That had meant that he was not upset with how she had left things last. The guilt had suddenly lifted off her only to leave her apprehensive. Anita realized that the decision had to be made. Again. She took a moment to consider, but Anita had already known what she was to do. She took a gulp of breath and swiftly took a step towards the outer gardens.

She collided with her sister. Belle squeaked ever so slightly before bracing against her. "Annie!"

Anita gasped, "Oh Belle, are you all right?"

Bella righted her dress, and cast her sister a concerned frown. "Are you? That man just frisked you onto the dance floor. And now you look as though you are to faint."

Anita mentally shook herself. Her sister was right. She was about to hastily run across the ballroom to meet with Bram, alone. Only to just realize that she was in no normal gathering, but her family's. Their reputation she had to uphold. She told herself that she had to focus on what mattered. Anita bit her tongue slightly; *I cannot bring scandal to the family. Not again...*

"Annie?" Belle asked once again.

Just when Anita was about to reassure her sister, Christina spoke. "That is an old acquaintance of mine, little Belle. A considerate gentleman, whom I asked to offer the waltz to our lovely Annie."

Both Anita and Belle cast her an awestruck look. Christina simply grinned and gave them both a charming giggle. "In fact, how about we all make our way out to the gardens. I will introduce him."

"Oh, Chris..."

"That sounds lovely!" Belle nearly shouted before wrapping her arm around Anita's. Christina had already turned to lead them through the ballroom.

Anita was stunned, not only was she to face Bram, with her heart thudding out of her chest, but now she was to meet with him with her sister. She was still bewildered that she had not noticed the sudden laughter between the two women leading her, and the fact that she was already outside, approaching the gardens. The gardens were lit with melted candles placed upon bronze lanterns. The lanterns hanging off tall rods that lined down the pathway. Bushes of jasmine and moonflowers filled in the walls of the garden maze that opened and closed upon the pathway they were walking.

Once they passed the bronze opening of the maze garden, Anita looked down and around. It seemed they were not in a complicated maze; halls of tall bush went straight around in one large circle. They walked straight down a quick path to the center with no delay. When they neared it, Anita's heart skipped. Bram was standing in profile, in front of a rock scaling fountain.

To Anita's surprise, he was not alone. Bram was talking with another gentleman, who was dressed in a fine dark navy coat, and tan bottoms. The man looked young, younger than Bram, but still charmingly dashing. But as they drew near, and Bram noticed their approach, Anita had to catch her breath. He was exquisite. In the way his eyes had widened and warmed as he narrowed his gaze upon hers. His body noticeably relaxed.

His friend had also glanced at their coming, as he gave a knowing smile first to Christina, and then to Anita. For a fleeting moment, however, Anita caught the man's eyes widen as he gazed at her sister, Belle. Once they fully approached them, the men had bowed perfectly, with Bram never taking his eyes off her. All ladies had graciously curtsied in return, with Belle bringing her hands together happily. The man smiled.

"Good evening, gentlemen," Christina said.

Both men nodded in agreement. "And a good evening to you too, Miss Godfrey Rose," Bram's friend returned.

Anita nearly froze, knowing that name was Christina's other identity amongst the outer circles of the Ton. However, Christina paid it no mind as she breathlessly laughed. She casually poked the man with her fan in a friendly manner.

"Mark, just as charming as ever. It is good to see you. How goes the science and agricultural lectures?"

"They fare well, I must say. Such new wonders that are soon to be created. Looking to change the preface of all things crop and grain." Mark answered in such a way that clearly showed his interest in the subject.

All three women listened as Mark began to tell in detail of all the new inventions being discussed to replace manual labor amongst farmers and cattle. He ended the subject with shortness of breath, as he quickly tried to express the importance of such a decree. Anita could not help but smile and admire the man. He had passion for the welfare of men and the economy. Strange that she could not recall ever seeing him in any other function that she was taken to in the past month. The man before her was a remarkable conversationalist. Although, the conversation had not distracted her away from the reality that Bram had not once taken his eyes off her. Anita tried hard not to stare back, but the way his eyes had heated at every movement she made left her feeling breathless and needing more of his gaze.

"But do you not consider that the men who work these fields could possibly lose their way of life?" Belle surprised Anita by asking Mark. Anita didn't realize how engrossed her sister was in the conversation.

For a moment, Mark stood motionless. A slow smile drew across his face. He took a step forward and bowed ever so close to Belle. When he glanced at her, it nearly caused Anita to blush. Mark's eyes were a shade of sparkling copper that caught the nearby blaze of a candle behind them. His smile was now partially opened as he drew Belle's hand to his lips. "May I have the honor of making your acquaintance, my Lady?"

Anita was only half surprised, compared to her sister, who simply stood there quiet as a flower. But something in the way her sister breathed deeply gave Anita pause. The expression on Belle felt familiar to her. After neither she nor her sister spoke a word, Christina coughed quietly into her fan. "Mark, this is Miss Annabelle Henderson, daughter to the Viscount of Hemmingway."

Upon introduction, Belle traditionally curtsied. Her golden curls falling forward, nearly brushing Mark's still raised hand. Belle cast Mark an expectant expression. Mark glanced to Bram, who observed them curiously. When Bram showed no sign of speaking, Mark cleared his throat, only to have Bram raise an eyebrow.

"Introduce me, Bram!" he whispered loudly.

Bram made a noticeable o shape with his mouth before grinning. "Ladies, I give you Mark Ford, Viscount of Trent."

Mark leaned forward once more to place a kiss onto Belle's hand. As he rose, he had the keenest of expressions. "Tis an honor to have a lady such as yourself pay great consideration over a topic that has no importance to you."

"That is not so, my Lord. I take great care over the topic. Our father cared for his lands for most of mine and my sister's lifetime. Right down to the very hands that he stands beside when the harvest is set. So, I care, my Lord."

Just when Mark smiled, and was to speak, Bram asked abruptly, "Your sister?" He glanced at Anita, just as she held her breath.

Belle seemed to have broken from her daze, as she looked as though she saw Bram for the first time. "Oh! Oh yes, Annie! I am sorry, this is my sister. Miss Anita Henderson, eldest daughter to the Viscount of Hemmingway."

Anita curtsied, but as she slowly brought her gaze up to Bram, there was no mistaking the haze that cloaked his eyes. Was that disappointment she nearly witnessed? Anita tried her best to ignore the sudden drop in her stomach. It surprised her to see such a reaction. She thought he would be pleased to finally know who she was. After all, he had come so far to look for her.

Mark turned to smile back at Bram. He swung his arm out in introduction, "My ladies, this is Bram Will- "

"Mark!" Bram suddenly interrupted.

Mark looked surprised as he cast his friend a confused expression. Everyone was silent. The scaling water fountain grew in sound as it splashed and cascaded down the marble rock stones. Anita's stomach had fallen. Something in Bram changed. No longer were his eyes brimming with heated desire. Rather instead they were glanced down at their feet. Anita quietly released her pent-up sigh. She should have known better to have hoped that he was as needful for her than she was for him. Her arms dropped as she too looked down before her.

"Well, there's a sudden chill in the air. Why don't we warm up? Belle, Mark, would you be interested in chasing in the garden maze? Annie, let us go too, and get lost. Bram, be a lamb, and be the one to find us!" Christina announced as she snapped Anita out of her slum when she began to pull at her arm.

"That sounds like a marvelous idea!" Belle answered joyfully. She began to follow, but quickly slowed to look back to check if Mark followed.

With a short glance to his friend, Mark nodded, smiled, and quickly rushed to step beside Belle. Anita heard the two laugh before she saw them step into one of the rows of hedges and disappearing. Anita knew she should have spoken out to her sister that she needed to be accompanied, but as she looked at Bram just before stepping inside the maze, froze her. He was looking at her with the most heated of expressions; Anita nearly tripped while trying to believe what she saw.

Chapter 8

B ram watched as the others made their way into the garden maze. His thoughts were in turmoil as the worst of his suspicions finally came to light. She was of the Ton. His Annie was no ordinary woman, but Anita Henderson, the eldest daughter of a Viscount! Everything they had done came crashing across layers of his thoughts.

He had deflowered a noble's daughter. Though he had all sorts of encounters in the past, strangely this felt different. What was this feeling? Was it shame? Bram was bewildered, and that only left him feeling suddenly furious.

It was not right. Bram should not be feeling this way. He reminded himself that she too had wanted it. That it was a mutual desire. But as he caught her gaze just before she stepped into the maze, the intensity of his thoughts stabbed his gut. She deserved better than what he had done to her. A better gentleman would have married her right after such an encounter. To save her reputation.

Again, furious cinders raved in his gut. Bram was not the sort to fall into such an ordeal. He had promised to never find himself trapped in a situation like this. And yet, he could not back away. Despite his screaming thoughts to run from there, Bram was slowly walking towards the direction of hedges Annie was dragged into. Tightening his grip, Bram had to end this, before anything more bound them closer. Or worse, she found out about his title and wealth.

Entering the maze, he heard laughter and music in the distance. Upon first coming out here, Bram knew the maze was not large enough to get lost and would be easy for

Annie to come find them. But as he wandered down the dirt path, he realized smaller rows of hedges hid within the larger ones. He felt himself walking in circles.

The darkened path did not help matters either. As he strode deeper, lesser candle lamps filled the space. Bram stopped. He decided to make his way back the direction he came from, unwilling to lose his way. But as he turned, he felt warm hands steady his coat.

Bram froze as he turned full around. Annie was staring into his chest, her features stunned, as though she surprised herself for catching him. Bram was just as impressed that he had to remember to take a deep breath. As he did, Annie's gaze widened, and she observed his expression. He half smiled as he watched her take in the sight of him.

She noticeably softened, and strangely her body felt closer than before. Did he imagine it? Being this close again, after so long, caused Bram's cock to stiffen. Just when he wanted to kiss her, Annie began to pull her hands away from his coat. He caught them just before.

"I thought I was the one to come find you?" Bram approved, as he lifted her hand to his lips. The sweet aroma of roses and honey faintly lingered on her skin. Bram found himself intoxicated once again, which surprised him. After all, he had just been thinking of ending things with her. He ridiculed the thought now. How could he have even considered doing that when she had such an effect on him?

"I…" Anita hesitated, just as Bram nipped the tip of one of her fingers.

"Yes, my sweet?"

"I…almost did not come. I had planned to go back into the ball. Back to reality. But then I realized that this is real, you, and this maze. Everything that happened between us. I know now I need to make a choice."

Suddenly Bram felt cautious. As though he feared what she was about to reveal. Or more like, end herself. Everything within Bram told him that it was for the best. That she deserved more, like a proper courting. Not a life of debauchery that Bram was so used to giving. Strangely, however, Bram realized he was not ready to give her up. He knew who she was now, but his desires fought against his logical reasoning.

"Bram, I feel that we shou-"

"I'm not going to let you go, Annie. This cannot end between us when it has only begun. I know you wish to end this, but I swear to you that you will not regret it. I will show you unimaginable pleasures. I will protect your reputation. I promise you; no one will know of this."

Bram was nearly mute when he finished. This was the first time he ever felt like he had to convince a woman to be his. It felt odd, but strangely challenging. His thoughts quieted, and his mouth went dry when Anita looked down. Her gaze was distant as though she was coming up with a reason to end their time together.

Just when he was about to bite his tongue, he spied the slight smile hovering above her lips. A quiet giggle escaped. When she lifted her gaze, there was a shy blush across her cheeks. Her smile only grew when suddenly she leaned forward to place a gentle kiss to Bram's lips. Bram almost felt dumbfounded, but his chest felt lighter.

"Did I miss something?" Bram asked with a grin. "What were you going to say?"

"I was going to say that I felt we needed to continue this. That it was my wish, and I wanted to know what you felt towards the matter." Anita's eyes crinkled as she observed Bram's relieved expression. "Your answer was more than welcomed."

Bram released a huff of air, smiled, and caressed Anita's cheek. "You truly do surprise me."

Her eyes softened as she leaned into Bram's touch. "Just as surprising, like when you found out who I was?"

Bram stiffened, but tried to keep his touch tender. He watched his hand slip down to the ridges of her neck. His thumb caressed the silk lacing of her collar. When he did not answer, Anita's brow knitted, as she noticed his faint scowl.

"You do not like that I am a Viscount's daughter. I saw it in your eyes, Bram."

"I...do not like to associate myself with the Ton," Bram responded.

"And yet, they seem to know you," Anita observed

softly.

"They know OF me," Bram answered distantly. He fought the urge to pull away from her. Old feelings erupted, and the anger burned in his chest like acid. He tried to tamper it down, advising his thoughts that it was not her doing. That Annie's statement only proved that she really did not know anything about him. How much he suddenly wished to keep that from her.

Bram gazed into Annie's eyes, and found no judgement. No suspicion, treachery, or scorn. No, she merely admired him. Her eyes soft and kind, and the realization struck his chest. Bram did not want her to look at him in any other way.

He sighed and leaned his head against hers. When he opened his eyes, he found her watching him through her lashes. Bram half laughed, raised his head, and said, "Come see a play with me next Thursday."

Anita laughed, "What play?"

"That's a surprise. But I have no doubt that you will love it."

"Which theater?"

"Le Opera Magenta."

"I do not know where that is," Anita scowled.

Bram caressed her wrinkled lip, and grinned, "The Godfrey Rose will know. Ask her. I will also send a letter to you through her if you do not mind."

Anita briefly looked away, and gently bit her lip. "You know of my friend?"

"She is an acquaintance." Bram stroked the worry from Anita's eyes. He could see her thoughts so clearly now. He loved that she was so easy to read once she was calm and relaxed with him.

Anita smiled, "I look forward to our next meeting then, and to your letter. Shall we make our way back to the ball?"

"Yes, but first I must have something to tide me over till next Thursday," Bram said in a low tone.

"What do you-?"

Anita's voice failed as Bram moved closer and pressed

her back against the hedge wall. To his satisfaction, his Annie was relaxed but breathless to be as close again. Her eyes were soft and low as she waited for his affection. Bram took in the moment, as he felt her warmth seeping through his chest. He smiled as he heard her silent urgency for his touch. It was a faint sound, but it was more than enough to encourage Bram's desires.

He kissed her. Bram kissed her with all the passion that had been pent up from the many days he had not seen her. She tasted like sweet warm wine, and before long Bram had his arms wrapped all around her. She too hung to him as though her knees were to give. Bram opened his eyes briefly only to see hers closed as if in a soft dream.

His lips released hers, but he still held on to her. Anita was breathless, but as she opened her eyes she was in a daze and smiled. "Thank you."

Bram chuckled, "Why is it that you're always thanking me?" He kissed the tip of her nose.

Anita hummed, "I suppose, I am thanking you for how you make me feel. This is all quite new to me," she confessed.

Bram took a small step back to observe her expression, and found pure honesty and content. If only he could take her right here, at this moment. The sensation pulsed in his groin. The memory of her face lost in pleasure nearly sent him over the edge. He gulped a deep breath and held out his arm. "It probably would be best that I escort you back to the ball. Wouldn't want your sister wondering where you have gone."

"She has gone ahead inside actually. To dance the second waltz with your friend, Mark," Anita said as she fitted her arm into his and began to walk with him up the path.

"Good man." Bram spoke with a smile. "And the Godfrey Rose?"

Anita looked straight ahead with a slight grin. "I sent her inside. I wanted to have the opportunity to speak with you." Her voice sounded almost proud.

Indeed, her actions were not what he had expected she would do. What no ordinary honorable lady would do. But Bram was beginning to suspect that Anita seemed to be different from them. With that thought, his chest felt lighter. Though he had dreaded that she was of the Ton, he now strangely felt hopeful. For what, he was not certain. He simply wished to spend more time with her. To pleasure her. To give her the experience she had never known. Who better to show her his world than him? The thought satisfied him.

As they approached the lighted path, Bram could see the opening doors to the ball, patrons and gentlefolk were upon the porch above the stairs. Though his gut cringed, he stopped them both. Turning to grasp her hand, he delighted in the way she moved closer to him.

"How much I wish I could take you inside, but it may be for the best that I let you go ahead of me. If they see me, it will most certainly draw unwanted attention upon you, my sweet."

Anita's smile softened, and she nodded. Gently pulling herself away, she turned to face him. "Will I ever get to know who you are, Bram?"

He simply grinned and touched her cheek. "Perhaps. When the time is right."

Anita looked as though she wanted to say something but thought better of it. Bram wanted to reassure her; however, the truth was he didn't want his reputation to deter her from him. Stroking the inside of her palm, he simply said, "Soon. Be expecting my letter."

She nodded, and with a final glance, turned to make her way up to the ball. As he watched her go, an impulse screamed for Bram to capture her once more for another heated embrace. It was not until he saw a herd of patrons step out from the ball, with their colored feathered fans, that he stopped. He could see them eyeing Annie as she approached them. Every one of them, with their beady eyes, judging the way his Annie walked, dressed, and how she greeted them.

His temper waned, however, when he saw she had not bothered to pay them her time. Anita simply walked past them and into the ball, their heads following behind her. Anita had the grace of a lady, but a will all her own. Bram admired that. *Perhaps there is hope yet...*

Chapter 9

A nita sat, waiting for Bram to arrive at the theater box she was in. The dark velvet covered chairs were gripped under her fingers. She was breathless. L'Opéra Magenta was astonishing! Never had she sat in a theater house with exquisite architecture. The polished woodwork spiraled across each of the balcony boxes, where they held heavy embroidered curtains. Anita surprisingly observed that these curtains could close, creating a private box, hidden from the audience below. What if Bram closed them in? A sudden thrill ran up her spine, the thought only leaving her ever more anxious for his arrival.

She focused her attention back to L'Opéra. The high vaulted ceiling distinguished such refinement, a grand mosaic painted. Multicolored rings encircled over a choir of spiraling designs. She was in awe of its beauty. Looking down upon the stretched rows of the audience, she saw the faces of every sort that could be seen in London. Ages of all classes sat amongst each other, laughing, boisterous together.

Closer to stage, the orchestra were already in tune, playing the faintest of music. They were aglow, surrounded by candlelight in the pit below the stage. The violins were soft, like a whisper. The basses were humming alongside. Anita found it fascinating how it reminded her of the sort of music one would hear in a dream.

The stage was closed off by a large velvet curtain. She

was excited to see the play. Christina had told her she was going to love it when she delivered Bram's letter. Christina was as thrilled as she, once the mystery of who Bram was became known. Christina confessed that she knew Bram. They were associated within the same circle, and he was one of the good friends to Richard, Christina's gentleman.

The two of them had come together, excited. Christina had insisted she wear the ruby red gown she owned, versus the sea green she originally had chosen. She said that red is the color for theater, the blood of art. Anita simply giggled at her friend. Looking down now at the curves of her breasts pressed against the fabric, Anita had the suspicion there were other reasons why her friend had chosen this dress.

No matter how much Anita had tried to prod her friend into telling her who Bram was, it only led Christina to simply say, "There's a reason Bram hasn't told you, though silly that it is. But I do know one thing about Bram. He doesn't like to be judged for his title."

Anita found that intriguing. Never had she met anyone who so fiercely rejected the ways of entitlement than him. It was easy to assume that he was of the Ton but hated to be introduced by it. Even his letter had only his initials signed. *B.W.* Anita was riveted and wanted to know more. *Why was there so much mystery surrounding them?* Anita thought.

The candles around the theater began to dim out, at the same time the orchestra quieted. People filled in their seats, as couples in the balconies moved forward to the railings. Anita wondered if Christina was in one of the balcony boxes. She knew her friend was in attendance, after she dropped Anita off. Probably with Richard, Anita thought with a smile.

Suddenly, warm lips brushed against Anita's neck. His shadow of a beard scraped delightfully across her nape. Her eyes fell as she took in Bram's warm spicy scent. His hand wrapped around her cheek, moving her face upward as he trailed his lips to hers. Anita faintly moaned to taste him again. It was a gentle kiss, lasting.

When Bram sat down beside her, she was glowing. All

the anticipation, worry, dissipated into sweet comfort and pleasure. Anita was awestruck with how Bram always made her feel. He smiled at her, a genuine grin which showed his clean white teeth. He looked rugged with his shadow of a beard, but his eyes were in delight. Filled with nothing but her, and Anita soaked it in.

It was not until she realized where she was, that she began to glance around, the tiny worry that someone may have seen their embrace. Bram's warm hand caressed her gaze back to him. His head bent, and his eyes deep into hers. "There's no one here that will pay us mind, Anita."

She took a steady breath, comforted by his words, and by the pleasure of hearing him speak her real name for the first time. "Are you certain?" she still could not help but ask.

"Quite. We are in my world now..." Bram said just as the orchestra began their intro, and the velvet curtains opened.

Anita's eyes widened. The stage was grand with an enchanting setting of vibrant colors, floating candles, and a woodland forest. The background had a rising full moon with tinted blue light giving it its glow. When the actors arrived on stage and began their songs, Anita realized which play this was. How too familiar this all felt.

"A Midsummer Night's Dream..." she whispered.

Bram was watching her every expression, smiling when he heard her words. He saw the memory of their first encounter cross her features. This was what he was waiting for, the fulfilled satisfaction of having his Annie here, in his theater. In his own private box. The thrill only excited him more. However, Bram could not ignore the glances being cast their way. He was speaking the truth when he told her she need not worry, but that didn't leave onlookers to not notice that Bram had a woman with him in his private balcony, something he had never done.

Before diving too deep at that thought, Anita looked to him then, and bestowed upon him the most glorious smile. His mind immediately quieted, his body growing both hot and relaxed. The second act began to perform, and her gaze shot back to the stage. The same scene in the book she left off at started, and Bram noticed that this was her favorite part. Her face lightened, and her eyes danced.

Bram used this moment to marvel at her beauty. The blush lingering at her cheeks. Her silky dark brown curls were pinned on top of her head, few wild strands falling across her nape. That ruby red dress hugged every curve of her body, making her look succulent and ripe. Her breasts called to him, their soft sun kissed color enchanting him. And again, Bram realized how he had never been with a woman like her.

Anita was fresh as the sunrise in Spring. She was pure and kind, and honestly expressed her feelings without a single word. He rested his arm on his knee, watching her behind his hand. They could have a momentous affair together, Bram thought with a hidden smile. He had no doubt a liaison with his Annie would be both fruitful and secure. In no way was she like the others, or worse, like the ballerina. Seeking his title, or fortune.

Although Bram did not want to admit it now, Anita was of the Ton. There still was the risk that she be exposed or become with child.

Strangely, Bram did not feel concerned. He felt assured that he would be in control. In fact, Bram prided himself with his history of not losing sense in the throes of passion. Indeed, gazing at his Annie only left him with the same longing she had on her expression at this very moment. He needed to have her. Now. If not, just a taste of her.

Bram slowly reached for the tie that held the heavy curtain open. He knew what he was about to do; she would wish for privacy. When Anita noticed the curtain move, her eyes fluttered. She took in a gulp of breath, and Bram saw the realization dawn on her face. She had expected this, and Bram felt satisfaction fill his chest.

The box darkened, save for a low-lit gas lamp next to the door. The sounds from the play muffled, and Bram could hear the deep quick breaths coming from Anita. Kneeling before her, he grazed his hands up to her knees, feeling them tremble. He shushed her calmly, easing her body to relax. Bram reached up to caress her cheek and deliver her a kiss.

"Be still, Annie. I merely wish to taste you..."

Anita expelled all her breath as she licked her lips. Excitement built in between her legs as her fantasies became reality, with this man bent low at her feet. This rogue that radiated passion in his fingertips. She was not shaking because she was nervous. No, Anita thought. She was trembling because she needed this. Had longed for Bram day and night since they have last seen each other. Since their last passionate embrace.

Bram's hands slowly gripped at her hem, his face calm, but his gaze burning. His brows knitted slightly. "Say yes, Annie. Say that you want me to taste you."

Anita felt faint. His request was exquisitely sensuous. His words rang through her belly as though he was already stroking her. With a soft moan, she nodded.

"Say it..." Bram glided his hands beneath and up her ankles gently. So gently, Anita felt the gooseflesh shiver up her legs.

Closing her eyes to thrive in his touch, Anita whispered, "I... want you to taste me."

Bram groaned, licking his lips as he lifted the bottom of her dress and petticoats over Anita's thighs. She had gone without her drawers, only leaving her chemise bunched at her knees. Slowly spreading her legs, Bram rubbed the stubble of his beard across the inner skin. Anita's breath hitched as her head fell back.

By the stroke of his touch, he made her come alive, just as the orchestra's music rose in choir. Bram glided his fingers across the lips of her core, delighted in the sleek wetness that awaited him. He touched the swollen nub that had aroused and tormented her so for many nights before seeing him again. Her body jolted as she felt his warm silk tongue, and she moaned as he swept it across her center. Bram essentially drew in her scent and taste.

He ravished her, in no way that Anita could have imagined. Even compared to their first embrace, this was far more urgent. Bram was hungry for her, and she needed him just as much.

When he knew she was wet enough, Bram slowly pushed in a finger to the hilt. Just as he began to move it,

Anita's eyes squeezed shut and her body exploded in waves of pleasure. Her cries were tuned out by the character Helena's song. When Bram did not stop, Anita weakly pushed at his head. She felt his laugh vibrate against her now sensitive skin.

"Enough for you?" Bram grinned from her knee.

"I cannot feel my body. It feels as though it has flown away from me." Anita lazily smiled.

"It has. You are as sweet as I remembered," Bram said as he licked his lips and rose to give her a long kiss, her taste filling her senses. Anita could not help but deeply blush.

"Did you know that this would happen?" Bram indicated the curtain with a tilt of his head.

"The thought did cross my mind. I just had not concluded that you would. Especially here, in such a theater." Anita gave a laugh. "My, what would the owner think? To know what things were done in this beautiful velvet box."

Bram grinned wide. *If only she knew...*

The thought caused him to realize just how much he wanted her to know that this theater was his. That he had put in the work to build this place from the ground up. Straightening her gown, Bram rose to take her hand, his decision clear. Kissing her soft scented fingers, he smiled. "Follow me."

Bram's chest swelled when she trustingly grasped his hand. Then he smiled when he saw her brows knit, as she glanced towards the dropped curtain. The choir was now singing. Bram kissed her hand, bringing her attention back to him. "You'll be back to see this play, as many times as you like. I promise you."

Anita looked like she was curiously thinking what he meant. But Bram then took a step back, to which she easily followed suit. She smiled, and Bram could see the honey gleam in her eyes. She was excited to explore with him, which gave Bram a warm feeling in his gut.

They shortly crossed to the wooden enameled staircase. The way up the flight of stairs turned darker, as it rose above the balcony floor. Bram felt Anita's hand tighten in his. From fear, or excitement, Bram wondered. But as they reached the final landing, to a hall lit with Moroccan lanterns, Anita relaxed softly. He glanced to her and found her face in gentle curiosity and wonder.

As they walked down the hall, Bram caught her stroking the velvet walls gently, her smile growing. He smiled to himself, but then back to her when they reached the closed door to his office. Anita looked on curiously, she stopped just before he opened it. They stepped in together, and she examined Bram's office.

"Welcome," Bram said, with an open hand placed on top of his desk. A proud feeling filled him when realization crossed her eyes.

"This is your office...?" Anita asked, amazed.

Bram grinned, "This is my theater." He nearly chuckled when he saw the look on her face. Closing her mouth, Anita hummed, glancing around. He wondered what she thought of his wide yet quaint wood walls. Shelving covered with play books and blueprint scrolls lined the far east wall. A stained-glass window with mosaic design hung to the west side. The rest of his office was simple, save for his large wood carved desk, that had claw carved foot stands, and red lining spirals at each corner of the surface. It was surely big enough to fit a couple upon it. The thought of seeing Anita there, face lost in bliss, nearly sent his cock into a frenzy.

"How extraordinary. This is one of the most beautiful theaters I have ever been in," Anita expressed as she slowly moved around Bram's office.

Sitting down now on the corner of his desk, Bram watched her explore his domain innocently, unaware of his heated desire. Despite the ache in his nether regions, he found himself soothed to see her in his space. "Have you been to many theaters?" he asked curiously.

Anita shook her head slightly, as she stopped at the opposite corner from him, tracing the red spiral on the edge. "I had been in one once, during my coming out season. But that was a shoebox compared to this place." She laughed softly.

"I'll take that as a compliment, then." Bram chuckled as he leaned slightly closer. "You lived in the Americas?" He stated more than asked. Bram already knew since Mark had already informed him. In fact, Bram had come to find out much from Mark, and his adoration for Anita's sister. Like when and where all the soon-to-be parties were to be, and if the sisters were attending. But he wanted to hear her speak about herself, and her time living in another country. Something he could understand, since he lived in Morocco for a good while. He surprised himself for feeling that way, even when he simply enjoyed watching her quiet serenity.

Anita's eyes went soft, as her hand found one of his pen quills. She stroked its black dotted feather, as she seemed to reflect a fond memory. "Yes. For most of my life. We moved there when I was a child."

"Did you enjoy the wild?" Bram smirked softly, then stood and walked to the wooden coat rack by the door. He unbuttoned his jacket to get comfortable and hung it up by one of the hooks, all the while soaking in the way she was devouring the sight of him. He smiled genuinely at how captivated she easily got.

She glanced back down to the feather quill with a flushed smile. "It was the most beautiful place. We have farmland there, so we lived quaint and by the land. My favorite time of the year there was the spring. We had an apple tree that grew beside our home. And every year, it filled the rooms with the smell of fresh apples. It was good there. Peaceful..."

Bram noticed her stop short, still staring down at his desk. He could see the faintest scowl upon her brow. "I heard the news of what is happening there. If it is true of what has been talked about, then it is a good thing that your family moved back here when they did. War seems to be on the horizon."

Anita drew in a deep breath, turning her face away, and that caused Bram's gut to drop. He stepped closer to her, lifting her face to look at him. There were no tears, but the deep sorrow was present in her gaze. She gave a sad half smile before saying, "I'm sorry. I try not to think about it. I have dear friends still living there. To think that if war broke out, then they could get caught in it. I cannot bear the thought of them being hurt."

Bram stroked her cheek. He could hear the honest fear in her words, and something within him wanted to immediately soothe her. Leaning forward, Bram stroke her lower lip with his thumb, tempting her closer to him. When he finally kissed her, they shared a breath. Leaning into her, all Bram wanted was to give her peace. Pleasure. Satisfaction. He knew he could give these to her. But what gave him pause was that he wanted to make her feel safe, and happy.

In that moment, Bram knew without a doubt that he wanted her all to himself. To always see her smile, and to be the cause of that joy. Pulling back, he saw no more worry in her now longing gaze.

"Thank you..." Anita smiled gently.

Bram chuckled, his desire only growing more definite. "Annie, I brought you up here because I wanted you to see my theater. To get to know a piece of me. This is something I don't normally do," he said as he stroked the curve of her back.

Anita gazed at him, openly relaxing and smiling. "I deeply appreciate that, Bram. I do." She answered sincerely, leaning her head against his shoulder.

Bram grinned, and nodded. "Yes, also, amongst other things. We need to discuss our meetings." He turned to lean against his desk once more and pulled her closer to his hips. "I'm certain that we both wish to see more of each other. However, because of your status, it poses a serious risk to your reputation. We must think smartly about our meeting arrangements."

"It seemed we were fine all this time before," Anita said, focused on the closeness of each other.

"We were lucky before. But since I showed my face at that ball, eyes will start looking around for scandal. Especially on you, I'm afraid, since I danced with you."

"Only from a dance?" Anita asked, surprised. Bram could not help but grin.

"Especially from a dance. They say the waltz is as close to love making than the actual act." Bram emphasized the point by rocking his hips against hers.

Anita laughed, slightly blushing. "I suppose that could be true." She looked down for a moment, and it seemed like a thought crossed her mind. Anita suddenly had a serious frown. When she glanced back up, her expression lightened slightly. "You are right, however. We should approach this cautiously. What do you suggest?"

Bram could see the sincerity in her eyes. The moment that made her different from all the folly women he had encountered. Reaching up, he stroked the curl of hair that had fallen forward. "We enjoy it, that's for certain." When she smiled softly, his chest lightened. "We can meet either here at the theater, or...at my home."

At her astonished expression, he realized the words that left his mouth. He had suggested his home? Never had he asked a woman to his home before. They both stood for a moment in silence. Would she be too appalled at the thought of coming to his home? Should he take it back? But before he could, Anita leaned in and placed her hand on his chest.

"Would that be safe?" She asked quietly. Bram smiled, releasing a breath.

"I guarantee it. I live on the South Bank of Newington. It's quiet, with its own private drive, and few neighbors," Bram answered. He felt proud to talk about his home now. A home he built on his own, which was not passed down by his father. His father's home was given to Bram's mother instead. He had found the perfect land, and it was away from London's high society. And right across the river Thames, this theater stood.

"Oh my, across the river. But I live near Hyde Park. How would I be able to cross to your home?" Anita asked, her eyes showing her mind trying to find a solution. She looked captivating... "I suppose I could take a cabby."

Bram was so engrossed at the thought of her in his home, it took him a moment to realize what she said. "Wait... you will not. I will send for my man, Jefferson, to get you and bring you there."

Anita's lips parted slightly, "That is exceedingly kind of you. But I would not wish to impose on Jefferson. I could find my own way."

Bram could not help but chuckle. Anita was being a lady without masquerading as one. To think her capable of handling herself in this sort of situation left him feeling proud of her. "It's no trouble. Besides, I cannot trust anyone but Jefferson to deliver someone so precious to me."

Anita looked down as she slightly bit her lip. When Bram touched her cheek, she leaned into his palm. He kissed her then, unable to resist. Her lips melted like butter against his, and her quick moan nearly set his loins on fire. The kiss lasted for only mere seconds, but they parted breathless.

"How will I know to meet you?" Anita asked blushing, her eyes low on his lips.

"Shall we meet every Thursday? Three o'clock?" Perhaps Bram was ahead of himself, but he could not help it. He knew deep down he wanted to see her at every chance he could. To have been denied so long before, ached him. Seeing her now smile grow, only excited him further.

"I suppose I can tell my family that I've joined a club," she laughed.

Bram smiled, "Yes, a quilting club."

That made Anita giggle more, clear excitement flushing her cheeks. She reached for them now, feeling how warm they were against her cool palms. "I must confess. I cannot believe I'm doing this."

Bram brought her delicate hands to his, looking at them joined. "Neither can I, to be honest. I've always had a solid rule not to get involved with ladies of the Ton."

Anita frowned, "Why?"

Bram looked at her, part of him contemplating whether to explain. But he was curious as to how she would respond. "Perhaps you can remember. London ladies are often only after wealth and title. Seemingly do anything to fool a man into marriage."

He paused, observing her eyes. She did not flinch or hide anything. She simply nodded. "I understand, I am familiar with women who are exactly so. It must be difficult not knowing who to trust."

Bram blinked, unsure of what to say. Was he expecting her to fail his test? Had he assumed less from her? But at the same time, he was relieved. But what she said next surprised him, for her tone was serious.

"I am not looking for marriage, Bram. I want you to know that. I am well past the age for it, and not expecting it either. What we will have will be purely friendship, and pleasure."

When Bram processed her words, he could not help the slight chuckle that then turned into a laugh.

"What's so funny?" Anita asked, her face baffled with a confused smile.

"My apologies. It just occurred to me that I've never had a woman who was a friend before." Bram grinned, kissing her hand, and bringing it to rest on his mid chest. Anita smirked, slightly shaking her head. She then grabbed his hand in a firm handshake.

"Well, sir. Then tis my pleasure to be your first female companion." Anita had on the sweetest yet sincerest expression. Bram could not help but soften his grip. She certainly eased him enough to be counted as such. No other woman had such an effect on him in that way, that is for certain.

"So, shall I write my address down?" Anita asked pleasantly. Bram smiled, and moved aside, giving her room to reach for his ink and spotted quill. When she leaned over his desk to write, Bram could not help but place his hand over her left hip, her warmth seeping through the dress fabric. He recalled the way her silken hips looked wrapped around his. His grip tightened.

When she finished, Anita handed him the sheet of paper. Bram knew where her home was. "Very good. I shall have Jefferson wait for you closer to Kensington Road. That is not too far for you?"

Anita shook her head. "No, that works perfectly. But how will I know Jefferson and your carriage?"

"I will introduce the both of you later tonight when I take you home. It will be dark, no one will be about, so it shouldn't be a risk." Bram squeezed her closer to him, pleased by their plans. He could see that she was as well, for when she turned to him, she had sweet desire in her gaze.

"Now that we have sorted everything out, may I ask for a favor?" she asked shyly.

Bram grinned, feeling a little uncertain. "What sort

of favor?"

Anita looked down, rubbing her lips together. Suddenly Bram felt a warm chill cross his nape. "I... would like to give you something."

Anita could see the slight suspicion in his eyes, and immediately she wanted to wipe that look from his gaze. She wanted to give him something that showed how much she desired him. To show how she appreciated all that he had introduced to her. Looking down at his white shirt, her eyes trailed to the opening of his trousers. Taking a deep breath of courage, her fingers reached for the fastenings.

Almost suddenly, Bram tensed then relaxed once he realized what she was doing. His eyes darkened, and he leaned back further to better help her reach for the buttons. His mouth opened, then closed, and he released a breath. Bram's entire demeanor was almost nervous, which caused her to smile. "Speechless for once, Bram?"

He chuckled, "Well, I can't help it when you surprise me so." Bram's chest dipped when she unbuttoned the last of his trousers. His eyes were drawn to her hand that was slipping inside the opening. His breath caught the moment she touched his cock, and he dropped his full weight on the desk. Anita felt excitement build in her belly at what she was about to do.

Dropping down on to her knees, she gently drew out his member. His warm length pulsed within her hand, and again she was amazed at the sheer size of seeing it again. Licking her lips, she leaned forward. But before she could kiss his tip, Bram stopped her, caressing her cheek. "You are...amazing for doing this."

She smiled shyly, "I'm returning the favor."

Bram stared at her for a moment, with a look that stirred her heart. When he drew away his hand, he lingered his touch on her lips. Licking his own, Bram smiled and leaned back. "This is more than a favor. It's a gift."

Anita smiled, understanding that all they had shared was a gift to one another. And this act of passion was another moment between them. She leaned in and took him into her mouth, the contact causing them both to moan. She was pleasingly stunned when he jolted in place.

She suckled his tip, amazed and in wonder with the taste of him. When her grip tightened, Bram groaned. Anita pulled away, worried that she hurt him. Bram bemoaned, reaching for her hand. "No, don't fret. That felt good. Continue what you were doing. Please."

Feeling assured, Anita held fast onto his shaft, and as she continued, Bram fell back into a relaxed state, the ends of his fingers stroking her hair. After a while, she noticed that his moans grew louder as she took him deeper into her mouth. She found the right rhythm that was both comfortable for her and intensified his groans. His hand grew urgent as it curled in her hair, as his whole body tensed. For a second, it almost felt like Bram was trying to pull away.

Anita did not want to draw away, however. The act drove her into a state of sweet delirium. Her senses swam in delight against the delectable scent of his heat. Suddenly, the essence of his very loins filled her, as if the earth seemingly rocked her to her core. Anita then noticed the excitement that had built within her own body, the pulsing ache that arose between her legs. Chills rolled across her skin.

She found him watching her, his eyes low and dreamlike. Anita smiled. "That was amazing."

Bram's chest rumbled with a lazy laugh. He lifted her and pulled her against him. "Yes, you are." He kissed her, deep and longingly, the embrace adding flames to the ache within her. The taste of him was still on her lips, and Anita was astonished at how amazingly erotic their kiss was.

A kiss, Anita thought, she wanted to last forever.

Chapter 10

Anita smiled into her teacup. Even she could not deny the glow that she was feeling. Three months had passed since she and Bram made their arrangements clear, and during that time, Anita never felt as free as she did now. Well, to a certain extent. She was still needed to attend this small gathering for tea with ladies that she had no interest in. But she passed the time by reminiscing her sensuous memories with Bram. The heat of them caused her to blush and sip on her tea a little more enthusiastically.

She recalled the night at L'Opéra Magenta when she had first tasted Bram. That being the beginning of Anita's sensualist journey, she thought with a laugh. He had been surprised by her actions, which matched her own. But he was entirely impressed by them as well. Later that same night, he took her to meet Jefferson. The coachman that was to transport her to Bram's home, and later, to anywhere she desired.

At first, Jefferson seemed aloof. Refusing to really look her in the eye, he had only nodded politely when Bram introduced her, along with his instructions. Even that first Thursday, when she met Jefferson along Kensington Road, he had said nothing more than, "Good afternoon, miss." And swiftly let her in the coach without a moment's delay. Anita knew the situation they were in was not the most comfortable of arrangements. Especially considering how important it was to remain out of sight. But Anita wanted to befriend the loyal man. Find what made him a trusted companion to his master. And perhaps, even soothe her nerves on the way to Bram's estate.

That was not entirely easy, however. Jefferson kept to himself for most of their earliest encounters. Either not saying a word or answering with a shrug if she had asked about his morning. It was not until the fourth week in, when Anita made a breakthrough. She decided to bring him a basket with a roasted beef and watercress sandwich, and a small decanter of aged red wine. At first, Jefferson was stunned, loosening the reins to the horses to uncork the decanter and savor the sweet-scented wine.

A slow thankful smile spread across his face, and for the first time since their meeting, he looked her in the eye. Nodding, he quietly thanked her for the meal. From that moment on, whenever she met with him, he greeted her politely, and commented on the weather. They soon began to have light conversations, but not about Bram, mainly on himself. Jefferson told her about his home life growing up in Kent, how he was but a child of sixteen when he took over the coach for the late master, before Bram. This gave Anita pause, for only a family of title would have attendants that span for generations.

She did not comment on this, however. Anita knew that when the time was right, Bram would indulge her curiosity. Already she and Bram were making leaps and bounds from when they first met. The past three months nurtured their companionship in ways Anita never thought would. It had the moment she stepped into his home.

Upon arrival, Jefferson promptly let her out of the carriage. They had ridden down a long driveway, and before that Anita enjoyed watching the river flow down the bank. Bram was honest about there not being any neighbors near. For most of the area was bare, save for a few shops, and port merchants. She found it thrilling to be so far away from Hyde Park, and what seemed like the rest of the world. Beyond the bridge, she finally felt like she could breathe.

That is until she stood before Bram's home. Her mouth dropped with how extraordinarily designed it was. It was not like any other Victorian home. The front façade was a light sandy masonry, with gold and wood trimmed diamond-paned windows decorating the first and second floors. A pointed arch window at the center between them, and a portico supporting the balcony above the entrance way. Unlike most Victorian homes, Bram's was mixed with English and Mediterranean aspects. But what stuck out to her most was the front wood doorway. It was engraved with decorative gold motifs, spiral designs that reminded her of L'Opéra Magenta.

By the time Anita brought her eyes down to ground level, Bram was standing at the now open entrance, grinning at her. She bashfully smiled as she walked up to him.

"You look wonderfully surprised." Bram sounded proud.

Anita chuckled, "How can I not be? Bram, your home is amazing."

Bram nodded, clearly pleased by her response as he knocked on the door's solid trimming. "I'm glad you think so. This here is by far my greatest achievement."

He welcomed her inside, immediately placing a hand at her waist. "Oh? What about L'Opér-?"

Anita went speechless the moment she walked inside. The interior of the home was even more astonishing than the outside. The ceiling showed exposed wood rafters and met with decorative trim molding. At the entrance, four columns opened the foyer, a large oriental rug on the floor warmed the area with its maroon and yellow spirals. By the far-left column, the dark wood staircase led to the second floor. But before that, an open dining room was exposed to the sunlight by the multicolored diamond-paned windows. To the right, she could easily see a cozy sitting room, lavished with more colorfully printed rugs, and pillows. Cherry wood furniture adorned the area and was placed close to a surround fireplace with blue and white tiles.

The home was breathtaking, and nothing like Anita had ever seen. Even the central hallway felt as though it went straight through the building. Something caught her eye, as she continued looking down the hall. Her gawking must have amused Bram because he suddenly broke out with a laugh.

"Your curiosity is beyond captivating. Would you like to see more of my home?" Bram asked, as he took her hand. Anita was thrilled, nodded soundly, and followed.

Walking down the hall, Anita detected the fresh scent of water, and plants. To her extreme amazement, they entered a small atrium that had entranceways from each direction. The ceiling opened through the middle of the home, leaving the clear sky free to see. The middle of the floor had a flat circular pool, with more of the same blue and white colored tiles decorating its bottom. This was what had caught her eye earlier. The walls were teemed with plants and a few chairs sat by one corner.

"This is breathtaking," Anita said as she moved closer to the pool of water. "How does it not overflow when it rains?"

Bram smiled, and much to Anita's surprise, went and placed his bare feet in the shallow water. He indicated the small holes around the ridge of the pool, and the one at the very bottom. "The impluvium is designed to hold only a certain amount of standing water. Once it reaches the maximum capacity, it filters through these holes, and the rainwater gets carried away to a gravel and sand filtering chamber underground."

Anita was impressed, smiling as she bent forward to stroke her hand through the water. "This is so beautiful. You designed all this yourself?"

Bram let out a quiet brief chuckle and looked around the room. When he nodded, he almost looked humbled. "This was the first thing I've ever built. Something that I knew I had to accomplish, or rather prove that it can be done."

When Bram looked at her, she had a questioning frown. "Can be done?"

He nodded. "That it is possible to succeed without the Ton's help." That was all he said.

Anita suddenly understood. He had built all this to prove to himself that it was possible. That despite the Ton's influences, Bram was able to accomplish his dreams. Deep down she appreciated his confession to her and found it relatable. Lately, even she wished that she were brave enough to follow her dreams, and travel, but could not see it likely. However, now she felt inspired. Because of Bram, maybe there was hope yet.

Anita felt warmed by his openness, especially when she looked at his bare feet, and realized that he had been like that the moment she arrived. Stepping to one side, she kicked off her shoes, lifted the bottom of her skirts, and stepped into the little pool with him. Bram's smile grew, and he reached to steady her. Despite the cool water, standing together under the sunshine warmed Anita to her toes. Bram stroked her cheek and leaned down to place his lips over hers. The first of many.

Their meetings began to weave themselves into each other. Their days ended when they parted and started when they met, each bringing joy and pleasure to one another. There was one memory Anita loved to recall. A month had passed, both she and Bram were embraced in his large wood canopy bed. His bedroom, much like the rest of the home, was exquisitely designed. The only difference being that his room smelled of spices and fresh wood.

Anita had grown to love the exposed rafters, especially in Bram's bedroom. There between the beams, dark blue and yellow stars and moons were painted. A large stone fireplace covered the other side of the wall from them, now crackling with a burning fire. She had sighed with contentment and stretched. Her body was still wonderfully sore from their lovemaking. Bram reached forward, caressing her offered breasts, down to her navel. Anita could not help but purr happily.

She loved the way he touched her, as if he knew just how much she wanted him to. Smiling, Bram pulled her to him, and gently suckled her bottom lip until she started kissing him back. The way he liked it. Anita did not stop until he started groaning, to which she laughed.

"If you keep that up, we may just go again," Bram said under his breath, stroking one of her fallen strands of hair.

"I don't believe it when you say 'may', anymore. It's either we do, or we do," Anita said with a laugh.

That had Bram laughing, which caused Anita's stomach to flutter. She placed her head on his chest as he stroked her back. They were quietly resting. Enjoying the silence. One of the logs in the fireplace popped.

"I can't remember the last time I've felt this relaxed," Bram said.

Anita smiled inwardly and hummed her agreement. She could not have been happier, especially when she got to lay beside Bram, taking in his warmth. Perhaps it was because she did not answer, or Bram was curious. He smoothed his hand over her cheek, bringing her to look at him.

"Are you enjoying yourself?" he asked.

Anita smiled, kissing his palm, she nodded. "I've never felt so free." She answered honestly. To make her point, she kissed his chest, and was tickled by the strands of hair there.

Bram chuckled, his expression pleased, but soon it changed to deep in thought. "You'd think you would be a lot more nervous of our meetings."

Anita's smile turned soft, as she shook her head. Laying her head back onto his chest, she said, "You soothe my nerves, Bram. The moment I cross that bridge, I know that everything is going to be alright."

For a moment, Anita thought she heard Bram's heart quicken, but soon he grinned and laughed. "I mean, of the Ton ever finding out."

Anita sat herself up, her hair falling to cover her breasts. She thought about it, before saying, "I suppose I'm not worried... I guess it's because no one has ever really noticed what I do. I mean, even saying I was joining a quilting club wasn't a surprise to my family."

That only made Bram grin more, showing his dashing smile and clean teeth. That look always made Anita want to sigh. "Somehow, I find that hard to believe. After all, I noticed you."

Now it was Anita's heart that raced. "Yes, well that was different. I caught you when you were raging with male need."

He laughed, "Male need?"

Anita nodded, "Yes! Or have you forgotten that woman in red?"

Bram grinned, sitting up, he reached for her face, and looked at her. "The moment I saw you, I knew." He paused, as though he wanted to choose his words wisely. "I knew you were going to be mine."

Anita went speechless. Swallowing the blush that was soon to spread across her chest, she smiled and looked down. Caressing her hair, Bram pulled her back down to him, and sighed.

"It will be a somber day indeed, when the Ton ever finds out of this," Bram said under his breath.

Anita frowned, "Bram, no one will. Besides, it's not like members of high society are innocent either. I know they have affairs as well."

Bram scoffed, "Yes, that is true. But ours is different. It stands out more."

She looked up at him confused. "Not as dissimilar to Christina and Richard. And yet, no one has found out about them."

He sighed. "It is unlike ours, because Richard is a pure breed, no one would dare defy him. While you are with a very desirable Mutt."

This time Anita scowled and looked at him hard. How on Earth can Bram call himself such an offensive word? When he glanced to her, he smoothed the wrinkle between her brow. He continued to do this, seemingly thinking about his words. Once her frown was gone, he stopped, and closed his eyes. "The Ton does not accept scandalous mix bloods. But they certainly eat up that sort of gossip."

Anita remained silent, but inside she was trying to quiet her raging thoughts. She could not deny the intense animosity she felt towards the Ton at that present moment, and even when Bram looked at her with a thoughtful expression, she still couldn't relinquish the feeling.

"Calm yourself, Anita. I can feel your rancor from here." He smirked.

"I just don't understand how bad that is. It's not like it brings ruin or ill luck to be with someone from another culture. I rather think that it creates union," Anita said straight-forwardly.

Bram's smirk slowly disappeared, as he contemplated his thoughts. "It did bring ill luck to my parents, though." After considering what to say next, Bram sat up and walked to place another log in the fire. He stared into the flames, all the while poking at the embers. Bent there, he was glorious to Anita. Naked, and toned, he looked like someone right out of her fantasies, and yet, she felt the thoughts that burdened him.

When he finally looked to her again, his eyes had soft-ened. He reached his hand out, calling her to go to him. She sat down in front of him, on a soft fur rug. They watched the fire, his arm around her waist, gently stroking her naked thigh. When he spoke, his tone was low. "My father had grown up around rumors the Ton created. They'd say that he wasn't truly a Williams, but rather, the late Earl of Kenwood's bas-tard heir."

Anita could not see his eyes, but she felt as though he was waiting. Expecting what she would say. But Anita leaned her head back, and rested it gently on the nook of his neck and shoulder. She felt him take a deep breath in, as he leaned his head to hers. "When he grew up, the rumors dimmed. At least until he met and married my mother."

She gazed into the fire and innocently asked, "How did they meet?"

"At a theater house." Bram let out a breathy laugh. "She was the main actress in the play. Something you don't normally see, especially with a Moroccan actress on an Eng-lish stage."

That was when Anita finally gasped and sat up. She smiled wide. "Your mother is from Morocco?"

Bram smiled and nodded. "Too bad no one else saw it the same way as you." He looked back to the fire. "Once they married, most of the Ton shunned them. If it was not for the lands and title, they might've ended up in the gutter."

They were quiet again. Anita leaned back against him. It suddenly all made sense to her. Bram's extreme dislike of high society, why he remained out of sight all this time. And his extra caution for her safety. All of this, and she just realized that he finally told her who he is.

Bram is an Earl!

Her head was spinning. Anita told herself to remain calm. This was an important moment. That in some way, Bram had felt this was the time to tell her. She smiled warmly, thankful that he finally opened to her. But when she nudged her head against his, Anita could detect his body was tense against hers.

Looking up at him, Bram had a faraway gaze. She sat up and turned to face him. When he glanced to her, Anita smiled. "Your mother must be beautiful. Do you resemble her?"

Bram's brows knitted slightly, but then they relaxed when the corner of his lips lifted. He nodded. "My father used to call her his precious gem. When I was a lad, he would say that I was cut from her same stone."

Bram fully smiled then and caressed her cheek. He did this softly, all the while gazing at her every feature. Anita shivered. His eyes penetrated hers. His touches grew warm and slow, and when his hands reached for her breasts, Anita was already panting under her breath.

"You really have no idea just how much peace you give me," Bram whispered in her ear. Anita could not do more but gasp for breath, her heart aching.

He lifted her and placed her over his lap. His hard cock pressed against her pelvis. When he kissed her, their moans were intertwined. Anita soon felt herself rocking against him, her need growing urgent. But Bram only ground against her in return.

She was wiggling by the time he finally entered her. They groaned together, their need sated, if not for a moment. Bram helped her move against him, lifting her in pace with her thrusts. When Anita began to moan, near her release, she closed her eyes.

"No, open them," Bram rasped.

The instant she did, her body quivered with her orgasm. She felt herself tighten around him and heard Bram's sharp breath. He grunted and moved harder against her.

Their eyes met, and she watched Bram lose himself in his climax. She gasped, feeling the shooting warmth of his seed within her.

After that they kissed each other hard. Almost urgent, if not for the fact they had just found their pleasure. They stayed there, on the floor in front of the fire, curled in each other's arms. Bram told her more about his life, and the world he grew up in. The lows of his childhood, to the adventures he found when he lived in Morocco for most of his adult life. Up till he found his passion for architecture. And even when he began to express the bitterness he felt towards his father, Anita listened soundly until he was done.

Nothing had seemed the same after that day. Bram and Anita felt closer in ways she could not explain. Whenever she came by his home, there were new stories, plans, or places he wanted to tell or show her. Even his promise to her that she would be able to come and watch *A Midsummer's Night's Dream* whenever she desired came to be. She probably had gone to see it at least three times. The play was exquisitely done, which she surprisingly found out was directed by The Godfrey Rose, who was thrilled to finally tell her and was as ecstatic to see how things were going between Bram and Anita.

"It was Bram that gave me my first directing position," Christina had told her. And when Bram nodded, commenting how small their world was, Anita noticed a tall broad man walking into the theater box. He was dressed gentlemanly, with a sharp black coat, gold cuffs, and an out of place scarf. Odd for an August night, Anita thought.

He took off his top hat, exposing his salt and pepper hair. He was rugged with stubble but held an aura of dominance. His eyes caught hers, and for a moment Anita saw a cold winter's morning within them. When Christina noticed his entrance, her smile beamed. That had seemed to melt the ice around his eyes, for Richard then smiled and politely grasped her hand when they were introduced.

Finally meeting Richard was almost surreal. She

learned how he and Bram were close friends, amongst others in their group. When he and Bram stepped to the side to speak, Christina pulled her over to whisper in her ear and laugh, "Isn't this amazing? Who would have thought that we would be with two of the six Rakes of Springfield?"

When Anita looked at her confused, Christina grinned, and said in a low tone, "Richard and his group of friends are rather known in society as such. They did not intend to be called that, but each one of these men have held up a certain reputation. Springfield was given because that's Richard's title and club where they all like to meet."

Glancing over to Bram, Anita asked under her breath, "Does Bram know that he is called a Rake of Springfield?"

Christina half laughed, "Of course. They all know. It's not a kept secret."

Looking down, Anita mumbled, "How do you feel knowing Richard is one of them?"

Christina then noticed Anita's hesitant worry and lifted her chin. "Annie, you should know better than anyone, Bram is yours now." She continued to search her eyes. "Besides, a silly nickname doesn't take away the fact that Richard cares for me. As I do for him. And believe me, most women they have had never received something like that."

That left Anita wondering for the next week about her and Bram's relationship. Was it something truly special? Was Bram really hers, like Christina said? But even if that were the case, it wasn't like it was something that would last forever. To her dismay, Anita faced the reality of their situation. She and Bram were only having an affair. Affairs did not evolve into anything more than what they were. And even if it did, would it feel right to force Bram back into the Ton? A society he's long felt resentment towards?

She continued to feel this way up until they saw each other again. Bram had surprised her the moment she walked through the front door. Candles were lit across the dining table, and two places were set up at the end. He escorted her to one of the seats, and after scooting her closer to his own seat, sat down as well. They partook of authentic Moroccan cuisine, most being Bram's favorite dishes. They laughed whenever she tried a bite of something different, and Bram enjoyed every moan she made when he fed her a spoon of dessert.

They made love right there on the table. Some of the food, Bram said, carried aphrodisiac properties. Which she now believed. She still felt hot and tingly long after they finished. That was when Bram suggested she take a bath.

She sat in the large copper tub that was in the adjoining room to Bram's bedroom. Her knees were bent close to her, her head resting on them. It was moments like this that left Anita's heart aching. She had to remind herself that they were only having an affair. This was not anything more. Her emotions would do nothing but ruin the joys they were having with each other, despite it being only a matter of time when they would eventually have to say goodbye.

Anita choked back a silent sob when Bram entered the bathroom. He did not seem to notice when he gave her a glass of wine, while holding on to another filled with his drink of choice, cognac. The sweet aroma warmed her body and soothed her heart. Bram then sat beside her, a cloth in his hands. He began to wash her back, slow languished strokes across her skin. Anita closed her eyes, trying not to notice the dull ache growing in her chest again.

"I thought you loved the dinner?" he asked quietly.

He did notice. Anita scolded herself mentally. She remained silent, however, not knowing what to say. So, she had only nodded, and gave a small smile. She did not want to look at him, afraid she was to cry if she did, but Anita felt his gaze on her.

"Anita. Look at me," he said calmly, but she detected the command in his voice.

She shook her head and continued staring at the glass of wine in her hand. He had stopped washing her back and lifted her chin to face him. Fresh tears barely brimmed in her eyes, but she refused to let them fall. Bram observed her and stroked her cheek. His expression unreadable, he looked deep in thought.

He did not say anything and released her. Bram picked up the cloth once more and continued to clean and knead her shoulders. They stayed silent, Anita's worry easing as she closed her eyes, focusing on the circular motions of Bram's touch.

"I find it hard to believe that you've never been courted before," Bram suddenly said.

Anita's heart jumped. What a thing to say, as though Bram had read her thoughts all along. When she looked at him, his face was serious, and focused on the washcloth against her skin. Glancing away she thought about how to answer, her mind immediately going back to when her family still lived in America. To her own debutante ball and coming out season. She had promised herself to never speak of it again, but when she looked back to Bram, he was staring at her. And that look always undid her.

Taking a sip of wine, she took a deep breath. "I had been... once."

The moment she said that Bram had stopped moving. "What happened?"

Thinking back to that time, Anita now knew how naïve she was. But nonetheless, it had been a painful lesson to learn. "It was after my debutante ball. I was introduced to a man that showed great fondness for me."

She could not help but smile slightly. That time was so new and exciting for her. She was a shy wallflower, but the moment she met Clark, she thought she was finally being seen for the first time.

"At that time, he always had a smile on his face. He used to say how he found it hard to make me laugh. But it was because he was terrible with jokes." Anita chuckled softly and shook her head.

"He would come to call on me twice a week. My mother was just over the moon by that. My mother always felt that it was dire for us to marry. So, I was glad that she was happy." Anita took another sip of her wine.

"It took him less than a month to propose to me. Of course, now that I think back, we probably only spoke no more than a hundred words to each other. And shared two kisses."

At the mention of kisses, she caught Bram swig back a gulp of his cognac. "Are you all right, Bram?"

He nodded, taking a breath. "I hope he wasn't a good kisser."

That had Anita smiling. Shaking her head, she said, "No, on both accounts they weren't good. The first one he took me by surprise, we bumped our heads. The second time everything was moving all at once, I thought he was going to fall off the carriage."

Bram let out a laugh, and smirked. "That's better." He leaned over the tub's rail and caressed the water against her lower back. "What happened afterwards?"

She recalled the memories that pained her the most. It was her sister Belle who came to her. Thirteen at the time, Belle used to love running around the home and village, playing with the village girls and gossiping about the farm boys. She idolised Anita during her coming out season, and especially was in love with the fantasy of love. So, when Belle overheard from the village milkmaids the rumor that was spreading about Clark shocked her to no end. She immediately ran home and told Anita.

"There was a rumor that my betrothed had only wished to marry me for my title and dowry. When I confronted him about it, he did not bother denying it. After that, I ended the engagement..." Anita paused, her thoughts in the past. It was not the plot to marry her for her money, or title. It was what Clark did next that hurt her the most.

"Why does it feel like there is more to that?" Bram asked, stroking his fingers up her back.

She sighed, "A month after, we started getting looks from villagers in town. Eventually we found out that he told others that I had thrown myself to him and expressed to him my wanton ways. He had said that he was the one that ended the engagement, due to him not knowing whether or not I was still pure."

Taking in a deep breath, Anita surprisingly felt relieved to be talking about what had happened. She had not fully expressed the true story to anyone. None but her sister and herself knew about it. Even her mother was wary of what to believe. To this day, Anita still was not certain if her mother ever truly believed the story.

"We decided to simply ignore it. Finding that rumors were as stale as lies. Although, after that, I wasn't approached by any more suitors." Anita swallowed, feeling both relieved and deplored.

"I wasn't heartbroken that I lost all marriageable chances. But I felt bad for my mother, and sister. Because of me, they were looked at disgracefully as well." Anita paused. "I suppose it was a good thing that we returned to London. Otherwise, my sister would have lost all chances too."

Bram was silent the whole time she spoke. It was not until she finished that Anita noticed Bram had both hands on the tub's railing, and they were white from him gripping it. She touched his knuckles, which brought him back from his thoughts. He stood and walked out of the bathroom.

When he returned, he asked. "What is his name?"

Anita looked at him curiously. "Clark Thomson, his father ran Thomson & Johnson Trading Company. I suppose they thought it would gain business if the family inherited a noble title."

Anita shook her head, the reality of that experience so clear now. When she looked up, Anita found Bram writing on a small note.

"Are you writing down his name?!" she expressed.

Bram smirked, and pocketed the note. "Maybe. And maybe I also have friends who trade to America."

She was shocked. "You mustn't. That was a long time ago."

Bram shrugged. Standing over her, he helped her up and offered her a towel. "It is important that businessmen know who they are negotiating with." Pulling her close to him, he curled a strand of her hair between his fingers. "Besides, he ought to know that those who wrong what is mine get what is coming to them."

Anita was aghast. Even at the time this had all happened, she did not have anyone defend her virtue. She had to learn to ignore and cope. But now, even after all these years, Bram made her feel fortified. Anita smiled thankfully, in which he returned with a kiss.

Before their kiss could deepen, they heard a knock at

the door. Bram stepped back, grimaced, and helped her out of the tub. He left Anita there to dry herself, while he went to answer the door. She was smiling to herself, despite how she felt earlier about their affair. For the first time, Anita was free of the past, and she was thankful for Bram at that moment.

"I told you to send these letters to my study, Willard." Bram's muffled voice came through from the door. Curious, Anita stepped forward, being sure not to appear by the doorway.

"Yes, my Lord. But I thought it best to tell you that this letter did not come from L'Opéra. It was delivered here," Willard, Bram's butler, said nervously.

Bram was silent. Anita did not hear his reply to Willard, and when she heard the door close, she peaked around the doorway. Bram was standing there looking down at the letter. His expression was blank, the only sign of his emotions was when he crumpled the paper in his hand. When he looked up, he found her watching, and for the briefest moment she witnessed a shameful look cross his eyes.

To this day, Bram did not reveal anything about the letter, and despite how she felt about it, Anita could not bring herself to ask him. She understood his privacy, and if he had wished to tell her, then he would have. However, something about that note had made her feel worried. Anita hoped that whatever it was about, Bram would be okay. And if he needed her, he would confide in her.

"Is that the dress you will be wearing to Hedgerow Ball, Anita?" a shrill voice called her out of her thoughts.

Anita found curious eyes staring at her, which brought her back to present. She sat on a chaise sofa, Belle next to her. The two women to their right were cousins from the Robinson family, Diane, and Lillian, Diane being the daughter to the Marquess of Bristol. They were cheerful girls, about the same age as Belle.

Much to her annoyance, Miss Kenyon and Miss Crane sat to her left. Somehow, they always ended up at the same gatherings, perhaps it was because their mothers were close associates. It was Miss Kenyon who asked about her dress. Anita still had not answered her yet, not really wishing to. She could tell Miss Kenyon was not thrilled by that either.

Belle cast her a confused, worried look. When she realized that Anita was not going to answer, she responded for her. "Oh no, of course not. We are going to wear custom ball gowns our mama ordered. They are richly tailored; I am so excited to try them on. Anita's gown will be especially exquisite. With hers, they are going to do a new silhouette."

The cousins echoed Belle's enthusiasm, asking questions, and crooning over the details she was telling them, whereas Miss Kenyon and Miss Crane were whispering amongst each other. Anita tried her hardest not to roll her eyes. Leave it to these two 'proper ladies' to perform the definition of rudeness. There are better things to do on a Tuesday, Anita thought. *Like, going to see Bram...*

They had not discussed the idea of meeting more than once a week, but Anita could tell they both wanted to. Bram would ask of her plans, and when she had nothing to do, he would almost look sheepish, considering whether to ask her to come see him again. But in the end, they left it that way. Neither one of them wanted to press the other. It appeared on the surface, they really were only having an affair, Anita thought with a sigh.

The clinking of teacups drew their attention. Miss Crane looked embarrassed, whereas Miss Kenyon only grinned. "My Belle, would you be a dear hostess, and refill my cup?"

As if they were twins, the cousins raised their brows in unison, clearly seeing the ploy Miss Kenyon was doing. They knew she could have easily refilled it herself, but what Miss Kenyon wanted was to make Belle feel inferior. However, Belle did not look the least bit phased by the question. With every ounce of dignity, Belle gleamed and scooted forward to serve her guests.

"Of course, Miss Kenyon. I'm sure that it is no easy task for you to do, considering the restraints you are wearing," Belle responded, grasping the teapot calmly.

A quiet gasp escaped Lillian, but she squelched it

before it left her lips. Miss Kenyon heard it though, and cast her a glare. She did, however, prove Belle's point by unsuccessfully trying not to pull at the poorly fitted tight lace collar around her neck. When Belle was about to pour the tea, she noticed it was empty. She stood with a smile.

"We're out of tea, but not to worry. I shall go brew more. I will be back shortly." The cousins nodded, while Miss Kenyon and Miss Crane looked as though something vulgar just occurred.

When Belle was out of the room, Miss Kenyon announced, "Well, such a shame the dear child has to get up and get her own tea. There are servants for that."

Miss Crane nodded, while the cousin looked surprised by her words. Anita on the other hand was furious. "My sister is being courteous of our cook, who is working hard in getting our dinner ready."

"I mean no harm; I'm just merely stating that a proper Lady needs to have a firmer hand with her help," Miss Kenyon declared.

"I believe the proper word for that is dictator, whereas a Lady is an example of politeness, virtue, and courtesy. Anything less than that is but a charlatan," Anita stared directly at Miss Kenyon.

The cousins nodded and smiled, while Miss Crane and Miss Kenyon were aghast. But Anita did not care, she was through being polite to others who did not deserve it. And she felt better for it. She grasped her still filled tea cup and sipped on it.

Miss Kenyon took in a deep breath and glanced to her companion, Miss Crane. Suddenly a slow grin grew on her face. "Shall we lighten the mood with a little gossip then?"

All three ladies, except for Anita, answered excitedly. Miss Kenyon gave a cheeky smile. "Well, I've heard the most scrumptious news about one of the six Rakes of Springfield."

The ladies gasped and sat a little closer, while Anita tried to look undisturbed. Her heart began to race. She told herself it probably was not of any importance. Christina had said that most of the Ton's younger ladies loved creating new gossip about Bram and the other men. This should be no different.

"I'm sure you ladies remember my tales about The Lover of the Opera? Bram Williams, the Earl of Kenwood?" Miss Kenyon said this slowly, as her gaze landed on Anita.

"Ooh, will this be anything like the stories of The Scottish Hound?" Lillian asked enthusiastically.   "Not him again, we've heard all about the Marquess. I want to hear about Blue Blood Philip!" Diane announced.

"Silence, you two. Let her speak!" Miss Crane exasperated.

Miss Kenyon grinned, "No, this won't be like those stories. But rather, I've heard that our Lover of the Opera may be taken from our tales."

The ladies gasped, and each had a disappointed look. "What have you heard?!"

"An acquaintance told me that she saw the Earl with someone in his theater box." When the ladies answered how that did not really mean anything, Miss Kenyon promptly replied, "He has been seen with her on more than one occasion."

This time the ladies exhaled, stunned. "Who is she?!"

Miss Kenyon shrugged and grinned, "No one knows. She didn't seem to recognize her, but my girl did guess that this woman is most likely a Lady."

That left the cousins to giggle wildly, "Oh dear, for shame!"

"How do they suppose she's a Lady?" Miss Crane asked.

"My source says that she dresses and carries herself like one. You know, filled with virtue, and grace," Miss Kenyon answered, her gaze straying to Anita.

The whole while, Anita felt frantic. She kept her expression calm, but her mind was whirling. Someone had perceived them! All along, others had kept notice of Bram and his exploits?! Anita was disgustingly shocked, but she still found herself wondering, how did she not realize by being with Bram on more than one occasion, it would draw attention from others? Especially, when it is with one of the Rakes of Springfield?

Anita sighed softly; it was because she really had not known. She did not let herself fully grasp the extent of Bram's reputation. Until now, as she reluctantly listened to Miss Kenyon's tales of him. Her heart dropped all at once. Anita had felt so confident that nobody would notice, but perhaps she was still that naïve girl from Pennsylvania. This was London after all, and the eyes of the Ton were everywhere. More so, compared to a small township. Surely, Bram had known that as well?

Suddenly, Anita replayed all her memories with Bram once more. She thought of every moment, from when they came together, to when they last parted. And all she could hear was Bram's fateful words. *"It will be a somber day indeed, when the Ton ever finds out of this."*

Dread filled her lungs. Bram had known all along that this was to be. That is why he often brought it up and seemed overly protective. That day, Anita foolishly thought he meant they would be noticed because of their cultural differences. When, it was really Bram's reputation they should have mentioned.

Anita almost wanted to laugh over the irony. Despite how she felt, she still found something that brought her and Bram even closer. She realized then that Bram had understood her pain all along. How he sympathized with her when she confessed to him what had happened in America. The very same had been happening to him, and still.

"Anita, do you know who the Earl of Kenwood is?" Miss Kenyon asked coolly.

Anita remained unmoved, she did not so much as blink as she chose her words wisely. "I don't follow gossip. And I don't have any interest in being a part of them either."

The cousins straightened a little at that, but Miss Kenyon still held her grin. "Really? Well I was only curious. After all, didn't he dance with you at your parents gathering ball?"

Diane and Lillian glanced at each other curiously, while Miss Crane and Miss Kenyon looked smug. "It was really an uproar to see him there. No one knew who invited him, and to have him there after all these years was truly a wonder."

Anita simply shrugged. She told herself to remain calm. She knew what Miss Kenyon was trying to do, but she would not give it to her. Anita handled worse gossip in America. And she damn well was not going to contribute anything to slander her Bram any further.

When Anita did not reply, Miss Kenyon simply laughed and carried on her tales for the other ladies. She moved on to telling them about the Insatiable Kent, and the Cold-Hearted Lake, all of which the girls squealed and enjoyed. Anita was in disarray however, and not just because they were speaking about men she knew. The realization came crashing down on her. Bram was in the same position that she was in America. If they continued to see each other, eyes would fall on them. New fresh rumors would spread, and it would be her doing, because she did not do anything to stop it. Anita felt sick to her stomach; she had to come to this painful awareness.

More than anyone, Anita knew how Bram felt towards the Ton. If these rumors were proven true, and society found out about it, that would push him into a corner. She told him from the start, that she was not expecting marriage, and that much was true. But if they were caught, then honorably, Bram would have to marry her. Or he would not... and Anita would face being shunned. Her family cast out once more. She could not bear if that happened to them again, or for Bram to hate her by forcing his hand.

Her heart skipping a beat, Anita knew what she had to do. What she wished she never had to do, but the decision was inevitable, and time was against them. Belle came back through the door, smiling, with a pot of fresh tea, unaware of the tragedy filling the room. Right before she sat, Miss Kenyon whispered to the other ladies, "I'll tell you all about the Lucky Mark at a later date."

The ladies giggled.

Chapter 11

London
The Earl of Kenwood's Estate
Thursday

This is hard for me to do, but I feel the time has come where we should end our meetings. In no way have you done anything that has made me make this decision. But rather, we have reached a point that if we continue this, it will undoubtedly draw the eyes of others. We have enjoyed our time together, that much is true. I will never forget all that you have done for me. I hope you will understand, Bram. Know that you are a dear friend to me, and I thank you.

Yours faithfully,
A.H.

This was not the letter Bram was expecting. Jefferson was still standing at the porch, apprehensively grasping his straw hat. When Bram opened the front door, he was eagerly awaiting Anita, only to find Jefferson slumped over, briefly making eye contact. When he asked what the matter was, Jefferson hesitantly gave him the letter.

At first, Bram assumed that it was another note from the ballerina. He was about to toss it when he realized the writing was different, and he found Anita's initials signed at the bottom. Bram had to reread the letter at least three times to fully comprehend what it meant. She was ending the affair with him. His gut twisted, and a sour taste filled his mouth.

"Did she give this to you?" Bram demanded.

Jefferson stuttered for a moment, as surprised as Bram was. "Yes, my Lord. She met with me at the usual place, but when I opened the carriage door, she stopped me. She told me to give this to you and to send her sincerest apologies."

Bram was trying to remain calm, but when Jefferson backed away a step, clearly it did not show. "How did she look?"

"The Lady looked saddened, my Lord. I felt her pause right before she gave me this here note."

This was absurd. Why so suddenly did she send this letter? And why look upset while doing it? It did not make sense to Bram. He nodded to Jefferson and released him to go. But not before telling him, "Continue to go there every Thursday, in case she returns."

Closing the door, Bram forced himself to his study. Slumping onto his chair, he stared at the beautifully written note. The thought of ending their affair was always far from his mind. He supposed that if the conversation did ever arise, they would discuss it together and choose the best course of action. At least, it would have given Bram the chance to convince her otherwise to not end their time together. But Anita apparently decided to take that decision into her own hands.

Bram slammed his hand against the desk and stood to get a drink of strong cognac. Holding the note, he read it again, and again. And one more for good measure. By that point, he finished his glass, and poured himself another. Bram gulped it down, exhaling a deep breath.

Sitting at his desk, he now found himself analyzing each sentence. Trying to find the answer as to why. Why this, again? Bram found himself unreasonably laughing. This was happening again. His Annie, his runaway wallflower, was trying to disappear once AGAIN.

Thinking back these last three months, Bram felt assured that what they had was perfect. At first it astonished him how well they fit. Besides learning how to pleasure each other, which was utterly amazing, they shared how to talk to one another. Even with the others at Springfield, Bram had never been able to fully express his passions, or bitterness. But with Anita, they talked about everything. From their lowest lows, to greatest hope.

Bram still smiled when he recalled the time he had taken her on a trip to see Trafalgar Square. Their first outing together. He could tell she was thrilled, if not just a bit nervous. But once they arrived, she was awed by the newly finished architecture, and the numerous western European paintings from the middle ages. When they explored the halls, she would longingly stare at each painting, like she once did at Sebastian's estate.

When they were in a hall amongst themselves, he wrapped his arms around her and whispered in her ear, "What do you see when you gaze into these paintings?"

She smiled, holding his arms to her belly. "Travel. Freedom. Beauty."

"Is that what you wish to do?" he asked.

She nodded but looked away shyly. "It isn't common for women, especially Ladies. But that would be my greatest dream. Would be lovely to travel the world."

When they left, Bram found himself fantasizing the world he wanted to show Anita. Her dream had him want to take her anywhere she wished. Including Morocco, and all along the Mediterranean, he thought. She would have loved it. But now, Bram sat alone, in his study, drinking back another glass of cognac.

Bram peered at her letter once more, the liquor soothing his frustration. "This is hard for me to do." *Then why do it?* "But I feel the time has come where we should end our meetings." *But I did not get a say in this, Anita.* "In no way have you done anything that has made me make this decision." *Then why does it feel that way?* "But rather, we have reached a point that if we continue this, it will undoubtedly draw the eyes of others." *We have reached a point? What could she mean?* "We've enjoyed our time together, that much is true." *It went beyond enjoyed, Annie...* "I will never forget all that you've done for me." *What about what you had done to me?* "I hope you will understand, Bram. Know that you are a dear friend to me, and I thank you. Yours faithfully."

Leaning back in his chair, Bram covered his face with his palms. A dear friend to her? Would only a friend measure what they shared together? Staring up at the wood beam ceiling, to the moon and stars Anita had loved so much. What had happened?

We have reached a point. If we continue this, it will undoubtedly draw the eyes of others. Did that mean that she felt people had started to notice? Thinking about it, there could not be any other reasonable explanation he could think of, unless she felt endangered. And if that was the case, then Bram wanted to know who had threatened his Anita. Or at least, know the reason why she abruptly ended them.

It would not be good to send her a direct letter, that alone would create havoc in her home. Nor could he ask Christina to deliver it for him. She and Richard had been gone for nearly a month. And as for Mark and Anita's sister, Belle, they had not yet made it official for him to call on her. *Leave it to Mark to take his time with a woman he clearly loves*, Bram thought grudgingly.

Bram sat there frozen, suddenly realizing his own thoughts. But perhaps, Mark did know about the next ball the sisters would be attending. He chuckled deep in his throat and closed his eyes. *Here we go again.* Back to the fray of the Ton. Something Bram never thought he would find himself going back to. But the difference that shook Bram to his core was that, now, he knew he was in love. Opening his eyes, he glanced back down to the letter. Stroking his fingers over Anita's *yours faithfully*, he knew that she was too.

The orchestra was low, its harmony gradually growing louder. Soft harps swayed alongside the bass of rafting cellos. The violins tentatively leaped into the melody, their course soon taking the lead into a moonless dream. At least, that is how

Anita envisioned the sound of the ball's music. Gowns of numerous colors and ribbons floated across the dance floor. Large hooped fabrics swaying and colliding with the softest of sounds. The air was cool from where they stood, but Anita could feel the warmth of hot breaths and laughter dancing together at the center of them all.

The Hedgerow ball was held in the great Hillingdon house in Middlesex. From habit, Anita found herself gazing up at the home's lovely architecture. A grand crystal chandelier hung overhead from the dancers on the main white marble floor, burning oil lamps lit each exposed wood column, circulating the majestic ballroom. The home was commissioned by the third Duke of Schomberg, but it now belonged to Mr. Richard Henry Cox, the present proprietor to the wealthy Cox & Kings. With a quiet sob, she felt Bram would have enjoyed the construction of the house.

The family, like many others, had to make way from London, a trip that lasted over an hour, just to meet the highly anticipated, and marriageable Mr. Cox, who was said to have newly arrived from his business travels in India. All of which Anita's mother, was now repeating back to none other than Mr. Cox, himself. Much to Anita's surprise, Henry, the name he said he preferred to be called, was taking the gossip quite well. He laughed cheerfully, even when the Viscountess still had not removed her hand from his offered arm.

"I must say though, Mr. Cox. Your dancing has thankfully not gone to hell on your travels! You can still lead an old Lady like myself across the dance floor." The Viscountess laughed.

"Oh, I wouldn't say it hadn't, my Lady. On the contrary, I am thankful to have had a good leader, like yourself, to help me." Henry grinned, good humored. "And please, call me Henry."

Anita's mother laughed once more. She opened her white lace fan and quickly cooled herself to hide her blush. "My, my, what a gentleman you are, Henry."

Henry bowed ever so slightly to the Viscountess, and then cast a warm smile to Anita. They were introduced before he and her mother had gone onto the dance floor. He was much taller than Bram, but Henry was slimmer. Whereas Bram had a natural darker hue to his skin tone, Henry was sun kissed, and had red blemishes across his cheekbones. He was clean shaven and kept his hair short. Although Anita could see that his hair was a chocolate brown color, she detected short wisps of blond and red, which illuminated his dark blue eyes.

However, Anita was longing to see dark onyx eyes. It was now three weeks since she last saw Bram, and her heart ached every day. Her mother worried that Anita had come down with illness, and that was why she stopped going to her quilting club. But Anita gave her no explanation. Her color had gone, her eyes sunken from tears, and she rarely ate.

Thursdays were the cruelest. Every ounce of her yearning to run to Kensington Road, hoping to see Jefferson and the carriage there, and be taken over the bridge to Bram's home. To freedom. But instead, she would stand next to her bedroom window, staring out, and releasing her tears. Only Claire, Anita's maid, knew that she suffered from heartbreak. Having no one else to talk with, Anita confided in Claire on more than one sickly night.

Anita had not heard from Bram, not that she was expecting it. He too knew how risky that was, that and she had not made it easy for him either. Anita knew she gave him no choice in the matter. Or written any clear reason; that being because she feared anyone finding the letter and realizing that it was she who Bram had been seeing. She could not write that an informant of Miss Kenyon's knew of them, in case somehow that someone was in direct connection to Bram, could see the letter, and run away to report back to her mistress.

Thinking how Bram could have felt upon reading her letter broke her more than anything else. Because she had no doubt that he would hate her after that. Not once had she run away, but three times now! Anita knew that this was it. Bram would think her crazy and forget her all together. Choking back another sob, she knew that that was probably for the best. To save them both.

"Henry, what do you think of my dear Anita's ball

gown?" the Viscountess asked enthusiastically.

Anita inwardly cringed, not wanting attention to herself. She was near tears, so she forced her eyes down.

"Oh, Anita! Don't be bashful." Her mother patted her with her fan.

"I believe your daughter looks radiant, my Lady. It is not often you see a brave woman stand out with a new style of dress. I find that admirable," Henry responded, admiring Anita with a cunning smile.

By that point, others joined them, clearly hearing Henry's response. Belle, Diane, and Lillian stepped into their inner circle, bringing with them Lord Brunswick. Belle was beaming in her rose-pink gown, while Anita's was a dark magenta color. Layers of ruffled fabric cascaded straight down from the bodice. A white lace train fell from the delicately woven drapery that sat high on what was called a bustle behind her.

Both Belle's and Anita's dresses were custom made together by a seamstress from Paris. The design was highly different from any other ladies' large round ball gowns. They were immediately noticed when they arrived, the style unheard of. But contrary to their mother, she insisted that it was good to stand out. At that moment, Anita felt like the complete opposite.

She wanted nothing more than to fade into the cream-colored walls, or into a library, Anita thought with a grim laugh. But it was too late, she was already being inspected by both her mother and Mr. Cox. "I must say that I was rather worried that their dresses would be taken out of context. But I do believe they are going rather well! I've been seeing other ladies admiring the design."

Diane and Lilian nodded in agreement, as they regarded the gowns. Lord Brunswick looked rather bored, stepping to the side, he drank back the rest of his champagne. As Belle and her mother were exchanging words and details about the seamstress from Paris, Anita caught Mr. Cox fervently looking at her. At first, she thought she was imagining it, figured he was admiring the dress. But Anita watched as his gaze slowly caressed down her body. She momentarily gasped, when they stopped shortly at her bust, then to her hemline, and once back up again.

Anita sensed his esteemed confidence. When his eyes met hers, to Anita, they showed an intended promise, and heat. She suddenly found herself without breath. As though acknowledging her thoughts, Henry grinned warmly. Biting her lip, Anita's eyes fluttered away, trying to bring her focus elsewhere.

The hairs on the ends of her nape rose, for she still felt his eyes on her. Telling herself to breathe, she felt abashed. Stunned to notice the intentions of another man, Anita's stomach flickered. Her memory brought back the first moment she and Bram met. Then her heart fell, her body turning cold.

"You are right, my Lady. Your daughter is certainly ravishing in magenta."

The group went silent. Anita's mother jolted on the unsuspected voice and waved her fan closer to her bosom. Anita heard a rush of breath leave the cousins, and Belle delightfully gasped. Lord Brunswick nearly choked on his refilled glass, and Mr. Cox glanced sharply to his left, his expression shrouded. All the while, Anita's eyes had closed the moment she heard Bram's low commanding vibrato.

Her heart gasping for air, Anita turned her gaze to the man that wielded it. She choked back her sigh. Bram was more handsome than she remembered. He had cleanly shaven, his dark hair only slightly shorter than it was. He wore a gray tailored gentleman's long coat, with a high white collar, and a navy bow tie scarf perfectly matching his leggings. His tan color vest was immaculate with silk gold embroidery.

Bram was a gentleman. Anita smiled, despite her feelings. She had never seen him dress his title. Yes, Bram always dressed exceptionally well, but never so much like a Lord as he did now. It pleasantly surprised her, and for a moment her stomach soothed. That is, until he looked at her.

There was a gleam in his eyes, a knowing. It went beyond determined. Past promises. But a clarity and focus like none other. How Anita wished she knew what he was thinking.

"Oh, pardon?!" the Viscountess released, fanning herself faster.

"Bram!" Belle exclaimed. "How good to see you. Is Mark with you?"

Eloise whirled on her daughter, tapping her on the shoulder with the fan gently. "Belle, don't call out a gentleman's name in a mannered ball, until proper introductions are established."

Belle's delicate brows knitted, and she said in a lower voice, "I'm sorry, mama."

"Please, my Lady Hemmingway. Do not fret on your dear daughter. Allow me to cordially introduce myself." The Viscountess turned back towards Bram just as he grasped her gloved hand. Perfectly bowing, he gently placed a kiss. "I am Lord Bram Williams, Earl of Kenwood."

The air seemed to have gone silent. The group glanced at one another, the rest of the ball unnoticed. It felt as though a spotlight shone on them. All waiting on the Viscountess's reaction. Anita imagined her mother fainting from shock for talking to Bram. She knew she almost did when Bram introduced himself for the first time. He sounded confident, and precise.

Much to her amazement, Eloise gleamed. Grasping Bram's hand, she patted it. "Good tidings, my Lord Kenwood. I've heard great rumors of you."

Bram grinned, "Let's hope they didn't make you blush too harshly, my Lady."

"Oh, not terribly. I am an old flower now, you see. Nothing surprises me anymore, Lord Kenwood."

"If only all the other flowers remained as spirited as you, my Lady Hemmingway. The fields would remain eternal." Bram gave a full smile.

That made Anita's mother laugh, but soon they heard a scoff leave Lord Brunswick. He had a sneer the likes that made his chin seem lopsided. "I beg your pardon, my Lady. But this Kenwood, should be ashamed to show his face here."

"I should? Why is that?" Bram asked in a low tone.

Lord Brunswick gutted out his chin, "As if you aren't aware, Kenwood. You make a mockery out of all things noble."

"How so?" Bram's voice lowered to a guttural sound.

"Everyone knows how demeaning your heritage is, and the vulgarity of your theater opera," Lord Brunswick answered assuredly.

Bram's expression directly hardened when he set his gaze on Lord Brunswick. "I am not the one who should be ashamed." He grinned coldly. "How is your brother? Still hasn't gained back half of the family's fortune yet? Or rather, shall I ask about your jaw, after your exploits in MY theater?"

Lord Brunswick sputtered, and coughed into his hand. The disdain was clear on his face. The ladies were left with wide eyes, glancing back and forth between them, undeniably curious with what Bram was referring to. But Anita guessed that last remark may have been connected to Christina in some way. The Viscountess, however, threw open her fan.

"Now, gentlemen. If you will please, calm yourselves. I, for one, do enjoy the gossips. However, I do not condone rifts being waged. Especially in front of our new host." The Viscountess patted Henry on the shoulder gently. Then turned her keen eyes towards the young Lords. "Lord Brunswick, while I do appreciate your moral outcry, you should consider your own doings before having it knock you back on the rear. And, as for you Lord Kenwood, no one likes a cornered cat with claws. You should do well to keep them retracted before others make an impression of you."

Bram half chuckled, pleasantly surprised by the Viscountess's mothering. If he did not know better, he would think that Anita had that very same ardent expression. He looked to her now, her beauty leaving him breathless. She was half smiling, both amused by her mother, and taken aback to see him. He grinned warmly, pleased to see her gently perturbed.

Bram had wanted her to be so; that alone told him how much she still longed for him. For if Anita genuinely wanted to end their affair, she would have been greatly upset at his presence. Not relieved.

"Well, now that is settled. My Lord Kenwood, what brings you to tonight's festivities?" Lady Hemmingway brought Bram out of his thoughts.

Bringing his arm around him and holding the other in front in a gentleman's pose, Bram told himself to look the part. He found it awkward, not having to focus much on his appearance before. Not really needing to. But now, Bram knew that to achieve his desired wishes, he had to impress the Viscountess. As well as the rest of the guests in attendance. Bram had to be the Lord he was born to be.

Bram realized long before arrival, that he needed Anita. The weeks were long and harsh without her. He found himself falling back to the empty void he had not realized was there. To the anger and darkness. Bitterness and blame towards the Ton. Troubled, he gravely discerned that he was no better than his father, by hiding away.

So once Mark had told him of this upcoming ball, Bram knew what he had to do. "Like many other young ladies in high society, there comes a time where it is needed for them to step out into the limelight. I find myself in that very same position."

"Oh, truly?" Lady Hemmingway asked curiously, with a fair and impressed expression.

Bram nodded, and bowed respectfully. "Yes, I find that I've stepped away for too long. And in doing so, left others to assume the worst of me."

Small snorting sounds continued to leave Lord Brunswick's lips. But no one acknowledged his presence, the ladies enchanted by Bram's ambience, instead. Bram glanced to Anita and found her looking at him with wonder. He smiled, trying not to give away his awkward stance. Much to his surprise, however, Anita's eyes suddenly looked qualm as she glanced away.

"Ah yes, Lord Kenwood. That is quite commendable."

"Thank you," he graciously said.

"Then let me formally introduce you back in civilized society," The Viscountess declared. She then went through the group, introducing each one, except for Lord Brunswick, of course. When she made it to Anita last, Bram stood straighter. He bowed closer to her gloved hand, and fighting back the urge, only briefly kissed her delicate sweet aroma.

Once he was upright, he found her refusing to look at him, and gently nibbling her lip. Before he could understand what that expression meant, the strings to the orchestra announced the upcoming waltz. Bram saw his opportunity. He cleared his throat and offered his hand to Anita. "My Lady, would you give me the honor of this waltz?"

A low hum escaped the other ladies, then a quiet hushing sound from the Viscountess. Anita glanced to them before looking back to Bram with an apologetic expression. She brought both her hands together, one gently tugging on the dance card bound around her wrist. Her eyes showing regret just before flashing to Mr. Cox. "My apologies, my Lord. But I have already given it to Mr. Cox."

As if by cue, Henry stepped forward and bowed. Grinning to Bram, he offered his hand out to Anita, who hesitantly took it. Gritting his teeth, Bram had to respectfully move to allow her to walk past him. Watching them approach the dance floor, he had to bite back the desire to lash out at Mr. Cox. The urge grew stronger once he saw the tall man pull Anita closer to him when the music began.

"Oh my, not to worry, Lord Kenwood." Lady Hemmingway stood beside him and expressed joyfully. "Often partners are set up before the festivities start. And Mr. Cox was highly adamant in readjusting back to English dances. This is the second waltz he chose my daughter to cavort with. Quite splendid for it to be Anita."

Bram inwardly winced but was able to still nod to the Viscountess right before she stepped away to the other ladies. Her words made his gut burn with the knowing of what had happened to Anita in America. Her mother was overjoyed by this occurrence, understandably so, perhaps. But Bram was seething. Anita did not deserve pity. She deserved him.

A delicate pull to his sleeve broke Bram's focus on Anita. Turning, he found Anita's sister Belle, at his elbow. She had a small frown, her rosy lips in a natural pout. His stomach now in knots, he leaned down, expecting what to hear her ask. "Lord Kenwood, did Mark come with you?"

Biting back the curse Bram felt towards Mark, he tried to remain calm when he decided what to say. "No, Mark told me to send his deepest apologies. But he had a matter to attend to."

Belle looked down, bewildered, clearly perplexed with questions she had no answers to. Again, Bram damned Mark, knowing full well the real reason his friend avoided coming to tonight's party. Mark was scared to death. And dammit, Bram understood that. But looking at Belle now, he could see how much she cared for him.

"Would you like for me to send him a message?" Bram asked with a smile.

That seemed to break her spell. Belle shook her head gently and tried to smile politely. "No. But thank you, my Lord Kenwood." She sighed softly. Looking back out at her sister and the Mr. Cox on the dance floor, that made her smile warmly. "I'm glad to see you here today, my Lord. My sister is happy. She may not look it, but the past few weeks had been hard for her. We've been puzzled by it, not knowing why."

Belle looked at him then, her eyes holding an inner wisdom. It occurred to him that she really knew why her sister had been down. Swallowing, Bram took an unsure side-step. "I'm glad to hear that your sister is well again."

"She is well, because you are here," Belle said in a low tone. "I truly hope you know what that means, and you use it wisely."

Bram was amazed by her honesty and protective statement. Nodding, he bowed over Belle's hand in thanks. "I intend to, little Miss."

With that, Belle nodded, and made her leave towards the other ladies. Glancing back out to Anita, Bram felt uplifted, as though he just received blessings from the heavens. A sign that he was missed, by Anita. Knowing full well what he must do, he had others to convince as well. But, he thought with a smirk, at least that was a start.

∞ ∞ ∞

Anita felt dazed. Whirling around the dance floor, she hardly noticed any others, or her dance partner, who had been making small conversation since they started. But Anita could not keep her focus, all thought on Bram. Each time they crossed, she found herself looking for him. At first, she saw him speaking with her mother, and then lastly to her sister. But once they made their way around again, she lost track of him.

Anita nearly fumbled when she thought she saw Bram by the far French doors leading to the veranda. Mr. Cox chuckled low in his throat. "He's not here anymore, Miss Henderson."

Anita flashed him a surprised look, and then blushed. "Pardon my distracted mind, Mr. Cox."

He smiled, turning her around another dancing couple. "Please, call me Henry." He drew her closer to him. For a moment, Anita gasped, thinking she felt his hardness, but she quickly pushed that thought away. She did not answer him.

Henry laughed once more. "You certainly are a mystery, my Lady."

"I am really not, Mr. Cox." Anita replied, seeing the disappointment cross his eyes. She again began to look around for Bram. Her instincts called out for him.

"Well, I disagree. I bet out of all these ladies here, you are different compared to every single one of them," Henry insisted. When Anita casted him a perplexed look, he grinned.

"I can tell you are a woman of means. That intrigues me," he simply said.

Anita suddenly felt her stomach turn. "I beg your pardon?"

"That won't be necessary. I'm speaking bluntly." When Anita did not think they could get any closer, Henry brought her close enough that she felt her bust skim his chest.

"Mr. Cox!" Anita exclaimed, her blush now devouring her. She quickly looked around, making sure no one saw. No one being Bram.

"There now, that is what I mean." Henry smirked. "My Lady, you don't act like one."

Stunned at his comment, Anita tried to break away from his grip, but he held her tightly. "I wouldn't, unless you wish to draw attention?"

Swallowing hard, Anita kept in pace with him. Biting her lip, she said in a low voice, "How dare you say such a comment, Mr. Cox?"

He smiled, continuing his dance. "I'm only saying that it would seem like you are a woman who enjoys pleasure." He said the word fervently.

Anita's eyes widened as she wrapped her mind around what he was meaning. She suddenly felt a cold sweat ache down her body. She had to grit her teeth to stop the nausea that abruptly arose. "I do not know what you mean, Mr. Cox. And I would greatly appreciate it if we are silent for the remainder of this dance."

She felt him chuckle, as she was pulled against him once more. "Then I will say this lastly. I would love nothing more than to appease your pleasure. And I shall have it."

Anita missed her step, and felt her face collide against Henry's chest. When she drew back, he had his hand intimately placed on her waist, close to her bosom. Two patrons closest to them drew out a gasp at the sight. Anita blushed fiercely and stepped away from him. He smiled broadly, and she thought her stomach was going to fall out.

Anita leapt away, past the onlookers eyes. She found her way up the staircase to the second landing, where the powder and resting rooms were held. Stepping into one of the rooms, two ladies jolly with laughter paid her no mind, as they exited the lounge. The room was empty then. Anita leaned over one of the washing bowls, pouring water from an offered vase into it, and splashed her face.

Her stomach plagued her, and she thought she was going to be sick. The dance only being a small portion of reason. Mr. Cox had planned a folly from the start. How dare the man, and his crude intentions. Breathing deeply, Anita loomed over the washing bowl. She heard her inner voice whisper how it was not as different as to when Bram and she first met. Why did she have such disdain for Mr. Cox, while he performed in the same manner?

Anita shook her head determinedly and grabbed a towel to dry her face. No, this was not the same. From the moment they met, what she and Bram shared was a mutual desire and respect. Their need for each other matched, like none other. Or at least, they did, Anita thought faintly. Their affair was no longer possible.

She lost track of how long she was standing there, until she heard a click at the door. Expecting to hear women laughing or talking, Anita straightened up, and drew in a sigh. She knew she had to step back into the party. Despite her stomach still feeling in knots, she had to hold her head high. Mr. Cox was undoubtedly with her mother still, reckoning her return. Anita grumbled under her breath.

"Are you well?"

Anita nearly fell over. She whirled around to see Bram at the end of the door. She paused, nearly pinching herself to see if she was not hallucinating. But the scowl at his brow looked real enough. She swallowed hard.

"Bram." She whispered. "What are you doing in here?"

Bram gestured for silence. He leaned against the door, his hand on the knob. Low muffled laughter came near, and for a moment, Anita felt her body begin to quake. The voices at the door paused when they tried to turn the knob, but found it locked. Bram and Anita heard their footsteps move away, and then quiet.

When Bram glanced to her once again, his scowl deepened. "Anita, you look faint."

He came to hold her, and she realized then that she nearly was. Bram caressed her cheek, only to find her ice cold, and shivering. For the first time, Anita saw worry in his eyes.

She then felt foolish, not wanting to ever cause such fuss, especially for Bram. She tried to pull away, but he did not let go of her.

"I'm fine, Bram. Please," Anita answered shakily.

"You are not. Stop acting like everything is well. I know you better than that," Bram said precisely.

At that, Anita nearly choked on her tears, but she bit her lip. "Bram, why are you here? It is dangerous for us to be seen together."

He half heartedly laughed. "Yes, well, that is quite right."

Anita's brows knitted. "Then why?"

Bram had a serious expression when he said, "What can I say? I wanted to see you in the arms of another man. It lessened the blow."

She lost all breath then and scowled. "It wasn't like that!"

He grinned wickedly, "No? It certainly seemed that way, by how you two danced together."

Anita yanked herself away from him, the memory of it causing bile to rise. "He did that on purpose! To make a point, and to make me desire him."

Bram's tone then turned cold. "What does that mean? Are you saying he tried to force himself on you?"

She gasped, "No! I mean, I'm not sure. The point is Bram, I did not wish for any of that to occur. For you to see that. In fact, if I had any choice in the matter, I wouldn't even be here!"

At that, Bram sighed softly. Grasping her elbow, he pulled her gently against him. Anita couldn't help herself; she willingly rested her head on his chest. Closing her eyes, she inhaled his warmth and familiar spice. After weeks of heartache, to be back in Bram's arms soothed her like nothing else. It also frightened her, for she now knew the truth at that moment.

"Bram, please. Tell me why you are really here," she said into his coat.

He waited a moment before answering. "I need to know, if you had been threatened in any way, that caused you to end us."

Anita bit her lip as she thought about the conversation with Miss Lucinda Kenyon. And to the letter she had written Bram. "A Lady of the Ton told me that she had an associate who kept eyes on you. The acquaintance told her that they had noticed you with the same female on more than one occasion. They started to guess that the woman was really a Lady, based on dress and manner."

For a moment, Bram felt tense beneath her. He took in a deep breath and touched her cheek. "Did this Lady outright believe it was you?"

Anita shook her head. "She didn't say. But she seemed rather keen to believe it was me."

"What is this Lady's name?" He kept his tone calm for her.

"Miss Lucinda Kenyon. Youngest daughter to the Marquess of Normanby."

Bram looked deep in thought at that moment, and Anita longingly stared at his handsome features. How she missed him. Her heart leapt back to life with him near. But the regret of her letter still burned her. She needed to know if he had not hated her for it.

"Bram, I am so sorry for how I'd written that letter. I knew how vague it sounded, but I was fearful of whomever that associate was. I worried that she would somehow get hold of that note and take it to her mistress." Anita looked down at his fine vest, unnoticing the intricate design. "I had planned to wait until the rumors settled, to write back to you with a more proper explanation."

Bram lifted her chin, his eyes focused. "I apologize that I couldn't wait for that proper explanation."

Anita's tears threatened her, for she recalled then, all the stories Miss Kenyon had told about Bram. She bit her lip, relieved anger forming to the surface. "Bram, you knew sooner or later, we would have been found out. Didn't you?"

Bram was taken aback for a moment. His eyes had shown surprise, but then the truth was evident. Taking in a sigh, he nodded. "I did."

When Anita looked down disappointed, Bram rushed to grasp her hands. "I had hoped otherwise, Anita. You must believe that."

"Then, why didn't you tell me? Why didn't you want to tell me who you were?" Anita pierced him with her pleading gaze.

Bram looked away, but Anita caught the shame in his eyes. His tone was quiet when he spoke, "I wanted to protect you." He sighed, then shook his head. "No, that's not true."

Bram closed his eyes, and after a moment, he opened them. He caressed her cheek, looking as though he would rather not speak. But he took in a deep breath, then. "Anita, I did not want you to know who I was. At first, I did not wish for you to know my title, but then, as we got closer, I wasn't sure how I would feel if you also knew about my reputation."

Anita was surprised. She had never seen Bram look as vulnerable as he did now. Or rather, as open to her. She took a step closer to him, their bodies nearly pressed together. "Bram, I hope you can know that I wouldn't have judged you for your reputation."

He released a small chuckle then, looking relieved from her words, and their closeness. "I should have known better. You are not like them..."

With that, Bram closed in and pulled Anita against him. They embraced each other, the sounds of their pent-up breaths winding together, their lips perfectly telling their unspoken word for the other. By the end of their kiss, they were grasping each other's clothing, both longing to get closer beyond them.

Distant voices came up to the door then, again finding the lock in place. This time they heard complaints, and footsteps walking away. Bram placed his forehead against hers and dropped a breath. They both knew they did not have long until more came to open the door. Pulling away, Bram had a torn look in his gaze.

"We need to get back to the party," he said. Anita could see the war Bram was battling inside. "I will go first. Wait for a while after that, and then make your exit."

Anita nodded slowly, her eyes fluttering to gain focus, and to draw away the tears she still refused to shed. The hole in her heart settled back as she watched Bram turn to go. This being likely the last time she would see him again. A quiet sob made it hard for her to breathe. Anita sniffed it back as she memorized Bram's every feature, not wanting to ever forget, and glad to have at least shared one last kiss.

At the door, Bram turned his face back to her. When Anita thought she was about to lose the fight with her tears, Bram smiled warmly. "I will find this associate that has been following me. And after I do, I will return. But this time, I plan to properly court you."

Bram left, leaving Anita stunned at the click of the door.

Chapter 12

B ram paced the room where he and the others always met in Springfield. Already, he partook two libations of cognac, and Bram was beginning to feel the
sweat build at his brow. For a week now, Bram mulled over,
day and night, what he had told Anita at the Hedgerow Ball.
He shocked even himself when he confessed how he was
going to court her! Those words flowed out of him after he
gazed at Anita for the last time. His heart twisted at the
thought of never seeing her again, and that's when Bram's
questioning was answered. He had to have her. More than he
ever felt before.

Despite how stunned he felt, Bram knew that it was
the truth. All this time knowing her, he realized just how
much they matched. Neither one wanted to be without the
other, and if their last kiss was of any indication, they were
desperate to be back in each other's arms. They trusted one
another. And as Bram learned, Anita was unlike any other
woman he'd ever come across. She was honest with him.

But that was half of the challenge solved. Bram knew
he had to face more to be with her. He had to win over the
Ton. Though that night had proved satisfactory with those in
attendance, there were still others that were repulsed by his
presence. Lord Brunswick being but one.

Surprisingly, when Bram had returned to the party,
he was met by Anita's mother. At first, he thought they had

been caught. But the Viscountess smiled, patted his arm, and took him around to be introduced to the older peers. Bram remembered how heartened he felt by her actions. She kept her word, much like his Anita would have. He found himself admiring the woman, as she so delightfully chatted with others, helping them forget who they were speaking with.

He briefly would catch others whispering and casting him glances. But the Viscountess would call to him and assure him to never mind them. In her own words, she told him that gossip will never stick, if you but show them the truth of their lies. Glancing to Anita, he wondered if this was how the Viscountess taught her to face the accusations in America. Bram commended her for that.

Perhaps there was hope that Bram impressed the Viscountess. With that, it would make courting Anita more likely. He stopped in his tracks. But there was still one problem. A risk he could not afford to threaten both his and Anita's fate. The associate who had been keeping tabs on his ventures.

This unknown assailant was a plague on his agenda. Not only did they ruin the cherished time he and Anita had together, but they also threatened the chances of their courtship ever being possible. If Bram didn't find out who this person was, then it would be likely that they would step forward and point the finger at Anita, once they saw the two of them courting. That, Bram thought determinedly, could not happen.

Bram already had an idea of one possible person, but to know for certain, he would need help. He paced over to the liquor and refilled his glass with cognac. Sipping from it, he suddenly grew hyper aware of the ticking clock on the mantle over the fireplace. The time nearly struck eight at night. Stepping back to the center table, between the furnished chairs, Bram lined the pieces of letters he had collected. Trying to ignore the tension that was beginning to pierce the crook of his neck, Bram placed his glass onto the table, and leaned over it.

The double doors opened, and Sebastian and Mark stepped through. They were murmuring about a subject

Bram could not focus on listening to. He was relieved that they came, but he stood still, staring at the letters in hopes of finding some sort of clue. When Sebastian came forward and smacked him on the back in a friendly gesture, Bram turned and grinned.

"I'm glad you showed," Bram said, genuinely thankful.

Sebastian's brow rose, as he said almost sarcastically, "You sounded actually serious in your note. One would think someone had died."

With a nod, Bram stared back down to the letters. "That may be true. But let us hope it doesn't get to that point."

When Sebastian gave a confused frown, Mark stepped in, and nodded to Bram. "Thank you for coming, Mark."

"Of course," Mark answered. His eyes shifted however, and a curious gloom overcame them. "How was the Hedgerow Ball?" He could not help but ask.

Bram nodded slowly, "It went good."

When it looked as though Mark wanted to ask another question, he held himself back, and looked down. Bram sighed, and inwardly shook his head. "She was there."

Mark immediately looked up, clearly his thoughts turning towards Belle, and not Anita. Again, he did not say anything.

"She was waiting for you."

Mark did not respond. He kept his eyes low, and after a moment, he finally nodded. Bram touched his shoulder "You should be there next time. Don't hold yourself back because of the past, old man."

Mark scoffed, but still chuckled under his breath. He grinned. "Old man? Look who's giving the sage advice."

They both laughed. Just then, the doors slammed open, and in walked Philip. Creating ever a grand entrance, Philip grinned, as he sipped on an already glass served with brandy. He looked around, seeing only the three gentlemen, and scowled. Checking his pocket watch, he swallowed his sipped brandy.

"Bloody Hell, has it frozen over? Did I arrive on time?" Philip asked, stunned.

Bram grinned, while the others chuckled. "Not quite. You're ten minutes late."

Philip frowned, but then gave a cheeky grin. "Have I finally surpassed the great Richard?!" he called out. Then laughed.

Mark shook his head, while Sebastian laughed and sat down by the fireplace. Bram could not help but grin, especially when he spotted Richard appearing behind Philip. Slapping him on the back, Richard smirked, catching Philip's humorous look. A glass of gin and tonic in his hand, Richard clanked his against Philips'. "We both know, that won't ever happen."

The two men laughed together and swallowed back their toast. Richard walked in and settled into his favorite chair, while Philip went to refill their glasses. When Bram stepped closer, he noticed the slight weary look that crossed Richard's expression then. But as he sat across from him, Richard shielded his eyes with a carefree grin. Much like his friend, who always chose to conceal his thoughts.

"Not like you to be late," Bram said jovially.

Richard smirked, and glanced down at his left hand. Bram did not see what he was looking at, but when his friend shifted in his seat then covered his hand, Bram suspected he was hiding something. Scowling inwardly, Bram could not remember when he ever saw Richard act in such a way. Collected, yes, but never peculiar. When Richard brought his hand back to the armrest, Bram still did not notice anything was amiss. Strange, he thought, but perhaps he was imagining things.

"I was detained," Richard said, as he received a new filled glass from Philip. Bram left it at that, knowing far too well that his friend was not going to go into any more details, despite how curious he felt.

Philip came around them and sat down across from Sebastian, who returned a toast gesture. "So, Bram, you have us all here now. What in Hell's domain caused such a fuss with you? Has someone died?"

A chuckle escaped from Mark, as Sebastian made a face that reflected what he had said earlier. Bram shook his head and grinned. He walked back to the letters lining the table. "That may well be the case if I am not careful. I've called you here to seek your guidance."

Richard and Sebastian listened to Bram's words closely, each carrying their own remarked expressions, while Philip cast a confused grin. Mark made his way over to stand beside Bram and observed the letters. "What are these about?"

"I confess that I am being plagued by an overzealous woman. She has been sending me threatening letters since April," Bram said aloud.

"An 'overzealous woman'? Come now, Bram. Like you would not know how to appease such a type. You have dealt with them in the past. Just give her what they all desire. You," Philip said.

Bram smirked humorlessly. "That is how I got into this in the first place, Philip." He shook his head. "No, this woman is accusing me of siring a bastard within her. And is now threatening me and mine."

"Did you?" Richard asked pointedly.

Again, Bram shook his head. "I do not believe I did. And based on the evidence of her letters, I believe it false."

Philip snorted into his cup. "You know who would give the best advice right about now? Sterling!" With a laugh, Philip held his side. "Where is the hound when you need him? Of course, he'd not be around when duty calls!"

"I believe Bram is right." Mark backed up. Picking up three separate letters throughout the timeline. "The way she leads each letter implies that she is only wanting money from Bram. While at first, she speaks of a babe, she later pays no mention of it, and begins to proceed in making threats."

"So, she hasn't followed through on her blackmail all this time?" Sebastian asked. Bram shook his head.

"Well, I say she is merely bluffing then. Don't falter from her threats, Bram," Philip said with a toast of brandy.

Mark wrinkled his brows as he read the last letter sent from the woman, the very same note that gave Bram pause. He took the parchment to Richard to read. After reviewing it, Richard's expression hardened. He returned it to Mark to pass to Sebastian, who also expressed a serious frown.

"What? What does it say?" Philip asked curiously.

Lord Kenwood,

Too long you have ignored my warnings. You have pushed my letters aside and decided to disregard my forewarning. You have even had the audacity to entertain another in your bed. Well believe me, Lord Kenwood, she will not be pleased to know that I am aware of who she is. I plan to expose her, and you. This is my final notice, if you do not meet my wishes, your Lady will have much more to worry about than a spoiled reputation. Pay me or face the consequences.
B.

"Well, that woman took it to a whole other level." Philip finished off his drink. "Not that it would do any good. It's clearly a farce. Bram would never go for a Lady of the Ton," he said with a wink.

The ones who knew better only gave Philip a tedious look, which left Philip confused. He exclaimed a sound when Bram did not agree with him, nor said a word. Then he laughed out loud. A whooping sound as he slapped his knee and fell back onto his chair.

"Settle down, Philip," Richard said firmly, however, there was still a note of humor in his tone.

"I leave the fray for a moment, and suddenly Bram changes his whole outlook of the Ton?" Philip joked.

"I did not change anything. But there is a woman who has," Bram expressed.

"Is this the same Lady the woman is threatening?" Sebastian asked from his chair.

Bram nodded, as his fingers tightened around the edge of the table. "I believe this woman is an accomplice, to another that has paid her to follow me. I fell to her whims, and now she's using that to blackmail me into giving her more." His knuckles began to whiten. "I cannot risk her to give away my Lady's identity."

"'My Lady'?" Philip repeated under his breath. His expression was amazed and serious. The others had noticed as well. The energy of the room turned astonished. It was Richard who stood then and made his way to Bram's side. Taking up a few of the letters, he examined them.

"Do you believe this is the ballerina from your last production?" he asked, not taking his eyes off the twenty-four notes of paper.

Bram nodded. "I'm certain it is."

"What of the person who hired her to follow you?" Richard began to stack each letter. Bram watched him curiously.

"My Lady mentioned another woman in her group questioning our acquaintanceship. I believe she may know more about this accomplice." Mark then brought Bram a refilled glass of cognac which he received most obligingly.

"Write down the Lady's name, as well as the ballerina's. I will look into them for you," Richard stated. He rolled up the letters and tied them together with a red ribbon. After Bram wrote the names down, Richard slipped the paper into his pocket, and gave him a nod.

"What will you have me do?" Bram asked.

After a moment, Richard smiled, and squeezed Bram's shoulder. "Go get your Lady, my friend." When Bram returned a confused grin, Richard winked. "I'll take care of this nonsense. No one dares harass any of my friends. Especially when it comes to their future."

For the first time in a while, Bram felt relieved. His trust in his friend lifting his spirits, he knew Richard was capable of great things. Especially when it came to getting tasks done his way. "You have my gratitude."

Richard nodded slowly, the weary expression he had earlier easing back into his gaze. "Just, don't do anything that may lose her."

Thrown off by his comment, Bram had the suspicion that something may have occurred between Richard and his Godfrey Rose, and he felt deep sympathy for his friend. What could have happened between the madly in love couple, he wondered. Nevertheless, Bram was thankful for his friend's words of wisdom. He clanked his drink against Richard's, and toasted the rest of the Rakes of Springfield, who returned the gesture.

∞∞∞

Anita exhaled as Claire tightened her bodice. It was not the corset that made her lose her breath, however. Time was the plague. It had been three weeks since Bram told her of his plan, and yet she still had not heard from him. Not that she would, she grudgingly thought. Anita straightened, telling herself to be patient. She knew the reality of finding whoever was following Bram would not be an easy task. The thought alone sent shivers down her spine. The disgrace of someone doing such a thing was vile.

"Are you cold, Miss? Should I stoke the fireplace?" Claire asked from behind her.

Shaking her head, Anita held fast. "No, thank you Claire. I'm fine."

Claire stepped away, returning soon after with a lapis color day dress. Once her garments were in place, Anita heard her door click open and Belle walked in. Smiling at her sister dressed in a lovely lavender color dress, Anita frowned once she noticed her sister's demeanor. Claire curtsied and excused herself, leaving the sisters alone together. Anita quickly embraced her sister, taking her to the bed.

Belle's tears fell as she leaned against Anita's shoulder. Anita stroked her head, pained that her sister was unwell. "Oh, sweet Belle, what is the matter?"

It took her sister a moment to speak, her breath catching with every sob. Sniffing back her tears, Belle looked up at her sister, her eyes like deep pools of sorrow. Never had Anita seen her sister in such despair. Fearing the worst, Anita held her sister closer, holding her hand.

"Annie-" Belle choked out. Anita shushed her softly, rocking her like she used to when they were young.

"It is all right, dear. Let it all out before you're ready to speak," Anita reassured her. It took a few more moments before Belle was ready. She wiped at her face, leaving streaks of red across her cheeks. Nevertheless, Belle still looked sweet and charming.

"I thought we were in love…" Belle was finally able to state. She let out a shaky breath, as she sniffed back her tears. Anita was surprised, not at all expecting to hear the words that her sister just confessed.

Pulling back, Anita observed her sister, yet still stroking back the curl that had fallen. "What happened?"

Shaking her head, Belle bit her lip hard. "So much, yet, nothing at all."

Frowning, Anita could not have been any more confused. "I'm afraid I don't understand, Belle."

Taking a deep breath, Belle sighed. "I can't understand it either, Annie." Grasping her own arms, Belle looked down at her slippers. "I thought I was in love with someone. He was everything that I ever dreamed of, and I thought I was his, but there was something that he is hiding from me."

"What was he hiding from you?" Anita asked quietly.

Belle had a deep expression when she answered. "He is afraid of me."

"That, that is ridiculous. Why on earth would he be afraid of you, Belle?" Anita said, astonished.

It was then that Belle's tears began to return, slowly spilling down her cheeks. Shaking her head, Belle covered her face with her hands. In a choked voice, she forced, "I just wish that he could give me the chance to prove it to him."

"Prove what to him?" Anita asked, feeling perplexed. She could not believe the state that her sister was in. Anita had never seen Belle this way, and it scarred her to see her in such pain. It nearly overwhelmed her, for it was not as different to how Anita felt not long ago.

Belle finished her tears, seemingly in deep thought. She accepted the handkerchief Anita offered her and wiped her nose. Before Belle could answer however, the door to the room burst open, and their mother hurriedly came inside.

Anita stood quickly to cover Belle as she wiped her face, though it had seemed as if their mother had not even noticed Belle there. Out of breath, Eloise cast a relieved look to her eldest daughter.

"Oh good, you are dressed," their mother expressed, fanning herself, and clearly flushed. Anita frowned, bewildered by all the fuss of the morning.

"What is the matter, mama?" Anita asked right when their mother approached her, trying to right her hair, and curl the sides. She flinched when Eloise pinched her cheeks next.

"Mother! What is going on?" Touching her cheek, Anita frowned.

"Sorry, my dear. I'm just merely trying to give them color." Eloise smiled wide. "I need to get you good and ready."

Anita stared at her mother questioningly. "What for?"

Her mother squeezed her shoulders, and with a laugh, nearly shouted. "There is a caller for you, my dear Anita! A gentleman caller!"

Frozen, Anita was surprised, uncertain of what to say. Her mother immediately dashed to the dresser, speaking of a brooch that would suit her gown perfectly. Anita's mouth went dry, and her stomach fluttered. Thoughts racing, her emotions danced. What was happening? Was Bram already coming to call on her? He must have sorted out the conflict with the persons following him, she thought.

Imagining him downstairs, amongst the bright plush cushions of the drawing room, Anita smiled wide. How out of place he would look there. That thought alone nearly made her laugh happily. Her mother rushed over to place the beautiful pearl brooch on her bodice. They both laughed together when she fumbled a bit with the clasp.

Her mother was beaming when she grasped Anita's hands. "You look lovely, my dear. I am so glad to see you happy. Now, despite what had happened in the past, we must not live in it. Remember, this is the time for new beginnings. And I do believe that this man is here to court you seriously."

Touched by her mother's words, Anita nodded. Smiling, her mother stepped out, but right before disappearing, she looked back to instruct her daughter. "Be sure to wait a moment before coming down. We mustn't let these gentleman callers believe we are desperate for their affection."

Once her mother was gone, Anita laughed quietly. She could not believe the joy and approval her mother showed. Her heart swiftly filled with excitement and rapture. She felt it beating rapidly against her breast. Catching her breath, her mind whirled with amazement. Anita was finally able to be with Bram, in more ways than one, and that made her smile blissfully again.

"I am so happy for you, Annie." Her sister's small voice came from the bed. Suddenly remembering Belle's presence, Anita frowned, and went back to sit beside her.

"Don't worry about me, I will be alright. I am sorry that I came in here bursting in tears," Belle said quietly.

Shaking her head, Anita lifted her sister's chin. "Do not ever be sorry for that. I am your big sister. I care for whatever is happening to you. I just wish I can help your ordeal."

Smiling softly, Belle shrugged. "I will figure it out. You know me, Annie. I often do." Nibbling her lip slightly, she seemed to consider her next words. "I suppose, I felt that you would know what I should do too. Since, you are in love as well."

Stunned, Anita did not know what to say to that. Clearing her throat, she kept silent. That is until Belle grasped her hand and whispered, "I believe Bram is a good man for you."

Always amazed with her sister's intuition, Anita quietly asked, "You know about Bram?"

Belle smiled sweetly, "You know that I've never followed gossip, unless proven true. But I have seen how he looks at you, and how you are with him. I am not blind. I feel that you both need each other. You shouldn't let gossip get in the way of that."

Anita gave a humorless laugh, "I'm afraid it is not that simple."

Belle gave her a stern smile. "You've always worried about our family's reputation. Held the burden on your shoulders. Well, this is the time to let that go, Annie. He is downstairs now, to properly court you. Mama was right, this is a time for a new beginning."

Anita slowly smiled and laughed quietly. "Who sounds like the big sister now?"

They both giggled and leaned against each other. Then Belle stood and imitated her mother as she gently pinched Anita's cheeks. Shaking her head, Anita sat up and hugged her sister. "Thank you, little Belle. I'm so lucky to have you as a sister."

Squeezing tightly, Belle agreed. "Annie, you need to remember too, that you can come to me if you're feeling heartsick as well."

Anita realized what her sister meant. Belle must have known about the time Anita was sick with heartache. Inwardly shaking her head, she truly was amazed with her sister's insight. Promising her she would, Anita agreed that they both will be there for each other when the need should ever arrive. They both walked out from the bedroom, and stepped downstairs. The drawing room door was closed, and muffled voices seeped through to the hall. Biting her lip, Anita squeezed her sister's hand. Belle gave her a warm smile, and an encouraging nod. Anita took a deep breath and exhaled with a smile. Ready to see Bram, she opened the door.

Chapter 13

Anita was stunned. She stood at the entrance of the room; the door was now closed behind her. She tried her hardest not to clench her gown, or to turn and run. Instead, her back was rigid, her breath shallow. Belle had not followed her in, her encouragement now dissipating. Her mother, Eloise, sat cheerfully chatting with the guest that stood over her proudly.

Mr. Richard Henry Cox grinned, and without stopping his conversation with her mother, slanted his gaze towards Anita and winked. That look alone made her skin crawl. Her mother casually glanced her way, and without missing a heartbeat, cooed at her arrival. Eloise launched herself to her daughter, smiling brightly between Anita and Mr. Cox. Wrapping her arm around her daughter's, she brought her closer to the center of the room. So much for her mother's discretion.

"Oh, my dear. You certainly took your time. I was afraid that Mr. Cox was getting tired of my boorish tales of our sleepy town in Pennsylvania," her mother voiced.

Giving them a dashing smile that did not quite reach his eyes, Mr. Cox chuckled. "I wouldn't say that my Lady. Your tales are filled with vigor and imagination, that can delight anyone."

"My dear Mr. Cox, flattery can get you anywhere," Eloise laughed into her gloved hands.

"I would surely hope so, my Lady." His chuckle was far too dry to Anita.

"Ah yes, isn't it nice that our dear Mr. Cox came to

visit, Anita?" Eloise smiled cheerfully. "He has declared that he came to see you, especially."

They both stared at Anita, waiting for her response. Silence was what only met them. Anita did not know what to say. It took nearly all her control to keep her expression calm. To ignore the rising nausea in her belly. She took a moment to speak, but nothing came.

Her mother laughed hesitantly, looking at Anita with confusion and urging her to speak. Forcing herself to swallow back the disdain of the situation, Anita was able to muster a small smile. She curtsied. "Good day, Mr. Cox."

A relieved breath left her mother, as Mr. Cox smiled wide, and bowed. "Good day, Miss Henderson. You look positively radiant today."

A pleased sigh escaped her mother's lips, while Anita simply looked down and away from Mr. Cox's steady gaze. They stood there in silence, Anita with her hands clenched together in front of her. Catching this strange stillness, Eloise guided her daughter to sit at one of the cushion sofas.

"Well now, I will leave you two momentarily. Would tea and sweets be to your liking, Mr. Cox?" Anita's mother said swiftly, much to her dismay.

Anita stood quickly. "Let me help you, mother."

"Oh no, no. I will return shortly, my dear. I am sure you two will do splendidly." Eloise waved her off, as she hurried to the door. But not before Anita caught the delightful wink her mother casted to Mr. Cox. Her heart dropped. This was planned all along.

Taking in a calming breath, Anita tried to remain still. But as she glanced to Mr. Cox, and found him studying her, Anita felt strangely hunted. And caught. His eyes were heated and calculating. She could not place his thoughts, especially when he began to grin.

"So, your mother tells me that you enjoy travel? Did you know that my company does trade through the coast of India? I bet you would adore the exotic sights there. Perhaps even be fascinated with their teachings of *Kama Sutra*. I have heard it brings delight to most of the women there."

"Is there a reason you are here, Mr. Cox?" Anita asked

steadily, unfazed by his attempt to shock her. Which must have intrigued him, for he raised a curious brow.

"Indeed, Miss Henderson," he only said with a wicked smile.

"Spare me, Mr. Cox. Tell me why." A sudden anger surged through her, not enjoying his tenacious attitude one bit.

He chuckled, "Could we perhaps drop the polite formality, and call each other by our names, Anita?"

"I'd rather not. That would imply that I would wish for your friendship. And after your stunt at Hedgerow Ball, I'd think not," she stated sternly.

He feigned woe, as he took a step closer to her. "I assure you; my friendship would not be something you would regret."

The way he voiced that made her feel on edge. Anita could not understand his persistence. Thinking back to the Hedgerow Ball, she made no attempt to show any interest in Mr. Cox. In fact, she rather had ignored him in the beginning, before her mother's insistence. She could not deny his handsomeness, but she also didn't regard herself as his type. He was conniving, charming, and talkative. He could not be trusted, especially after his actions when they had danced. What could he see in her that would gain this interest? Unless...

"I do not know if my mother has told you anything about my past, but I am no stranger to men who wish for a title, and an extra dowry. So, let me assure you, sir. I will not give my affection lightly to conmen. Especially to one who promises something that I would not regret."

Mr. Cox frowned, and for a moment, Anita finally saw the true soul behind his eyes. He was not pleased with her words and she could tell then that the Mr. Cox was not accustomed to rejection. As though it had never happened. However, he quickly cleared his expression. Easily smiling once again, he sat down beside her. His warmth so close, Anita detected his scent. A trace of sea salt and patchouli.

"I understand." He was looking down and let a moment pass between them before he spoke again. "I can see how difficult it would be to believe in a man who takes a fancy in you. Always having to suspect if they are only after your dowry, or actually interested in the intelligence you harbor."

His eyes warmed as Mr. Cox comfortably settled in closer to her. "Believe me, I will be perfectly honest with you. I am interested in all these things." Dipping his head lower, he caressed her with his gaze. "You are surely plucked, and that lessens the trouble of dealing with a fresh girl. Not to mention, how flushed you are with need. Not just any man could tell a woman who is in heat. I, on the other hand, could detect it from a mile away."

He seemed to be satisfied with himself, while Anita held her stunned emotions in check. Strangely, however, she was not surprised by the actuality of his persona. No, what shocked her was his insight towards her virtue. It unnerved her that he saw right through her. Which left her wondering if anyone else had noticed.

"Rest assured, your silence does not deter me. In fact, I rather enjoy it. Will make courting you even more relaxed," Mr. Cox said jovially. He reached out, attempting to stroke the curl of hair against her cheek.

That was when Anita stood, her anger erupting. She whirled on him, determined to end this now. "Mr. Cox, you have no right over me! I am the one who decides whom I wish to court. Just because you have charmed my mother, does not mean I do not see right through you as well. You are a leech. And trust that I will not be silent towards this. I do not want your affection."

"No?" Mr. Cox asked quietly. His eyes hardened as he stood. "You'd rather wish for the affections of a scoundrel? Someone that couldn't possibly fit into your world?" He stepped closer, nearly toe to toe, and said under his breath. "Lord Kenwood will never be accepted by your Ton."

Scowling, Anita held her ground. "What would you know about Lord Kenwood?"

Mr. Cox grinned, "Enough."

He left it at that, but his eyes held knowing, and a silent threat that Anita became familiar with. Holding her breath, Anita needed to step away from him. But right before she did, Mr. Cox grasped her hand firmly. She flinched and looked away as he forced it to his lips. He kissed her knuckles, and before releasing her, trailed his finger along the inside of her palm. Shivering, Anita wrenched her hand away.

Chuckling to himself, Mr. Cox turned towards the door. But right before stepping out, he glanced back, a forged smile in place. "I will return to call on you again. Perhaps by then, you will have accepted my proposal, and that there will be no more talk of Lord Kenwood."

He left the room. Anita heard the faint sounds of his farewells to her mother, who seemed upset that he was leaving so soon. Once she heard the front door close, Eloise came rushing in. Her mother looked cheery and hopeful as she grasped Anita into an embrace. But the last thing Anita felt was joyful.

What did this mean? That yet, another block kept she and Bram apart? Her heart felt faint. When Eloise drew back, she found her daughter pale and breathless. "Good heavens, what on earth is the matter, Anita?!"

∞∞∞

Bram sat at his desk, letters with addresses covered every inch of the dark wood. Ink residue marked his hands, as he had been writing out notes and arrangements all morning. Bram felt revitalized by his plans and set out on them the moment he woke, which was long before dawn. He was so engrossed that he had not noticed the door to his office opening.

"Don't you have anything better to do on a Saturday?" Sebastian said sarcastically, impressed, as he observed few of the addressed letters. He paused once he realized the names and invitations.

Bram leaned back in his chair, grinning. Lifting a half-smoked cigar, he lit it, satisfied with his progress. When he noted Sebastian's surprised look, he half laughed, smoke filling the air. "Awestruck?"

"Bram, these are invitations. You do know this, right?" Sebastian asked, half wanting to check his friend into a doctor's asylum.

Bram's grin widened, as he nodded. "I am well aware."

Brows knitting, Sebastian did a double take around the room. Sitting, he scoffed. "Did I enter into another world? Are you truly Bram Williams?"

"And obviously, the one and only, Lord Kenwood." Stacking the invitations, he sealed them in a wooden box. Rising, he went to pull the bell for his secretary, who entered momentarily. "Send these out, post haste."

Watching the interaction, Sebastian's jaw was slack. "Have I gone mad, then?"

This time Bram looked at his friend with a shake of his head. "Relax. You are still sane, well, as close as sane gets, that is." Bram chuckled.

Smirking, Sebastian leaned forward to observe his friend. "Then what am I witnessing here?"

Thinking for a moment, Bram smiled to himself. He had come to the decision; that to be with Anita, he needed to be a part of her world. Fully. Not the other way around. That was the only solution to keep her safe, and for them to be together. Bram knew how risky that would be. Many years of tarnished reputation kept the Ton and him at arm's length. But that still did not mean that Bram could not charm his way back in. At least, close enough to court Anita properly.

This morning's epiphany revealed that if Bram could not beat them, then he had to join them. Play them at their own game. Dazzle them with what they love to gossip, but in the end, expose the truth of their lies. Just as Anita's mother had advised him. Let the Ton perceive for themselves Bram's ordinary, yet accomplished life, then he would seem just like them. And if he can convince a few to his side, that should take care of the rest.

Satisfied with his thoughts, Bram leaned back once again, and puffed on his cigar. "The prodigal son returns."

Scowling, Sebastian examined Bram as he thought

over his words and actions. For as long as he had known Bram, never had his friend said anything positive about the Ton. So, to witness this now truly astonished him. "I understand that you've been going through a lot as of late. But is this truly what you wish to do?"

Lifting his head, Bram heard the concern in Sebastian's tone. Realizing his actions did not seem rational, Bram nodded seriously. "I know this is odd of me. Especially to you. I never thought I would consider showing my face to them again either."

"Then, why? Is it really because of Miss Henderson?" Sebastian asked knowingly.

Bram stared at Sebastian questioningly. "So, Mark told you her name."

Grinning, Sebastian shrugged. "He was speaking more about her sister, Belle. But Anita's name was brought up as well."

Chuckling to himself, Bram shook his head. "Well, I confess that I am as besotted to Anita, as Mark is to Belle. So, yes, I am doing this, so I can have her."

Sebastian's expression turned serious. "But, at the expense of your own morals?"

Bram scoffed. "My morals? They were nonexistent before I met her."

That left Sebastian speechless. Leaving him to recall the years they had been friends. Sebastian had never seen Bram with a woman for long to trust, nor attend parties other than their own. He knew his friend to be a good man, a loyal comrade, and hardworking. Looking around now, Sebastian grasped that Bram was the most concentrated in his work. But above all, he knew how the Ton functioned, and for that, Bram kept himself away. Establishing his own world in his Opera House. Sebastian truly knew what Bram was sacrificing for this woman. The mentality that he was shifting within himself. That alone told Sebastian the severity of Bram's desires, and this woman's effect on him. He only hoped that it was true.

"Well, you were there for me, so I am going to support you now. If this is truly what you wish," Sebastian honestly expressed.

Genuinely smiling, Bram nodded. "Thank you, Kent. I appreciate that." Grabbing an invitation, he handed it to Sebastian. "Come, it should be fun. In a stuffy coat, and tight knickers sort of way."

Sebastian laughed, "Just be sure to serve plenty of liquor and sherry. That should solve the problem." He snorted once he glanced at the invitation. "Especially if it's going to be a masquerade. Now that shocks me."

Bram laughed, and scratched the back of his neck. "I thought it only right, considering the ball is going to be hosted here in the Opera house."

"Well, I suppose we'll have to see who's brave enough to appear at the Lover of the Opera's domain," Sebastian said with a sarcastic laugh.

Scowling, Bram put out his cigar. "That is a godawful nickname."

Laughing, Sebastian said, "Use it to your advantage. The ladies seem to like it."

Shaking his head, Bram stood and adjusted his coat. "Well, be sure to let the others know, and bring whomever you wish. This should surely be an interesting event. For now, I'm off to make arrangements with the decorators and house hands."

Nodding, Sebastian joined his friend. Impressed by the hopeful expression on Bram's face, Sebastian walked out of the theater with thoughts on his own future. He wondered if one day, Sebastian too, would ever feel as alive again. Anything, like it was when he was a young man, and in love. Breathing deep the cool night air, Sebastian used it to ease the ache in his soul. A sadness that had never healed. And he stepped into the sightless evening, in search of pleasure that could never be fulfilled.

Chapter 14

London
Earl of Silverton's Estate
November

A nita quickened her steps as she approached Christina's front door. The day was cool and gloomy, which had Anita hurrying over to her friend's home before it rained. When Anita heard Christina had finally returned from her travels, Anita wasted no time. She desperately needed to speak with her friend. She was the only one to understand Anita's ordeal, and perhaps could advise her on what to do when it came to Bram and the new unwanted courtship with Mr. Cox.

The weeks had quickly passed, with still no word from Bram. However, Mr. Cox had shown his face at least daily, consistently insisting they get together to attend events. No matter how much Anita declined, her mother would end up coincidentally bringing them together. Mr. Cox was relentless with his flirtation, bringing Anita to fear being left alone with him. Already twice, he had attempted to hold her close. But thankfully, she was always within reach of the exit.

There was nothing Anita could do to deter the Mr. Cox, and she needed a skillful plan from an expert. The front door opened just as a light drizzle touched Anita's white shawl. A large man dressed in a butler suit stood at the door. He carried thick dark brows, deep pooling eyes, and an aura that said he would rather be out in the fields than standing at the door of a three-story townhouse. Anita did not recognize him, so she waited to be addressed before speaking outright. Funnily enough, neither did he. They stood there together at the door, seemingly motionless, while a cool wet breeze swept past his built frame.

"Uh… is the Lady of the house receiving today?"

The butler noticeably sucked on what seemed to be chewing tobacco and shook his head. Just before he was to close the door, Anita put her hand out. "Wait, this is the Godfrey Rose's home, is it not?"

Pulling the door back, the butler leaned on its wood frame, before speaking in a low throaty voice. "Aye."

"Then I am in the right place. I am sorry, but could you please ask her if she may see me? My name is Anita Henderson."

The man's brow rose as he contemplated her words. After a short pause that seemed to only allow Anita's shawl to dampen even more, a light and familiar voice sounded from inside, just beyond the pillar from him. With one last chew of his tobacco, he stepped back, and offered her the open space. Once inside, Anita followed his slow bridled pace to the next room over. Anita's newfound instinct was to scan the architecture of Christina's family townhome.

The last time she had visited Lord Silverton's estate, Anita was still a girl. The room they entered had once been the parlor to which the late Lady Silverton, Christina's mother, used to host her tea parties. The air had always smelled of fresh roses and lavender. Vases filled with bouquets of them, placed all around the room. The large stained glass window would have been opened to allow the light in, in different hues of blue and red. Steaming pots of tea and sweet chamomile cookies were always offered at the table seated between the soft cushioned couches. It was a bittersweet memory, a time when Anita knew Christina's heart was carefree. Though she had always been spirited, it was only after her mother's passing when Christina had become teasing and rebellious. But nevertheless, Anita was the only one who knew deep down the anguish Christina had truly faced every day without her mother.

She had known this by just looking at her dear friend.

By the way her eyes ached longingly when she thought no-body was looking at her. Or by the shortness of breath when she had no words to tell. Anita knew this because she saw it right at that very moment. Anita's immediate attention drew to Christina. She was lounging on a new plush chaise, a quilted blanket covering her lap. Her long hair was loosely swept and braided to the side. She wore an easy white garden dress, which told Anita that the butler had been right when he said Christina was not receiving any guests. What troubled Anita the most was how pale Christina looked. Her lips dry. Her eyes swollen.

When Christina caught Anita's surprised look, she smiled weakly, then nodded to the butler who had been standing there unmoving. "Thank you, Georgie. We are fine here."

Once Georgie stepped out of the room, Anita gasped and fell beside Christina on the chaise. "What has happened? Are you all right?"

Christina chuckled softly to herself, yet no humor was there. No teasing gleam in her eye. "That is quite a long story to tell, and something that I really don't have the energy to discuss. But I am as well as I could be."

Pulling back a strand of fallen hair, Christina smiled sadly. "I must look terrible, though. I'm sorry for that."

Shaking her head, Anita scowled. "Not at all, there's nothing to be sorry about. You had gotten sick while on your travels?"

Looking away, Christina slowly nodded. She reached for the quilted blanket and lifted it higher around her arms. Despite her worry, Anita could not help but smile gently. Christina looked like her younger self once again, curled up sick. But what had happened while Christina was away? If she had fallen ill, how well did she recover? Anita nibbled on her lip, trying not to think of Christina's mother's ill fate and looked down. Noticing the blanket, however, Anita's eyes widened. Touching it softly, she traced the gold and blue interlocking rings.

"Your mother's wedding quilt."

Smiling sadly, Christina nodded. Tracing the same

rings, her other hand balled into a fist. Her voice was quiet when she spoke. "Do you remember when she would tuck us in with this blanket?'

Anita smiled, remembering clearly. "She would tell us fairytales and use the rings as a path into each world."

Nodding, Christina's eyes looked far away. "And she would tell us about the good and evils in these worlds. How princesses were always captured by the monsters. But at the end of them all, they would be saved by their loving princes." Christina shook her head softly. "I think my mother forgot that monsters could disguise themselves as princes as well."

Her brow furrowing, Anita looked up at her friend. She hesitated before asking, "Did something happen between you and Richard?"

Christina swallowed hard, not yet answering. But Anita saw it in her friend's eyes. They grew wet, but no tears fell. Clearing her throat, Christina covered her face with a humorless chuckle. "Let's not get into that bag of bones."

Sniffing back, Christina pulled away her hand and conjured up a teasing look in her eyes. As though nothing had occurred, Christina smiled. But Anita only frowned more. Once Christina realized her friend was not easing up, she sighed. "Just let it go, Annie."

Looking ever more worried, Anita leaned in, but was stopped by the sincerity in her friend's gaze. "I promise, I will tell you. Just, not today."

Anita forced herself to nod. Despite how she felt, she knew that whatever had happened must have been painful between her and Richard. She could tell by the frailty of her friend's demeanor. Instead of pressing the matter, she simply took Christina's hand and squeezed it gently with a small smile. Sniffing back and clearing her throat, Christina gave her a lukewarm smile before calling out to Georgie for some tea and cookies.

"Oh, don't fret over me, I am fine," Anita quickly said after Christina's request.

"Nonsense. This will be the first in a long time since you have visited my home, Annie. Allow me to be a proper hostess." Christina sarcastically chuckled, bringing a small form of light back into her eyes.

Laughing quietly with her, Anita nodded. Then she settled onto the chaise alongside her friend. She could not imagine this being the right time to bring up her troubles with Bram and Mr. Cox. Not wanting to burden that load onto Christina. They must have sat there long enough in silence before Georgie brought in a wheel cart of tea and warm cardamom cookies.

Anita watched him curiously as he gently poured a cup of tea and gave it first to his mistress and then to her. His hands were big and roughened that he looked out of place in the feminine parlor. But his manner was patient, focused, and tender. He sat napkins out from his pocket, then turned and left. She suddenly heard Christina laugh, which brought her attention back to her.

"I know what you're thinking. Georgie is quite a sight when he is doing dainty tasks. But he means well and can make you a marvelous bloody Mary." She laughed.

Anita chuckled under her breath. "I believe that. What had happened to Rogers?" Anita referred to the late Silvertons' butler.

Christina shrugged and sighed. "I sent him to serve my father in the country. I had no need for a spy to report back every scandal I got myself into."

Anita nodded, understanding, considering how she remembered Rogers's biased tendencies even as a child. She sipped at her tea, warmed by its soothing flavor. Anita nearly finished her cup without saying another word. For some reason feeling awkward and uncertain of what to say; that is, until she felt Christina nudge her with her knee.

"So, what has been going on with you while I was away?" she asked teasingly, obviously not knowing how she and Bram had to end their affair, or the threatening theories from Miss Lucinda Kenyon. Anita glanced down into her cup and sighed.

"Come now, Annie. I know there is something you came here to talk to me about. I can see it clearly written on your face."

Anita shook her head softly. "I couldn't, Christina. You

199

should rest rather than hear my woes."

Christina expelled a breath and waved her statement away. "Oh, stop that, besides, it will be good for me to get my mind off things. Go on, tell me Annie."

Despite her worry, Anita knew that she needed to tell someone, and went on ahead to tell Christina everything that had occurred. Even the troubles she was currently facing with Mr. Cox.

Christina was frowning by the time she was done with her telling. Shaking her head, she placed down her cup of tea and sat up. "This is absurd. Lucinda Kenyon is as dense as a doornail. She was merely trying to provoke a response from you."

Anita shrugged. "Well it worked. I cannot risk any more unfavorable light to fall upon Bram. Nor I. I must consider Belle's reputation as well. It would break my heart to do that to her."

Christina shook her head once more, contemplating the situation. But just as sudden, a realization softened her expression. She smirked as she leaned back against the soft cushioned chaise. "Well, now I see what Bram is planning. Thank goodness too, I thought he had gone mad. But then again, I did think you had something to do with it."

Anita frowned, uncertain of what Christina meant. Her look gave Christina pause. "You don't know, do you?"

"What do you mean?" Anita was bemused.

With a grin, Christina reached to the table stand beside her. She pushed aside a few notes and letters and grasped the eggshell color card. It had blue pressed lettering and at the bottom Anita was astonished to make out Bram's initials. Her breath caught when Christina placed it onto her open hands. She felt faint when she read what the invitation stated.

"Bram is hosting a ball?" Anita was barely able to say out loud.

Christina nodded, assured of what that meant. "It would seem that Bram is stepping up his plans in courting you properly."

"Yes, but with a ball?" Anita asked in disbelief. "I can

hardly believe this. Bram hates the Ton, yet he's inviting them into his opera house?"

Anita stood, suddenly feeling like she needed to pace. She knew she should be overjoyed, but something within her felt concerned. How far was Bram willing to go in changing himself for her? Even if that were the case, would Anita be alright with his change? She did not want him to regret his choices. Because if he did, then there was the chance that he could regret being with her as well. Anita found herself wringing her hands together.

"Annie be calm. I can hear your thoughts from here." Christina shifted in her seat, but Anita had her back to her.

"Christina, this isn't like him. And that worries me because, what if he regrets getting involved with the Ton again." She sighed. "I, more than anyone, know how they treated him. Why would he do this for me?"

"Because he loves you..."

Taken aback, Anita stopped pacing. She glanced over to Christina and found her grinning at her. The truth suddenly warmed her, because despite her worry, Anita knew deep in her heart that Christina was right. Bram loved her, and he wanted to be with her. He must have realized that the only way for them to be together was to do things right. He knew about her past, and he wanted to keep that from happening to her again. Anita inhaled a soothing breath and smiled.

"Now, all you need to do is go to his ball, and simply let everything fall into place. Bram is a gentleman; he should know how to court," Christina said with a laugh.

Anita could not help but giggle with her. But she suddenly remembered her other obstacle. "But what about Mr. Cox?"

"Pish, once Bram charms your mother, there will be no more mention of this loathsome Cox."

Anita breathed in a sigh of relief at Christina's words, for she knew they were true. Bram was capable of such a task. Eloise was not the sort to judge Bram for rumors of his repute. Her mother would first see for herself what sort of man he was. Anita knew without a doubt that her mother would love him.

Convinced, Anita made her way to sit back beside Christina. She smiled wide, thankful to her friend. Just as she was about to lean in to hug her, Anita stopped short. Christina's mother's wedding quilt was lowered when she had shifted in her seat. At her stunned expression, Christina covered herself.

"Christina...?" Anita asked quietly. "Is that...?"

Nibbling her lip, her friend sighed and nodded. "Yes, Annie."

"You are with child," she stated breathlessly.

Christina rested her arms over her belly silently. Despite the concern tone in her friend's voice, Christina raised her head up unabashed. Though she did not think that Anita would judge her like others would, Christina still needed to show how unashamed she was. No matter what had happened between her and Richard, this babe was not a mistake.

"Your mother would have been so happy," was all that Anita said as she leaned forward and placed her hand over hers.

Astonished, Christina had nearly choked on a sob, but smiled, nonetheless. Swallowing the lump in her throat, she grasped Anita in a tight hug, and quietly thanked her.

"Now go, Annie. And be sure to have as much fun for the both of us." Pulling back, Christina added with a grin, "And don't let that pompous ass Cox get in the way." The two shared a laugh, like when they were young girls once again.

∞∞∞

Bram looked down below at all the hustle and bustle of his opera house. Plans were underway for the night of his first masquerade ball. Shaking his head, Bram was beside himself, almost unable to fathom the reality of hosting a party for the Ton. Grinning, this would be a night they will not soon forget.

Nor he, for finally he would get to see Anita.

He gripped the balcony rail, his excitement so intense that he nearly ground himself against the polished wood. His lust was unbound, he thought, perturbed. Remembering the restless nights of sweet tormented dreams, he found himself more than once thrusting against the mattress, pleasure unsated. Even stroking his sleepless member gave it no ease. Bram desired Anita more than she knew.

Bram needed Anita's laugh, her smile, her warm brilliant eyes gazing into his soul. The love he knew she had for him long before he even realized it. That love that filled the dark hole inside him. He was impatient to see her. It had been too long, yet the moment he saw her family's invitation among all the rest, his whole body warmed.

His feelings were unwaived, which still surprised him. But rather focusing on his personal self-change, he pressed forward, making sure that every detail of the upcoming ball was in place. Bram observed the rows of seating being dislodged and carried to storage. The polished wood floors were swept and mopped. Lady-hands hanging up wreaths of mantled masks and ribbons above the archways. The stage was decorated with hanging stars and Moroccan lanterns. Bram grinned; if any persons of the Ton had not accepted his heritage before, they sure as hell would have to deal with it now. Bram instructed his decorators to make certain that there were aspects of his Moroccan culture throughout the ball. He did not care either way if he was accepted, but he did want to impress his successes.

When he began to imagine the outcome of the ball, Bram heard footsteps approach him from behind. His secretary, Jane, handed him a note sealed with Richard's crest. Nodding to her, he ripped open the letter. It was short and blunt. Richard had wanted Bram at his estate at the soonest convenience. Bram thought it odd, normally Richard always set up their meetings at Springfield, but pushed the matter aside.

"Send word to prepare my carriage," he instructed Jane as he folded the note and placed it into his coat pocket. Whatever the reason for Richard's invite, he knew that it was always for a good cause. Looking over the balcony railing one last time, he just hoped that it did not get in the way of this week's event.

Bram arrived at Richard's estate shortly after. It helped that his friend lived close and within the city. Fitzgerald, Richard's butler opened the door and led him straight to his master's office. A room on the far east side of his friend's expansive home. The home was a traditional Georgian red brick three story building, long white frame windows, and wide-open rooms with pale painted walls. Bram thought of no comment towards the stripped walls and bare wood floors. He knew that the home once belonged to Richard's late father. Perhaps it had at one time been decorated with expensive furnishings, but Richard sought to be rid of anything from the past.

It was not until Bram stepped into Richard's office when a spark of personality adorned the space. The room was wooden, with a cool marble desk. Shelves of ledgers, contracts, and biography books covered each wall. Richard sat at his desk, a cigar in one hand, and a pen in the other. He was in the middle of writing when Fitzgerald opened the wide brown double doors. With the wave of his hand and without looking away from his work, they were invited inside.

"Bram, good of you to come as soon as possible," Richard proclaimed as he sat back and took a long puff of his cigar.

Bram smirked, a perplexed look upon his brow. "Of course, when is it often that you summon me to your home?"

Richard agreed with his statement. Standing, he nodded at Fitzgerald with a silent command, then stepped over to his collection of decanters. "I think it would do you good to have a glass before we proceed any further."

Bram suddenly felt unease. When Richard was to pour a glass of Bram's favorite cognac, he refused it. "I think I would rather prefer a clear head. What is this about?"

For a moment, Bram saw the surprise look cross Richard's expression before it turned to one of genuine respect. "Very well. My men found the ballerina that has been harassing you."

Bram was amazed. Richard had found her a lot sooner than he expected. "Where was she?"

"In Marie Howe's company for sheltered women."

"By the east district?"

Richard nodded, then walked to the door when a knock sounded. Bram was beside himself. The ballerina had been a lot closer than he suspected. The east district was not too far away from his opera house. Knowing how near she truly was roughly giving Bram an unsettling feeling. Bram heard Richard silently exchange a few words with Fitzgerald before closing the door.

"Look Bram, there's more. But I need you to be calm and focused before we move forward."

Bram scowled, "What is it?"

"She is here." Richard said quietly and bluntly.

Bram stood with a jolt, nearly knocking over the chair. "What?!"

Richard rushed over to him. "Quiet your voice. We mustn't alarm her."

Bram scoffed, "Alarm her? You must be joking, Richard. I hope you are. The woman is a fiend. She ought to be reported."

"That may be so, but we still need her," Richard announced sternly.

"What are you saying?"

With a sigh, Richard tasted his cigar. "We've had her since last night. She stated that she would only admit of her doings in your company. Bram, by the sound of it, I believe she is withholding far more than she is letting on. I need you to be calm enough to charm her into telling you everything she knows."

With a sigh, Bram leered at the decanters of alcohol. "Mayhap I should have had that glass," Bram said, then shook his head and tightened his grip.

Richard smirked, "I told you. Just remember, this will either go smoothly or straight to hell. But if it does run south, then at least we have leverage." Richard slipped Bram a folded telegram. Bram noted the message was from Paris. His eyes widened as he read the note before glancing back to

Richard. "Understood?"

Bram released a pent-up breath and nodded. He closed his eyes and imagined Anita there with him. Her presence gave him strength. The reality of the matter was hitting him like a ton of bricks. He was doing all of this for her. If not for Anita, Bram would have allowed this ballerina to ruin his name. It would have meant nothing to him.

"Bram? Are you ready?" Richard spoke over Bram's thoughts. With a nod, he watched his friend open the door.

She came through the door and for a moment Bram did not recognize her. The ballerina's hair had turned a lighter color, her skin was sun-kissed, and though that should have left her with a natural glow she still had bags under her eyes. Her clothes were stylish, yet Bram could not miss how worn the hemline and neckline were. She was slimmer than what he remembered, which proved that she was not as pregnant as she claimed in her farce letters. That still reassured Bram, nonetheless.

She did not come in quietly, rather instead she came in with a curse to Richard's men. But once she caught sight of Bram her face lit up, and a knowing grin replaced her sneer. She tugged her arm away from Fitzgerald and attempted to right her disheveled hair. Bram suddenly recalled all too well that crooked smile of hers, and he thought to himself: how in the world did he ever think to bed her? He was weary of the man he once was.

"Oh, my Lord. How good to see you again."

"How not good to see you."

The ballerina's face fell at Bram's comment, but that did not stop that wicked grin from returning. She helped herself to a seat nearby and crossed her legs as any theatrical person would. "I assume that you are here to discuss my letters. How do you suppose I should give you what you want to hear if you treat me with such disdain?"

"Assuming you know anything." Bram knew what the ballerina was getting at. He had dealt with plenty of people such as her who believe themselves smarter than everyone else. The best route to approach this was to make her think she had all the cards in her hand, and to call her bluff.

It seemed to work. The ballerina's lips pursed as her back tensed. Looking to Richard, she demanded a glass of gin before she was to ever divulge her secrets. Bram grinned, "I assume it's safe to say that you aren't pregnant?"

The ballerina gave him a dumbfounded glare. When Richard purposefully faltered in giving the ballerina her drink, she scoffed. "Of course, I am not pregnant!"

"Just checking." Richard said with a wide knowing smile.

The ballerina glared at them both before throwing back the whole glass. At least that was impressive, Bram thought. Leaning forward in his chair Bram pinned her with a stern frown. "Now, tell me what the meaning of those letters are. Why are you blackmailing me?"

The ballerina had a coyish expression with a mocking glint in her eye. "Do you even remember my name, Lord Kenwood?"

The question threw Bram, the answer now thwarting him. It must have been clear on his face; he heard her chuckle to herself before shaking her head. She leaned back in her chair and rested her chin on her knuckles. Of course, Bram did have her records from the last production, which had helped Richard locate her, he just could not recall her name at that moment. Blast her for this small win.

"You are far more in for a pound than I believed you would ever be. I mean, I had faith that you were smarter than you were handsome, but perhaps I was wrong. Clearly, you are oblivious to the schemes that others have against you." She nonchalantly peered at her nails, picking at an unforeseen spec before fixing him with a glare. "It is Beatrice, by the way. Beatrice Chevrolet."

Before Bram could detest her mockery, he caught Richard's frown. They both simultaneously realized her words. There were others that were calculating his downfall. If so, then who? Richard gestured to Beatrice from behind her, indicating to Bram on how to proceed with this. Bram inwardly grimaced. But he knew that Beatrice was the sort of woman that desired to be needed, to be charmed. Especially by men like him.

Squaring his shoulders, Bram took in a deep long breath. Trying to avoid biting his inner lip, he attempted his most charming grin. He raised his brows as though impressed. "I suppose you got me on that one. Forgive me for seeing you as nothing more than just some conniving twit."

Beatrice dropped her hand and scowled at Bram, while Richard cast him the same confused frown. Bram knew that his friend wanted him to woo her for information, but that was not in Bram's nature. "Listen, enough of these games. I know you were brought and kept here against your will. Perhaps it is the circumstances that is making it difficult for you to trust us." Beatriz pouted slightly as she glared over her shoulder at Richard, who stared back at her blankly.

"Come now Beatrice, though short as it was, we had a good time together. Who knows, it may have led somewhere. But we know the truth now. It was your choice to be a part of the blackmail. And it was because of this deception that ruined what we could've had."

Bram decided to speak the truth rather than seduce her. He was not lying when he said there had been a possibility that their encounter could have developed into something more. Not that he had intended it at that time, but fateful things happened every day. Look at him and Anita now. His words had the effect he hoped for, however. He watched her nibble on her lip, her expression casting a regretful sigh.

"Bram...uh," she caught herself. Indecision tore at her face. But soon it was replaced with a knowing hatred. "You are ridiculous! You think you can sap me up like you do with all the other women you have laid with? Well, my Lord, I am not a trollop fool. Clearly so, since you have no clue on what is coming to you." She grinned in satisfaction.

Shaking his head, Bram stood from his chair, and went to fill a glass. He returned with one for her as well. She eyed him over the rim, contemplating his motives. They sat in silence, until Bram indicated to Richard to leave the room. After some hesitation, his friend finally did so.

"I'm not trying to make this difficult for you, Beatrice. I'm actually trying to help you out of this situation," Bram said after taking a drink from his glass. "You may not believe it, but I want to see you walk away from this safely."

She scoffed, "Is that some kind of threat, my Lord? Because if you have not noticed, I am the one holding the cards, not you."

Bram leaned back, stirring the glass over his knee. "You would like to think so, wouldn't you?"

"What is that supposed to mean?" She glared at him.

Ignoring her evil eye, Bram drank back the remainder of his drink before answering with a question of his own. "Last chance, Beatrice. Who employed you into this scheme?"

With a click of her tongue, she kept silent. However, her body had grown tense. She swung her leg over her knee as she crossed her arms. Bram observed her attempts to hide the fidgeting. With one last sigh, Bram pulled out the telegram Richard had given him. She regarded it apprehensively, but still showed no indication to comply.

Unfolding the envelope, Bram proceeded to read the note. "*Adrianna Claudette Chevrolet. Age: Twelve. Location: Paris, St. Vincent-de-Paul Hospice.*"

Beatrice sat straighter, her eyes widening, her fingers clutching her inner elbows. When Bram glanced up from the note, he found her white in the cheeks, the blood draining. In a calm quiet whisper, Bram frowned, "She is your daughter, isn't she?"

The once collected woman in front of him now swallowed hard, gritting her teeth. She looked away from him without a word. Folding the note, Bram placed it back in his coat pocket. Standing, he collected his glass and indicated hers. Without hesitation, she gulped the remainder of her drink and gave him the cup. Bram returned with a fresh libation for her.

She stared down at the clear liquid for some time, picking at its glass ridge. Bram waited patiently, hating yet knowing this was the only route he had to take. The ticking mantle clock in the room began to blend into the silence, Bram could make out muffled voices down the hall. No doubt Richard instructed his men to a task. It was clear that Beatrice heard them too. Her lips were tight when she finally broke the stillness.

"Do you plan on harming my daughter?" she asked quietly. Bram detected the slight quiver in her tone.

After a moment, he sighed and shook his head. "You needed the money for her, didn't you?"

She glowered at him, her opinion of him clear on her face. "Well it's not like I am some noble Lady who can care for my bastard child in the country!"

Bram frowned and leaned forward. "I pay you no judgement. But even you should know that this isn't the way of caring for her."

Beatrice stood erect, her anger seething through her skin. "And how would you know what would be best to take care of a daughter? A child to a worthless whore? That anyone wouldn't give a bleeding fuck about? Who would have every door refuse her entrance and leave her to die on the streets?'"

Bram winced at the words he had once said to her. He felt sudden shame then, and it took him a moment to collect himself. He thought of the way he once was. To the man before he met Anita. Bram grimaced. Imagining what Anita would think of him if she knew how he had treated Beatrice.

"Beatrice..." Another pause. "I am sorry for how I had treated you before. I was not in the right state of mind to react gentlemanly. You should not have been placed in such a position in the first place. I'm sure you did not deserve it."

Bram meant his words, realizing how much he had changed just then. He sighed as he placed his glass on the side table next to his chair and moved to look out the window. Another moment of silence deepened the void between them. Until, "She promised to pay me if I seduced you."

"At first, it was only to keep you occupied until she was ready to get close to you. She wanted me to spy on your whereabouts and activities, your likes and dislikes. She wanted to learn to become the woman you would prize and desire. But that did not happen. She warned me that if I lost sight of you before she was ready, then she would refuse to pay me," Beatrice sighed harshly.

"I grew desperate and began to send those letters to

you. But she found out either way once she caught wind that you were seeing another. A Lady of the Ton."

"How did she know it was a Lady?" Bram asked from the window.

"She said that she knew her. Had seen her at other gatherings." Beatrice took a sip from her glass. "She concocted the plan for me to send you that last letter. Only then, would she pay me if you left that woman."

"Anything else?" Bram asked quietly, the anger within him slowly building to a roar. He tried not to direct it at Beatrice.

She sniffed before answering, "She plans to make her move during your masquerade ball. She will try to gain your attentions. She also spoke how if you were to deny her, then most likely, she will cause a scene. If she were to also see you seeking out the Lady, then she plots to exploit the two of you in front of all."

Bram ground his teeth, trying hard not to curse out. The plot was so clear, and yet, foolish. This was nothing more than the schemes of a lunatic child. It shocked him the lengths this girl was willing to go for her desired illusions of him. Inwardly sighing, Bram knew he had to prepare for the ball. Who knew getting back into the trenches of the Ton would bring such danger? Oh wait, he did, Bram thought as he stifled a sarcastic laugh.

Stepping away from the window, Bram reached into his coat pocket to pull out his papers. "How much did she promise you?"

Beatrice instantly straightened. Pouring back the remainder of gin, she swiped her lips with her hand. "Sixty pounds."

Her lisp told Bram that she was lying, but either way, he pulled out a hundred. Beatrice's eyes nearly doubled in size and reached for the amount with shaky hands. But before letting go, Bram bent down.

"Thank you, Beatrice. I truly hope this helps you with your daughter. But, before giving this to you, I need you to tell me the name of this Lady culprit first."

Chapter 15

Despite the unusually warm November day, Anita found herself wringing her hands. She followed closely behind her parents and sister, who chattered happily about the wonderfully busy season they had. Anita could not help rubbing her lips together, before inwardly sighing. It had been eventful, in more ways than Anita could have ever imagined. Thinking back to when they first arrived, she would have never imagined the choices she has made. The person she became. Did she even recognize herself anymore? Yes, yes, she did. This was the woman she always had within her. But was too afraid to release. To set free.

A boast of laughter caught her attention, as Belle and their mother clasped hands and practically frolicked in the grass. Their father merely chuckled, as he remained on the path, cane in hand. Anita once thought that she was much like her family, but how different she truly was. She was a free spirit. She suddenly realized that she hated being a trapped bird. She did not wish to be caged in one place. She wanted to explore. She wanted to travel. She wanted to just be herself. Away from prying eyes, and manipulative souls. Anita wanted to be her own person.

Being with Bram showed her what she was capable of. How limitless her desire was. She was strong, brave, and knew how to love. She wanted to embrace it fully and share that same passion with Bram. She smiled to herself; they were only days away before his ball. To which, to her surprise, her mother had gleefully accepted the invitation. Eloise spoke highly of what she remembered of the Lord Kenwood at the Hedgerow ball, saying how impressed she was on how he held himself among the gossipers. Reminiscent of Anita, she said heartedly. That made Anita blush, warmed by her mother's words. If she accepted what happened to Anita in America, would that mean she would welcome Bram when he decided to court Anita?

The thought made her pause and found herself gazing at a swaying willow tree. Would her parents receive their wedding with open arms? The idea of marrying Bram brought her arms around her, her heart skipping a beat. Would the dream truly become a reality? Would the fairy dust be cleared from their eyes, and love found?

"Annie! Come quick!" Belle shouted from down the path.

Quickening her steps, Anita was astonished to find her family surrounding a man she recognized. It was Mark! Who was beaming next to an equally blushed Belle.

"Mother, Father, I would like to introduce Mark Ford." Belle was beside him, embracing his arm.

Their mother smiled pleasantly, while their father cast him a familiar expression. "Are you the Earl of Cadogan's boy? Viscount of Trent?"

Anita watched the noticeable gulp Mark tried to hide behind a grin. "Yes, my Lord. That is my father."

Their father smiled, and slapped Mark on the back. "My God, my boy. I have not seen you since you were half my size. What a surprise indeed."

Their mother nodded approvingly and offered her hand to Mark. Anita watched the relieved smile pass between Belle and Mark, and for a moment she felt weary. She could not help but want that same easy acceptance, wished for it when the time came. If ever…

Her family continued their stroll through the park, Eloise happily chatting about the prospects of the future, and how wonderful coincidences were. When they rounded about a pond, Anita noticed Mark whisper something to

Belle. Her sister walked ahead between their parents to speak with them. Or distract them more like, for Mark began to hang back towards her.

"Good morning, Anita," he said warmly.

Anita smiled, and nodded. "Yes, a particularly good morning Mark. I'm glad to see you here with Belle." Knowing well how much Belle missed him. Anita and her sister spoke more after that day Belle had come to her in tears. Anita now knew just how close Mark and Belle were.

Mark blushed and nodded. "Yes, indeed. This day was long awaited by the both of us." He paused and cleared his throat. "Forgive me. It must feel the same for you and Bram."

At the mention of Bram, Anita nearly skipped a step, but maintained herself. She nodded quietly.

"I have something for you." He rummaged through his inner coat pocket, finally pulling out a folded note. Looking ahead to make certain her parents were not noticing, Anita accepted it. "Bram sends his love but wishes for you to read the note with an open heart."

That was odd, Anita thought, just before Mark walked ahead. Unfolding the note, Anita stopped short. Crumbling the note close to her, she glanced to see where her family was. They were rounding the pond still, so she sat down at one of the closest benches. Anita reread the note.

Anita, my love

Miss Lucinda Kenyon has been confirmed as the culprit. She desires to expose you and our relationship to the world. The only way to appease her is for me to yield to her wishes. She means to seduce me during my Masquerade ball. If she were to see me seek you out, she will create a scandal. I plan on going along with her farce, but I will stop it right then and there. However, it pains me to write this, you must not look for me that night. Nor I for you. This is not what I wanted for us, but it must be so. I will still make this count, my sweet. Whatever I must do to be worthy of your hand.

Yours faithfully,
B.W.

Holding back tears, Anita ripped the note furiously. Once she realized what she had done, her hands fell. Taking in ragged breaths, she wanted to scream. She wanted to run and confront Miss Lucinda Kenyon and shout out all her hatred for the woman. But above all, Anita wanted to be in Bram's arms. She knew too well that he must be in as much turmoil.

Suddenly, reality was becoming all too clear, the dream fading. Was this to be their fate? To be always looking over their shoulders? Always threatened? Bram promised he would take care of it. But how? When it seemed like all was against them? Looking up at Belle and Mark, talking happily to her parents, Anita felt a stabbing pain in her heart. Where would they be when the dust settles about them; would they be brave enough?

When they returned from Hyde Park, Eloise had insisted that Mark join them for tea. She stated that it was the perfect time to rest and learn a little more about Mark, and his family. Anita observed Mark's noticeable stiffness, as did Belle, who immediately spoke up against it.

"Oh mama, it is late in the day. I'm certain Lord Trent needs to return to his affairs." Belle was clearly trying to hide her disappointment with a warm awkward smile.

Mark patted her arm and shook his head. "It would be my honor to join you all for tea, thank you my Lady Hemmingway."

Belle looked astonished but then hid her blush under her bonnet. Eloise clapped her hands splendidly and wrapped her arm around her husband's as they continued to walk down the road to their home. By the time they got there, they all found Mr. Cox waiting at the threshold. Her parents politely welcomed him; at the same moment Belle glanced back at Anita, who was cringing and trying hard not to grind her teeth. The man was relentless, and it infuriated her how her parents did not see the disinterest she had for the man.

"I hope you would forgive me. I found it to be a lovely afternoon and thought it would be a fine day to call on Anita,"

Mr. Cox expressed, his crooked grin ever more infuriating for Anita to see. This certainly was not the day she wished to see him.

"Well, I don't see why not. We have invited the Viscount of Trent for tea as well. Mark Ford, this is Mr. Richard Henry Cox, his family owns and operates Cox & Kings." Eloise introduced him in a hearty manner.

Mr. Cox and Mark shook hands and nodded to one another. They entered their home and were soon in the drawing room. The ladies sat comfortably together on the chaise, as the men stood by them. Once tea was served, Eloise began a comfortable conversation. Or at least a convenient chat for her mother, Anita thought.

"Mr. Cox, will we be seeing you at Lord Kenwood's masquerade ball?"

Anita witnessed Mr. Cox try to scowl unnoticeably, but she and her mother still caught it. Before answering, he suppressed it with an awkward grin. "Forgive me, my Lady, but I found that question to be quite surprising. To know that such a well-mannered family such as yourselves would be attending this Lord Kenwood's ball is alarming to me."

"And why is that?" Anita watched as her mother casually raised her chin gracefully, knowing full well what that expression meant. Anita had seen it many times before, back at home whenever a lady patron was discussing her daughter's scandal.

Mr. Cox coughed into his balled-up fist. "Again, forgive me, my Lady. I meant no disrespect, I merely am stating that considering Lord Kenwood's reputation, one would think that appearing at such an event would cause a scandal."

Eloise tilted her head, as though considering her thoughts before answering. "Mr. Cox, though I do respect your concern, I find it out of place. This is a new time, a new era, and quite frankly, one should see past scandals as dust to the wind. Lord Kenwood is clearly trying to reestablish himself among the community, and I doubt my family will be the only ones there. But, of course, if you feel such a way about reputation, then perhaps, to save yours, you shouldn't go to this highly anticipated event."

Anita nearly hugged her mother tightly, so proud of her approach and defending Bram, just as she once did for her own daughter. She caught Mark's admiring expression, as he then held Belle's hopeful eyes. Her father simply stood staring out the window, a cup of coffee in hand, and a smile on his lips.

Mr. Cox sputtered, his face flushed, before adjusting his collar. "Quite right, my Lady. It would seem I am being untoward. Perhaps, it is simply my protective nature over your daughter. I'm sure you have already assumed that I am seeking for her hand, and thus, wouldn't want any undesirable attention brought her way."

Anita rolled her eyes, before realizing Mr. Cox's announcement. She froze in her seat, her gaze flashing over to her mother and father, silently pleading for the same stunned reaction. Unable to see his expression, she was only able to notice her father's back stiffening. Belle's mouth dropped, as Mark cast Anita a sorry look. Eloise simply batted her eyes at Mr. Cox before smiling slowly.

"Well, that is certainly good to know Mr. Cox. And why yes, Lord Hemmingway and I did think that is where your plans were heading. Though, I would have preferred you would have kept that to yourself until the time came when you would properly ask my Lord Hemmingway for his blessing. I suppose it is well that Anita knows of this now."

Eloise glanced at her daughter, clearly seeing the dread on Anita's expression, and for a moment felt pity. Her husband was silent, and Eloise knew that meant he wanted no part in this. Nodding to herself, she fixed Mr. Cox with a cool expression.

"Well, Mr. Cox, I suggest if this is truly the route you wish to take, then I advise that you accompany us to Lord Kenwood's ball, and prove that you can take care of my daughter's reputation. If you find yourself so wholeheartedly unable to attend, then perhaps you aren't fit for this family, because let me assure you, sir, we are a clan that do not take kindly to gossip and fear of scandal. Is that fair for you?"

Anita observed the discomfort Mr. Cox was in, but soon he nodded. He approached Anita, grasping her hand, he bent over it. "I will do what I must to show my affection for your daughter."

He said in such a tone, that Anita felt chills run down her neck, then he kissed her fingers. She immediately had the suspicion that he was not going to take this lightly, and she feared what was to come. Anita was going to need to be wary at Bram's ball. Mr. Cox dropped her hand and bowed to her family, announcing that it was past time to take his leave. Her mother and father nodded their goodbyes, while Belle and Mark stood and bowed.

Soon after, Mark spoke about taking his leave as well, and expressed how he adored their company. Eloise had her cheery disposition back and made Mark promise to call again soon. Then she was happy to hear that Mark was attending Lord Kenwood's ball as well.

"We will certainly be looking for you then, Lord Trent. So good of you to call," Eloise said, as her husband came forward to shake Mark's hand.

Mark politely bowed to Anita, before giving her a knowing nod. An expression that soothed her, leaving her to think that Mark was off to speak with Bram, and informing him of what had occurred here. Unfortunately, Anita sighed, not that that would help her. She and Bram were not to see each other at his ball... and thus she was left alone with the Mr. Cox for the duration of the party.

Anita was trapped in this world that was no longer a dream. What was she to do?

As Bram was counting down the days to his ball, he had an unsettled feeling in his gut. Now that the ballerina was no longer a threat, he still had to plan what to do about Miss Kenyon. She was the bigger threat to all his plans, but what could be done? Was Bram simply going to go along with her twisted plot, or did he have to resort to measures that Bram had wished to bury a long time ago? He knew he could tarnish her reputation by simply making a scene against her, but that would only continue to keep Bram's name in the dark.

And unfortunately, Bram could not think of a well thought out plan because Philip had decided to call on him. Not that he could not see that Philip clearly needed him. Bram never seen the man look so disheveled and drunken before. His friend looked as though he had not shaven for days, and his clothes were unkempt. It took Bram a moment to understand the inebriated speech Philip was spewing.

"-and she thinks that I can just change?! She is asking for the impossible! I cannot change, I am who I am, and you would think that be enough, but NO! She wants more. MORE, Bram! Can you believe this?"

Bram was watching Philip's already near empty glass of liquor spilling to the floor as his friend was exaggerating his words with his arms. Bram stood, grasping Philip's glass, offering to refill it, but really, he was setting it far away from his friend. There was no need to replace his office's rugs, not again. With a sigh, he urged Philip to sit, and with an even louder groan, Philip fell into the chair.

"Now she refuses to see me. She says I am a pompous child, with no responsibility and care of my actions. But who is she to tell me this? ME, Bram? It is not like she isn't just as much of a child. In fact, that is what I believed made us so perfect for each other. We had an understanding. Why? Why does she want to change that now?"

Bram paused when he thought he heard Philip's voice catch. He sat down across from him and was surprised to find the pain in Philip's eyes. This was serious, and Bram was astonished. Philip was always so carefree, never had Bram see him in this state. Just when Bram was about to speak, his office door swung open, and Mark walked in.

Mark had a serious worried expression, and Bram held his breath. What happened at today's meeting? Was Mark able to give Anita his note? Before either of them could speak, Philip launched himself to Mark, their drunken friend dramatically slurring, "She left me, Mark! She left ME!" into his shoulder. Mark looked at Bram confused, before patting Philip's back.

The two men unlatched Philip off Mark and sat him back down. Bram decided it would be best to give his glass back to Philip. Telling Philip to breathe and sip on his drink for a moment, Bram stood by Mark who looked genuinely concerned over Philip.

"Jesus, what happened to him?" Mark asked.

Bram shrugged, and lightly spoke back, "I was trying to figure that out myself. He only just arrived twenty minutes before you did. And he showed up in this state. But what I could gather, Miriam left him for reasons unknown. It would seem she is unhappy with his ways."

"But that is Philip. She ought to have known the type of man he is." Mark frowned, shaking his head. "Alas, Philip finally had a woman leave him first."

Nodding, Bram observed Philip drink back the full glass. "He isn't taking it well."

With a sigh, Mark decidedly answered. "I will take him with me, he shouldn't be alone right now."

Bram agreed, they have only ever seen Philip act out when he didn't get his way, which was rare. But when it did occur, it was often usually a rampage across London that would cost him a fortune. There was no telling what would happen now, being that a situation like this never happened before. They could only imagine the worst. At least with Mark, he would be the sound of reason.

"Bram, I gave Anita your note, but there seems to be another dilemma." Mark spoke quietly.

Hearing Anita's name gave him pause. He fully faced his friend, his brows knitting in anticipation. Something did happen, but what? Had Anita waited too long? Was she no longer wishing for his courtship? So many cruel thoughts raced through his mind.

"She accepted your note, not that I would say she took whatever was written in it happily, however. Afterwards, the family and I returned to their home. But there was a man there calling on her." Mark hastily added, "But it was clear that she was not at all pleased that he was there. In fact, she looked rather upset and faint."

Mark described him, and Bram instantly recognized him. "Cox."

Mark stopped short. "Yes, that is the name. He seems rather aggressive in my opinion. Went so far as to announce his plans on asking for Anita's hand in front of all of them. Including myself, a stranger."

Bram tried to tame the anger that was threatening to immerge, wanting to punch this damned Cox in the face, he balled his fists instead. Through gritted teeth, he asked, "And how did they respond?"

With a sigh, Mark scratched at the back of his neck. "It was clear that Anita was shocked and angry. I believe her father was not pleased either, but her mother was cool about it. She proposed that he prove his nature by attending your Masquerade ball, to which, I should add, she defended as well as your reputation."

When Mark worded the conversation between Anita's mother and Mr. Cox, Bram was beside himself. So, the blasted man was trying to court Anita all this time. Did he have a good chance in receiving her parent's blessing? Considering how Mark described Anita's father, it sounded promising that the man did not like Cox. But what of her mother? Anita told him before how much her mother would do anything to get her daughter married, would this be one of those instances?

Damnation, Bram thought. What a time for this to occur, especially when Bram had Miss Kenyon to worry about. If not for her threats, Bram would be by Anita's side during the ball, and properly praise himself in her parent's eyes. Bram would have done his best to be the perfect partner for her. And considering how Lady Hemmingway had previously received him, Bram believed it would have been prosperous.

"Being with her during your ball will be the right time to make your affections known, wouldn't it? Lady Hemmingway seems to speak very highly of you. I wouldn't be surprised if she would choose you rather than that cad," Mark said encouragingly.

Bram sighed, and explained the situation to his

friend, the telling only making him angrier. "So, you see Mark, it appears that both Anita and I are cursed."

Feeling nearly defeated, Bram shook his head. "It seems as though everything is trying to keep us apart. My reputation, blackmail, threats, and now this. A man who is nearer to marrying Anita than I ever could."

Frowning in sympathy, Mark patted his friend's shoulder. "Bram-"

"Bloody hell! Then cause a damn scandal, Bram!"

Mark and Bram swung their gazes over to Philip who was bent over in the chair. Lazily raising his head, Philip sniffed and wiped his nose with the back of his sleeve.

"What are you getting at, you drunkard?" Mark scowled.

"Bram, it is simple. Do what you're bloody good at and create a theater performance!" Philip answered, beginning to hiccup.

"And how, pray tell, am I supposed to do that, Philip? Isn't that the last thing I should do?" Bram shook his head at his friend. Leave it to Philip to speak such nonsense.

"Think about it. How many well-bred families will be attending your mysterious ball? Bring them all down to our level, and they won't be any bluer than my childhood scrumpet of a nanny, Georgina." Philip paused with a knowing smile and a clear memory in mind.

"Give them a true Rakes of Springfield ball, the kind that they are all dying to be a part of." Philip began to chuckle and try to lick out any last drops in his glass.

Bram scowled, and said below his breath. "Utter nonsense..."

Mark held up his hand. "Well, maybe not quite, Bram. Think about it. Getting everyone inebriated would surely lower everyone's inhibitions. It may even drive some to committing scandals themselves. All talk would be cast away from you, and potentially aimed at others. That would put everyone on the same field."

Bram considered it, though crazy as it may seem. "But what of Miss Kenyon? She will still be trying to seduce me in front of everyone. Drunk or not, people will still notice and talk. They are waiting for that."

"Unless you plan a coup," Mark expressed thoughtfully.

Bram curiously regarded his ingenious friend, who so effortlessly began speaking of a plot that could save both his and Anita's future. The plan was clever and could easily work in Bram's favor. No matter what Miss Kenyon could say, Mark's tour de force would put her threats to rest. Bram grinned, placing his hand on Mark's shoulder, he nodded his thanks. He also walked over and refilled Philip's glass with a laugh and offered him a dinner plate.

"Very good and all, and you're welcome. But can we now talk about MY woes?!" Philip exclaimed.

Chapter 16

Anita was overwhelmed to be back at L'Opéra Magenta again. Her heart raced, the familiar smells enticed her, the laughter almost deafening as she roamed the crowded foyer. A smile came to her lips as she looked upon the many masked faces. Her mother was right, Bram's ball was a hit. There was little shyness, everyone's aura exuberated curiosity and excitement as the crowd moved from the main hall into the elegant auditorium.

There were auditory gasps as guests witnessed the extravagant adornments, flickering candles among the chandeliers that made them look like diamonds, an orchestra playing dances, and from what Anita could see, there were already patrons dancing together under the shimmering mosaic ceiling. Servers were dressed in their finest, as they waited trays of champagne, wines, sherry, and appetizers of the highest cheeses and meats.

Anita was amazed at how grand L'Opéra Magenta was when there were not any rows of chairs. It almost seemed like a different atmosphere, save for the glorious theater stage. As Anita made her way closer, she paused and touched her cheek. She knew Bram had a hand on the decor. Floating candles dazzled the scene, a midnight background with glittering stars, and a large bright blue moon painted, rising gloriously.

Too well did it remind her of their first encounter

together, of Bram's fierce kisses, his dark longing eyes. In that moment, Anita longed to see Bram, and that pierced her heart. This whole event was supposed to be for them, was to be the beginning of their future. Instead, Anita had to swallow back her bitter tears for she knew this was not the time. She had to remain strong and see the positive. She knew, deep down, that this WAS the beginning. This ball was going to change everything for Bram, and that he did this just for her. She had to admire that.

Staring up at the painted blue moon, she reminded herself of when she first witnessed Bram looking out at that exact real moon. He had known then what he wanted, and Anita must do the same. No matter the time, or the cost. She reached her hand behind her magenta adorned mask to wipe the small tear that threatened to fall. Looking down at her matching gown, she smiled. Anita decided to wear the same dress and mask she did when Bram had first seen her, hoping that perhaps he would recognize her easily.

Suddenly, Anita felt a presence to her right. She was struck to find a woman beside her. What awed her was that the lady was taller than Anita, and lithe. Her gown held her snug as it matched her bejeweled black mask. She looked as though she was in mourning but was still equally dashing. But what astonished Anita the most was the soft hue of her skin. It matched Bram's!

The Lady smiled at her, before turning fully to face Anita. She curtsied, and Anita returned the gesture. She then caught the woman's eyes behind the elaborate mask and was taken aback by the bright golden color. Before Anita could think of a proper thing to say, the woman surprised her by reaching out and caressed Anita's cheek. Anita caught her gasp, as her mask was lifted above Anita's face.

The woman nodded pleasantly, a genuine smile touching her dark red lips. She corrected Anita's mask over her face, before again touching her cheek.

"I knew my son would find an honest and loving woman someday. Quite frankly, my faith nearly faltered, but when I began to see a light return to his eyes, my heart was restored."

Anita nearly lost her breath. This was Bram's mother! Anita was beside herself as her mouth dropped, to which she received a light laugh from his mother. Anita curtsied once more.

"My Lady forgive me. This is truly a moment I wasn't expecting," Anita announced.

She laughed once more, her voice a low soft hum. "My dear, if I were in your position, I wouldn't have expected it either. Please, call me Magenta."

Anita smiled gently, warmed by Bram's mother's sincerity. Magenta, the same name as the Opera house, a theater that Bram so lovingly built, dedicated to his mother. Anita truly realized the importance of this ball. Everyone, even his mother, was here for Bram's restitution. That left her heart beating faster.

"My dear, don't worry too much about tonight. All will be well, heed my words. As I know my son, he prepares for anything. Much like his father, he is. Always sets out for what he wants. But feels his emotions deeply. That he got from me."

Lady Magenta nodded, her thoughts pausing, clearly reminiscing on her departed husband. Anita could see the love in the woman's eyes, and the longing that was still within them. She reached out to grasp Lady Magenta's hands within her own. She patted them appreciatively, before casting her gaze across the grand stage.

Lady Magenta laughed happily. "Did you know that Bram actually designed this stage from the original theater that I used to perform? Yes, truly. Bernard had taken him as a child, often while I was still an actress. Oh, how they loved watching the theater together. I often wonder if Bram remembers that. He must in some way, after all, look at the details of this very stage."

Anita spoke reassuringly, "I do believe so. No matter what Bram may say, I have witnessed the love he has for his past and heritage."

Lady Magenta nodded, comforted by Anita's words. "I'm sure you had already known, but nevertheless, my son may confess how he feels about his father, but truly, that isn't what pains him. Bram never really got to know him. We had hard times, that is true, but Bernard always wanted the best for us. He worked hard to keep us secure, but unfortunately, that left him often not at home." Lady Magenta sighed quietly. "I suppose Bram saw it differently. He believed his father only cared about being accepted back into the Ton, but that was not true. Bernard loved us, dearly."

Before Anita could reply how she believed Bram really felt towards his father, Lady Magenta turned to her once again. "Bram told me to come find you. He wanted me to tell you how beautiful you looked tonight. I suppose he wanted you to be reassured that he was here and has seen you. In truth, I insisted on meeting the woman that has changed my son for the better."

Anita blushed, looking away. "Oh, that is flattering my Lady Magenta, but I- "

"Nonsense. You have no idea how Bram was before he met you. I honestly thought he would truly be lost. Be the man that everyone believed him to be. But now, look. Witness everyone that is here. High born, low born, it doesn't matter. They are all equals here, and Bram brought them all together. Because of you. Yes, you dear."

Anita was speechless, not knowing what to say, and yet smiled, nonetheless. Looking on at the crowd of attendees, Anita was amazed at the sheer amount of people. Knowing then, that Bram was not truly the pariah he thought he was. Everyone wanted to witness the brilliance of his success. They longed to be a part of his world. Was it truly because of Anita?

"Now is not the time to be modest, darling. As my old mentor Jamal Berdouni used to say, 'we must humbly live our lives selfishly by every moment. Or else, we will be poor.'"

The two women laughed together, when Anita heard Belle calling from a few feet away. It was almost inaudible, if not for her dear sister bouncing and waving her hand about to get Anita's attention. When Belle finally made it past the group of people that was blocking straight passage to her sister, Anita was pleased to see Mark following closely behind her. Any man that may have been glancing at Belle, was not doing it for long once they caught the towering Mark beside her.

"Anita! There you are!" Belle said breathlessly. Once she realized Anita was not alone, Belle quickly pardoned herself and curtsied to Bram's mother. "Oh, forgive me."

Anita smiled at her sister, and quickly introduced her to Lady Magenta, who smiled brightly and complimented on Belle's beauty. When Lady Magenta addressed Mark, it was in comfortable familiarity. Of course, Bram's mother would know his close and trusted friends.

"Again, forgive me my Lady, but I am in need of my sister's aid," Belle tried to say politely, but Lady Magenta understood and wished them a pleasant evening. Before walking off, she spoke directly to Anita about calling on her for tea.

"I have the most splendid stories to share with you, my dear. Call on me soon please." Anita nodded, but once more Lady Magenta grasped her hand, and said below her breath, "And remember, don't let the envy of others taint what you and Bram have. You both bring new hope to this time, and that is the kind of love this world needs."

Anita was speechless but was touched by Bram's mother's wise words. They smiled at one another and said their farewells.

Belle quickly embraced her arm the moment they began walking away. "Belle, what is the matter?" Anita could see the alarm in her sister's eyes.

"Annie, its mother! I have never seen her in such a state! Quick, I do not know how much longer I can keep her at bay." Belle was already dragging her in the direction to where Anita guessed their mother was. Beginning to feel just as frightened, what could Belle mean? She looked to Mark for any more information, but he simply kept his focus on Belle, and their surroundings.

As they found themselves a floor above the grand auditorium, Belle and Anita entered one of the balcony boxes. Anita found her mother resting in a chair, her dress hiked up to her knees, as her father feverishly fanned her.

"Good heavens, fan faster Stephan. I am nearly breathless!" her mother exclaimed; her cheeks flushed.

"What is the matter? What happened?" Anita rushed to her mother's side. When Eloise realized her eldest was beside her, she grasped Anita close to her bosom.

"Oh, my dear sweet child. Have I ever told you just how fetching you are in that color?" Eloise squinted at her daughter's gown and began to chuckle. "Oh look, Stephan, the color is magenta! Aren't we at the L'Opéra Magenta too?!"

Her mother began to giggle, her color a now beet red. Her father sighed, and passed the fan over to Belle, who immediately took up the position. "I'm afraid your mother is flushed, children. I've only ever seen her in this state on our wedding night." Their father shook his head. "Odd, I hardly saw her sip from her glass."

"Will she be all right, father?" Belle asked with concern. Her mother grasped her wrist, motioning to fan faster.

Stephan nodded. "Yes, in time. Your mother just needs to rest for a while. I will go get her some liquids, then perhaps encourage her to dance."

"Oh yes, Stephan! Dance with me! It has been SO long since you have. I do so miss it," Eloise gasped, and hiccupped.

"Please, allow me to fetch Lady Hemmingway her water. I would like to be of some help," Mark announced. Stephan clamped him on the shoulder in thanks, as Belle looked at him with great affection in her eyes.

When Mark turned to go, he had a warm knowing smile. An uproar from below caught Anita's attention. Leaving Belle to fan her mother, Anita rose to look over the balcony. That was when Anita suddenly noticed the majority of the crowd's demeanor. She felt déjà vu overcome her, as she remembered her time at Philip's soiree. Witnessing the drunken state of people at that party, she watched it occur again. Only this time, it was with people of the Ton. Anita was beside herself.

"What is happening?" Anita whispered under her breath.

At that moment, the orchestra quieted. The crowd's attention was drawn to a tall dark figure walking to the front of the stage. He was robed in a black cape, a white mask covering only half of his face, and held a large lit candelabra. Almost instantly, Anita recognized the man to be Bram. Hushed whispers filled the room but were soon silenced when their caped host spoke.

"My, how unexpected." He said the words slowly, eyeing the crowd before him. He then gave an exaggerated actor's bow, the flames to his candelabra flickering wildly.

"I bid you all welcome, to L'Opéra Magenta's grand Masquerade! A first to what may be many for you. That is to say, of course, if you find this dark rabbit hole not too frightening." He paused as the crowd laughed amongst themselves.

"Enjoy the festivities before you and take full advantage of the servers you come across. For there will be many delights to savor. Dance to your hearts' content, but please, do not jump on stage believing yourself to be the next Shakespearian actor. Though I do know how tempting it may be but let us keep that to the professionals."

Another wave of laughter flowed through the assembly. Anita was in awe as she listened to Bram. He looked so confident and comfortable, unfazed at the full attention upon him. She smiled to herself, wondering if it may have learned it from watching his own mother on stage. Then her heart skipped a beat when Bram suddenly unveiled his mask, the attendees growing silent once more.

"Ladies and Gentlemen, on behalf of myself, the theater is yours." Bram bowed graciously, as the party applauded and cheered.

Once again, Anita warmed as she watched the positive confirmation wash over Bram. She never felt so proud of him then at that moment. She could not take her eyes off him, but when Bram glanced up in her direction, Anita lost her breath. He smiled brightly, kissed his hand, and waved it towards her. He made his leave off the stage until Anita no longer could see him. The orchestra began to play again, and the crowd dispersed. Laughter and chatter filling the air.

"My, he sure is a handsome fellow," Anita's mother startled her by stating. Anita did not notice her mother standing beside her, Belle still fanning her from behind.

Eloise was blushed as she giggled gently and nudged into Anita's shoulder. "Wouldn't he be a catch, Annie? Can you imagine? Why, he reminds me of a younger version of your father."

Her mother laughed again, as her father grinned and cleared his throat. "It's true! He has an air of mystery and confidence. Much like how your father was when I was first introduced to him. Oh, don't you remember, Stephan? The Hadley's Spring Ball?"

Her father nodded pleasantly, as he rubbed on Eloise's back. "That was a special event one could never forget."

Anita was warmed by the affection between her parents, and then realized her mother's earlier words. "Mama, you like Lord Kenwood?"

Eloise grasped the fan from Belle, before patting her youngest cheek. She began to fan herself again, "Oh yes, I do believe he is a steadfast gentleman."

"But, what of his reputation? Wouldn't it bother you if he and I would marry with the kind of gossip to his name?" Anita tried to sound innocent with her question. She could not miss the side glance from Belle, her sister equally hopeful of their mother's response.

Eloise blew a raspberry. "Hogwash! Child, you more than anyone should know how I feel about gossip. Considering your own not so long ago. But now look, everyone deserves restitution."

Anita released the breath she did not realize she held. Feeling more hopeful than ever before. This was the answer. Her mother's response guaranteed that she and Bram would be accepted. Anita and Belle shared a glance and smiled deeply at each other.

Right then, a dance began, and Eloise perked up onto her feet. She grasped her husband's arm, and with a tug, encouraged him to follow her out of the balcony towards the dance floor below. Belle pounced towards Anita with a laugh. They held hands then joyfully embraced.

"Annie, this is wonderful! I just knew mama would be open to you and Lord Kenwood's relationship. Now, you two can be together." Belle sounded so hopeful.

Anita nodded. "It would seem so. I can hardly believe

it, but this is genuinely surprising news."

"You must tell him soon!" Belle said excitedly.

With a laugh, Anita patted her hand. "Not just yet, but yes, soon."

Mark walked in, carrying a glass of water, when he realized it was only Belle and Anita within the balcony. Belle giggled at him, gave him a kiss on the cheek, and took a sip from the glass of water.

"I suspect your mother has improved?" Mark asked jokingly.

"Indeed, the sound of music rejuvenated her," Belle said with a laugh.

"Would you care for a dance as well then, my Lady?" Mark asked charmingly.

Smiling softly, Belle nodded. Looking back at Anita, she gave her the cup of water and assured her that they would return soon. Anita shook her head and told them to have a good time. Once they left, Anita looked out from the balcony to find them below. She also wondered if there could be a chance to catch a glimpse of Bram anywhere as well.

∞∞∞

Bram paused around the corner of the stage after he gave his welcoming speech. He drew in a breath, amazed at the crowd of people his Masquerade ball had drawn. He expected a good number of guests, but the crowd before him was ridiculous. At least, he received a good reaction to his appearance. And nothing made it better than when he found Anita watching him from one of the balconies. That alone made it all worth it.

He wanted nothing more than to rush up to that balcony and grasp her into his arms, to kiss her warm welcoming lips. Especially when she looked so radiant in the mask and gown she had worn when they first met. It was as though she was recreating their story, and by the heavens above, he loved her all the more for it. How much he wanted her, it made his chest ache.

But burning rage filled him instead. Bram had to take care of Miss Kenyon, the sniveling child that thought she could rule Bram's affairs. Well, she had another thing coming. The plan Mark and he created would stop her agenda in its tracks; Bram just had to find her first. Miss Kenyon had not yet made herself known to him, and for that, Bram could not deny the frustration he was feeling. He was on constant guard.

Glancing around the corner of the stage, he observed the dancing guests. The laughter and drunken states that many were in. At least, this part of the agenda was underway. Philip had made a good point on getting everyone inebriated. Maybe then, if Mark and Bram's plan faltered, the scandal would not be as noticed. Philip's special decoction mixed in with the wine and sherry were sure to get everyone in a good state of oblivion.

Bram found himself searching the balcony rows for a sight of Anita again. Seeing her would strengthen his resolve once more. However, when he found the one she was in, Bram grew tense. She was turned away from the railing, facing a man that had just stepped into the balcony. Bram immediately could see the tension within her frame, her hands gripping the rail of the balcony tightly.

Without thinking, Bram rushed towards the staircase leading up to the second level. He tried to calm his breathing before stepping closer to the closed curtain of the balcony box. He began to faintly hear words being spoken and determined the sharp tone Anita was casting towards this clear unwanted man. The moment Bram heard the man's reply, he knew it was Mr. Richard Henry Cox. Right then, all Bram wanted to do was tackle the bastard. But Bram reminded himself that this was a good opportunity. He now knew Cox was here. Bram listened closely to what was being said.

"I do not wish to dance with you. I'm sure you could easily find another suitable lady that would be taken by your persuasive charm," Anita announced curtly.

Bram heard Cox chuckle humorlessly.

"And what? To start this whole boorish charade again with another?" Cox scoffed. "I already have your parent's blessings at hand. It's only a matter of simply making you say yes."

Bram gritted his teeth at the man. How dare him to think he can force Anita to his will? Bram's fists balled, every ounce of him wanting to bash Cox in the face.

"I will never say yes. I am promised to another. Nothing you do will change that," Anita said clear and precise. Bram could detect the calm confidence within her.

There was a moment of silence before Bram heard the rush of frustrated breath leave Cox. He suddenly feared the worst, imagining the man rushing Anita in the balcony for all to see. That thought alone gave him a cold sweat. That would ruin everything. Bram squared himself, prepared to intervene if it went to that.

"Anita, if you do not adhere to my proposal, you will regret it," Cox said through his teeth.

"Not as much as I would regret it if I were to marry you," Anita answered quickly.

Bram grinned. How proud he felt to hear her stand up for herself. His Anita was truly one of the strongest women he ever loved. Before Bram could hear Cox's response, he heard a set of footfalls approaching. Bram recognized the gleeful chatter of Belle and Mark, and swiftly ducked into the neighboring theater box before they saw him.

Bram listened as Belle and Mark stopped in their tracks as they nearly bumped into Mr. Cox. They all exchanged awkward greetings, as the couple pardoned themselves for intruding. Anita quickly used the opportunity for escape and announced to Belle to help her find the lavatory. But before Anita stepped out with Belle and Mark, Bram believed Cox had grasped her to whisper under his breath.

"If you do not meet me back here in due haste, I will tell your mother of your wanton ways. I will also tell her how I have tasted you as well."

"She will never believe you," Anita managed to sound

coolly, but Bram knew the anger seething under her tone. Matching his own. The bastard.

"No? Would you care to test that?"

There was rustling before Bram heard Anita take off away from the theater box. He guessed she must have pulled away from his hold. He continued to listen before stepping out into the hall. He peeked within the balcony and found Cox still there, wearing a white mask, leaning against the railing, staring down below. A moment later, he stepped back to pull the curtain close, darkening the box slightly, and sat down into one of the chairs checking his pocket watch.

Battling the rage within him, Bram forced himself away from there. He had to continue the evening, and the plan, no matter how much he wanted to toss the sod out of his theater. How much he hated to admit it, but he needed the man. Bram made his way down the staircase and entered the auditorium. As he passed guests, to his surprise, they were smiling and greeting him. A few caught him in conversation over the magnificence of his theater, others making innocent comments on how they would not have ever imagined it being such.

Bram would smile, hiding the scowl behind it, and thank them politely. Then he would make his leave onto the next couple that would stop him. By the time he finally made it to the refreshments table, he was exhausted. He ordered himself a cognac and drank it down quickly before he was interrupted once more.

Sure enough, Bram felt a brush against his back, and instantly felt tension cross his neck. Looking over his shoulder, a woman stood there in a dark purple dress, wearing a feathered peacock mask. Her bright red lips smirked, as she addressed him. Or more like admired him, from his head to his groin. Bram immediately expected who the woman was.

"Lord Kenwood," she stated in her best seductive voice. But Bram saw right past it. Grinning, he detected the reserve in her eyes.

Bowing halfheartedly, he grasped her hand. "Who may I have the honor of being in the company of such beauty?"

"I am Miss Lucinda Kenyon," she answered a little more reassuringly, her eyes now clearing of their reservation. Bram knew this moment was crucial, he had been waiting for this meeting all evening.

"The infamous Lucinda Kenyon," Bram answered in his most charming voice, as he bent down to kiss her hand.

"You have heard of me?" she said with mild surprise. However, Bram could not ignore the slight suspicion within her gaze.

He chuckled nonchalantly, "Forgive me, I meant that in jest. But, in truth, I could not imagine your name not to be infamous. Behind the mask, I could tell of the beauty that is hiding beneath."

Bram's tongue itched as he said what needed to be said. Despite his hatred for the conniving woman in front of him, Bram knew that the plan would not work otherwise. Unlike Beatrice, Lucinda Kenyon had to be fooled by her own game. As Mark had said, Bram must bring out all his charm. She believed him to be the Lover of the Opera, so, might as well fit into that fantasy.

Her eyes softened at his compliment, and Bram felt his charm was beginning to take hold. He took a step closer, near enough that he could smell her strong lavender perfume; it made his nose itch. But he still managed to grin. He thumbed the peacock feather that leaned near her left cheek. Bram heard her intake of breath and watched her slow smile.

"Would you care to gift a man such as myself the opportunity to gaze upon your radiance? If not, that is all right. I'll understand, considering my scandalous reputation."

She batted her eyes, "Lord Kenwood, are you asking me to take off my mask in front of everyone here?"

Bram caught the suggestion and went with it. In a low husky voice, he declared, "I would rather see you alone, so I may freely look upon all of you. But, if you are one that enjoys the chance of being seen in such acts, well, I can be accommodating."

He saw the twinkle in her eye, as she sucked on the

bottom of her lip. "You are quite forward, my Lord."

"I know what I want when I see the opportunity. That is only of course, you are giving me one."

"But aren't you trying to win back the affections of the Ton?" she asked innocently. Bram knew what she was really referring to, however.

He shrugged, unbothered. "Would be good for business, honestly. But, what can I say, I am a rake with old habits."

She looked satisfied with that answer and looked away in thought. Glancing back, she had a wicked glint in her eye. "Well, if that is the case, I suppose I could meet you in private. What do you suggest, my Lord?"

Bram grinned. "Meet me up in one of the theater boxes. That one," he pointed, "the one with the curtain closed. Do not dare make me wait. I love a woman that takes what she wants."

Miss Lucinda Kenyon's brow raised, as she smiled, "Well, my Lord, you will be pleased to know that I always go after what I want. And my sights have been set on you for quite some time."

"What took you so long? How I would have ravaged you properly." Bram tried not to cough at his words, the lie leaving his mouth dry. But it created the effect he wanted. Her quick intake of breath, the licking of her lips, told Bram that she was aroused and wanted him. He smiled and grasped her hand to kiss once more. Staring deep into her lustful eyes, Bram told her to wait five minutes after his leave before making her own.

"It would give me great pleasure to see the beauty beneath that mask as well, be sure to take it off before you come inside. And perhaps, I may let you remove mine too."

Leaving her flushed, Bram made it seem like he was striding towards the balcony staircase but switched directions once he was out of view. He quickly entered the backstage door, and found Edgar, his limelight man. Though the man was drinking when Bram approached him, he quickly flew to his feet the moment the man saw him. Patting his old stagehand on the shoulder, Bram instructed the man on what to do for him.

"The moment the curtain opens. Not a second later."

With an understanding nod from Edgar, Bram hastened his way to the balcony staircase. He had to hurry, for the life of him and Anita, he prayed that this would work. Bram could not help but wonder what he was about to do was the right decision. He did not give it much thought, but now as he was about to cause a scandal that would have been otherwise meant for him; he could not help but feel rueful.

By the time he made it to the top step of the balcony floor, he almost felt hesitant. But he continued towards halfway down the hall. It was now, or never. He must not pause, or he would lose the chance. Reminding himself of the months Bram was threatened, spied on, and thought a fool; it pressed him to move quicker. Miss Lucinda Kenyon must already be arriving, what if he missed the chance?

Bram stopped in his tracks, breath escaping him, unable to believe what he was witnessing; Anita was standing by the entrance of the theater box where Mr. Cox and no doubt Miss Lucinda Kenyon were in. She was peering inside, quiet, and unmoving. That is, until Bram watched her arm raise to the curtain's drawstring. Just as he was to call out her name, Anita pulled down on the cord.

Moments later, an uproar of shocked voices and laughter rang through the auditorium below. Bram could see the glow of the limelight illuminating the theater box. All attention was directed on to the couple within. Bram stood there stunned, his thoughts racing to understand what Anita had done. But before he could reason with his emotions, he saw Anita duck into the neighboring theater box, cueing Bram to do the same.

He heard Miss Lucinda Kenyon shrieking, demanding the man to leave her be, but much to Bram's surprise, it appeared that Mr. Cox was following her down the hall. Their voices began to muffle out, until Bram stepped out and saw that they were gone. The ruckus below started to die down, as the music began to hurriedly tune back in. Bram could not believe it. It would seem that the plan had worked, but not by his own hand.

"Bram...?" Anita whispered.

She was still standing within the theater box, her body only half peering around the edge. Bram watched her hands tightening around the frame. He could see the regret within her eyes, the quiver around her lips. It was then he knew that his Anita felt ashamed of herself. Scowling, Bram pulled her into his arms, her face digging deep into his coat.

"That shouldn't have been you. That cord wasn't meant for you to pull." Bram said sorrowfully, holding her tighter to him.

Anita pulled back to stare into his supportive chest. She spoke between breaths, "I saw them- they were- embracing. And all the while, I thought- here were these two people that wanted to ruin- what we have. I grew so angry- dear God, Bram, I was- vengeful. I couldn't stop myself..."

Bram watched as tears began to flow down her cheeks, and he wanted nothing more than to take her pain away. He grasped her face gently, and slowly swiped across her flushed cheeks. She looked up at him with her glistening sad eyes and felt his heart ache. Bram drew her lips close and their wet warmth met his every touch. They held each other as though they would never let go. Time stood still for them, for only a moment.

"Is it finally over?" she whispered close to his lips.

Bram was filled with a sense of gratification over that thought; it nearly brought a tear to his eye. Grasping her hair and waist, he brought her mouth back to his and kissed her hard. Her soft moans caused him to harden against her quivering belly. All he could think about now was to pull her into the closest theater box. But he knew it was too soon for that. Guests below would be looking for that. No, he would settle on simply kissing her lovingly to him.

He was so overcome with joy then, he had to pull away slowly from her decadent smile. Anita's eyes glowed with emotion; she never looked more lovely to him. Bram felt the moment was finally upon them, he needed to tell her how he felt. His heart longed for it. His Anita deserved to know.

"Annie—"

"Anita!" A shocked shrill voice screamed from the

end of the hall. It jolted them both, as Bram watched the dread fill Anita's expression. They both turned slowly to find Anita's mother standing rigid, her hand to her mouth. For the first time in his life, Bram felt grievous at being caught. But, not for his behalf, for Anita's. Anita's hand tightened around his, and he returned the gesture to reassure her.

"Mother, I can explai-" Anita began.

"No, Anita! You come here this instant!" There was no more shock to her voice. Bram heard the contempt instead. Anita looked between him and her mother, the hesitation clear on her face.

"Madam, please, this was no fault of your daughter's. I kissed her. Upon my word, I will owe it to her." Bram spoke out before he could stop himself. The truth of his words ringing in his ears.

But it was as though Anita's mother did not even hear them. She shouted for Anita to come to her once more. When Bram tried to speak again, she interrupted him.

"Lord Kenwood! I may have been courteous to you in our previous encounters, but do not for one instant believe I overlooked your reputation. I may have given you the opportunity to prove yourself otherwise, BUT that has clearly been demolished by what has happened here. How dare you take advantage of my daughter! To threaten her honor! You have no right. She is an innocent woman! Anita does not have anything to do with your world of depravity." Eloise was near breathless, her cheeks flushed with exasperation.

Bram was speechless, never being in such a situation. Her mother's words cutting him deep, Bram realized how true they were. He dishonored Anita in front of her own mother. The one person that was supposed to give him her blessings. It was then, Bram knew he had no right to put Anita in this position. To bring her down to his level of debauchery. He failed. He felt ashamed of himself, and was not able to fight the depleting emotions that overcame him. With great pain, Bram forced himself to let go of Anita's hand.

Anita turned to him surprised. "Bram, no..."

"Go, Anita. Go to your mother." He could not bear to look at her.

"But-" Her voice was ripped with emotion.

"GO GOD DAMN IT!" he shouted, startling her. Good, he thought. Let her see the real him for once...

He knew she was crying when she turned away from him and walked towards her mother. Bram finally looked up from his shame to watch Anita and her mother make their way down the staircase, and out of his life. Just like that, it was over...

Bram punched the wall beside him.

Chapter 17

London
Springfield Club
Two weeks later

Bram stared at the empty decanter at his side. Sitting at Springfield Club, he paid no attention to the discussion between Richard and Sterling. All he heard from before was that his friend Sterling had just returned and was now married. But the moment his friend began telling details of his adventures with his new wife, Bram tuned out. He was neither interested nor sober enough to congratulate Sterling.

Bram could almost grin to himself. Who was the drunkard now, he thought? How the roles have reversed between him and Sterling. Bram could not remember the last time he saw Sterling this sober, and Lord help him, Bram hated it. Sitting up, Bram stood and almost caught himself. The room nearly tilted, and Bram had to walk more carefully towards the other liqueurs. Trying to identify one that he would like, he felt a hand slap his back.

"I heard good things from your Masquerade ball, brother. Sounds like you are becoming a fan favorite among the Ton, Bram."

It took a moment for Bram to realize that it was Sterling talking. The man had a decent accent that Bram never noticed before. Scowling, Bram did not answer him. He blindly grabbed a bottle and took it back to his chair and empty glass.

Laughing, Sterling sat across from him. "I know. I do

not sound like my usual self, right? Well, that's the difference between a constant bottle of scotch and now."

Bram ignored him again and refilled his glass. He scowled when he tasted wine but drank it back anyway. There was silence in the room, but Bram paid it no mind as he poured another glass. He did not notice the concerned looks pass between Sterling and Richard.

"Haven't you had enough, Bram?" Richard asked. Bram detected that his friend tried to sound casual, but still could not hide the regard within his tone.

"Not nearly," was all he said. Bram drank the glass of wine.

Richard stood to ring for service. "Might as well get some food served then."

Sterling agreed wholeheartedly, expressing how famished he was. "Been too long since I had some good Springfield service."

When food was brought in, Richard began to plate food and tried to hand it to Bram. He scowled at it and refused. Bram heard a quiet sigh escape from Richard before his friend then yanked the glass of wine from his hand. Bram protested but was immediately silenced when he saw the look on Richard's face. He was enraged.

"I've been watching you come here, day in and day out, swallowing back more than you can afford. I kept quiet, but I cannot do that any longer. I know what happened between you and Anita pains you. But it doesn't mean that you should drink yourself to death!"

Bram became cold, his voice toneless. "Don't you dare say her name."

"Bram, this is ridiculous! You have done so much to better yourself, to save your namesake. You are just going to throw it all away and return to your old ways? That is not like you. You do not give up once you set your mind on something. That is not fair to you OR to Anita."

Bram looked up at Richard with a lethal gaze. "That will be the last time you say her name, Richard, or so help me..."

Richard hardened, knowing full well the threat Bram

just stated. "Or what? Are you prepared to ruin the closest friendships you have too, just because you won't face what you had with...Anita?"

Bram sprang up from his seat and grasped Richard's collar, the two of them nearly stumbling from Bram's imbalanced state but holding fast to one another. Bram saw red and wanted nothing more than to pour all his pain into Richard's face. Sterling jumped to get between them, placing one hand on both their shoulders, shouting.

"What is the matter with you two?! You are brothers! Stop this!"

"Say it, Bram! Say why you can't face Anita!" Richard cursed as Bram almost swiped his elbow into his jaw.

"You don't know a damn thing about it, Richard!" Bram bellowed.

"I know more than you think! But do you?! Do you know why you can't have Anita?"

Richard finally had Bram restraint by the neck and arm, shaking him. They were breathing hard into one another's face. Bram stopped struggling, despite still holding onto Richard's coat lapels. He was silent before dropping his head. He could not admit it to himself, he did not dare. The truth only slicing him deep. The memories with Anita, of their first time together, haunted him.

"I- wasn't brave enough..." Bram said sorrowfully. He gritted his teeth, his fists balling, wrinkling Richard's coat.

Bram stepped back, tearing himself away from Richard and Sterling. Walking to the fireplace, he stared into the flickering flames, but he did not feel their warmth. He probably never would, he thought. Bram felt dead inside. Speaking the truth only sealed it.

Sterling stood beside him quietly, placing his hand on Bram's shoulder. "I know that look, my brother. You must not think this the end. It is not. It is only the beginning. You must believe it so."

"How can I, Sterling? I have ruined everything because of who I am. Even when I tried, I was still looked at as some pariah."

"Aye, but, you're a dashing pariah." Sterling tried to

make light of it. Richard lit a cigar and offered it to Bram as a peace offering. He accepted it and leaned his drunken body against the marble fireplace. Ashes collected on the end of the cigar as Bram ignored it, too lost in his slurred thoughts.

"You must eat something," Richard declared, and turned to fix a plate.

Sterling nodded, "I suppose one small glass can't hurt at this point either."

Bram slowed his breathing as he tossed the half-smoked cigar into the fire. He ran his hand through his hair, then leaned his head forward against the marble. The coolness contradicting the warm hearth. At this moment, this was all he had. Himself, and the cool void behind his closed eyes.

A gentle knock sounded at the door. Bram heard Richard set down the plate of food, but before he could make his way towards them, the doors opened. Bram heard Sterling shout out a happy welcome to Mark, but then it was cut off soundly. Bram opened his eyes to glance over his shoulder. His arm slid off the fireplace mantle in shock. Bram thought for a moment that he was seeing things in his drunken state. But he knew he was not.

Belle walked in beside Mark. Her demeanor was shy and nervous, but the moment she saw Bram, it changed to determination. Bram literally watched her square up her shoulders. Belle lightly touched Mark's arm reassuringly, before stepping towards Bram. Despite the situation, and her absurd soundings, Belle could not stop herself from still curtsying. To his shock, the other men in the room bowed. Bram stood straighter and bowed awkwardly, hoping he would not tip over in front of her.

"Belle, you shouldn't be here. This is no place for a Lady. If your mother knew-"

"There is no time for that! Once I knew you were not coming for Anita, I had to find you," Belle declared.

The mention of Anita's name made him wince. He stepped away from her and grasped the small glass Sterling had prepared for him. He drank it back in one gulp.

"I don't know if you've heard, but your mother does not

approve of me or my debauchery. She would have summoned the hounds of Hell if I had shown up to your home."

"That simply is not true, Bram! Everything will change if you would just come with me." Belle followed him until she was toe to toe with him. Her eyes were pleading.

"You weren't there, Belle. You didn't hear what your mother said to me." He sighed in frustration. "She was right, I am no good for...Annie."

His heart clenching to the first time he dared to say her name nearly broke him. Bram moved to sit down. But Belle still paced beside him. Her voice was hurried when she spoke.

"You need to come. You must declare your love for Anita! Because she loves you too Bram!"

"That will not change anything, Belle. Please, let it be," Bram said weakly. He was exhausted, all his energy depleted from his encounter with Richard.

To everyone's surprise, Belle fell to her knees in front of Bram. Tears were welling up as she fiercely bit at her lip. Mark came closer, as if tied to her pain.

"She's been dead, Bram. Anita has lost all strength and hope. I have never seen her like this. Never." A tear fell. "She didn't even fight when mother told her that she would be returning to America."

Bram froze at her words. "What...?"

Belle nodded before releasing more tears. "That is why I came here as soon as I could. I didn't know until this morning when I found her packing."

Bram's thoughts were racing. It did not help that his head was pounding, however. Anita was being sent away? How could this be? How could their mother be so heartless, especially with all the talks of war happening over there? Bram was furious.

"When is she set to sail?" Bram said between his teeth.

"Four o'clock, today," Belle answered ardently.

Bram was beside himself. Stunned, he sprang up to search for the clock on the fireplace mantle. "It's ten past one o'clock!"

"I tried to hurry and have Mark bring me here! Please,

Bram, we must go to my home immediately."

"Shouldn't I be going to the docks?" Bram's head was spinning. He feared he would be sick.

"You first need to go and get Belle and Anita's parents' blessing. That is the only way you and she can be together. Once you have it, the both of you can marry," Mark said soundly.

Marriage. Finally, Bram's foggy head focused. Bram thought of seeing Anita again, but as his wife. Living together freely. Being accepted by her parents and by society. Making love at all hours of the day. Having children... A spark of life ignited in his heart. But a dark cloud of doubt faltered it, making it seem impossible. Especially with all that had happened. Bram was hopelessly dreaming again. Shaking his head, Bram stood very still.

"Your mother will never give me her blessing. She discovered Anita within my arms. She won't simply look past that."

"No! Bram, please list-" Belle tried to explain.

A cool glass of water splashed across his face so suddenly that Bram had to gasp for breath. Everyone swung their gazes on Sterling, who gently placed the now empty cup on the mantle. He shrugged and grinned.

"Someone had to do it. The fool was not thinking straight with all that liquor in him. Stop looking like you want to murder me, Bram. You need to get going, you don't have much time left."

"As if I can go drenched, Sterling!" Bram exclaimed. He combed back his soaked hair and wiped at his wet brow.

Sterling scratched his chin, trying to hide the wide grin. "Always worked when Mariela did it to me," he said under his breath.

"Here, you can wear my coat," Mark announced as he took off his and handed it over to Bram.

When Bram exchanged coats, Belle was wringing her hands. By the time Bram adjusted himself, she pounced towards the doors. Telling them to hurry, she led the way out of Springfield Club. Once they were in the carriage, she was explaining to Bram all the good things their mother had honestly said about him, and describing how inebriated her mother was that night, how Eloise was even expecting his call within the last two weeks. Belle was not clear on when the decision was made for Anita to travel to America, but she knew it had to at least have been nearly a week ago. That was when Anita became really withdrawn. She was not even taking dinner with them anymore.

Knowing this made Bram quiet. He leaned against the carriage window, deep in thought. Had he truly made the right decision to stay away? Did he have the chance to change their mother's mind all along? Closing his eyes, Bram was weighed by his regret. He had been so lost within his emotions, he allowed fear to overcome him. What Anita must think of him. Now, all he feared was not having her forgiveness.

The carriage stopped, and Mark stepped out first to help Belle down, but she did not move. Bram found her staring directly at him. At first, he thought she was not going to say a word, she was so still. But as quick as he could have guessed, she grasped his hands. Her grip was surprisingly strong.

"My mother will believe you if you tell her the truth about how you feel. She is not a blind woman, or an unforgiving shrewd that you think. She shares a love similar to yours and Anita. You just need to tap into that, and I promise you, she will give you her blessing."

Bram smiled softly, touched by Belle's words. Despite still feeling a little doubtful, he nodded, and patted her hands. They stepped out of the carriage, and Belle led them both inside her family's townhome. Bram was trying to seem calm, but his breathing was labored. Entering Anita's home was surreal, and he felt half out of his mind. His drunken state was gone, but it still felt as though Bram was walking into a dream.

Belle told them both to wait in the hall before she entered the drawing room. Mark elbowed his arm and gave him a reassuring nod, to which Bram was grateful for. At least, that proved he was still awake. A moment later, the door opened, but it was not Belle. To Bram's surprise, it was their father.

Lord Hemmingway looked at them both with an un-readable expression. When Mark bowed, Bram quickly did the same. Still without a word, Lord Hemmingway took a step back to allow them to enter. Belle and her mother were waiting inside. Bram walked forward and bowed to them.

Lady Hemmingway eyed him before looking to her daughter. "Belle, wait outside."

Frowning, Belle looked as though she was about to protest. But when her father cleared his throat, it was an obvious command to obey. Belle bit her lip as she glanced to Bram when she walked past him. When he heard the door close, Bram forced himself to stand a little straighter. He, too, cleared his throat when Lord Hemmingway came around to sit beside his wife.

"Thank you for a moment of your time," Bram began. He resisted the urge to pull at his collar that was still partially damp.

"I am surprised that you have come to show your face here at all," Lady Hemmingway stated evenly. Switching her gaze over to her husband, she waved her hand towards Bram. "Stephan, this is Bram Williams, the Earl of Kenwood."

Bram traditionally bowed to Lord Hemmingway, who nodded back. Bram could not guess what the man thought of him. But he must not falter, Bram told himself. He just needed to find the right words to say. However, it was Lady Hemmingway who felt like she needed to speak first.

"I am really quite curious as to why you have come to call on us, Lord Kenwood. Rather late, however. My daughter is not here."

"May I ask where she has gone, and to when shall we be expecting her return?" Bram asked as casually as he could sound. It seemed unsuccessful, however, based on the way Lady Hemmingway clucked her tongue.

"It is of no concern to you when my daughter will be back. In truth, you are the reason she is no longer here." Surprisingly, Bram detected her lament. It was not quite blame, but rather affliction that Anita was gone. But wasn't it Lady Hemmingway's decision to send her away? Again, Bram felt at a loss for words. He realized he never was in such a position before, in front of patrons that held his future in their hands. Bram was always the one to dictate his fortune. Taking the lead on his own businesses and architecture, he never dared put his decisions onto another. But here he stood, in his most vulnerable state.

"My Lord and Lady Hemmingway, first I must apologize for my actions. I am more embarrassed than you perceive, and trust, that is not so easily done for someone like me." Bram paused to release a sigh. "But you must know that Anita leaving is the last thing I want."

Anita's parents glanced to one another before Lady Hemmingway penetrated him again with her questionable gaze. "Pray tell, what is it that you want from Anita then?"

Bram took a deep breath before answering, "I wish to marry her."

Lady Hemmingway scoffed before sitting back into her seat. "Out of the question! You sir, are overstepping your boundaries."

Bram swallowed back the bitter taste of disconcertment. Remembering Belle's words, Bram remained firm. "May I ask why you feel this way?"

Beginning to flush, Lady Hemmingway sat forward. "Lord Kenwood, I believe you already know this answer. To put it bluntly, you do not come from a reputable background. Your name is written on many of the gossip pages. And quite frankly, being titled as the Lover of the Opera does not place you as the marriageable type. How can I subject my daughter to that life? She would be pitied for all her days."

Bram resisted the urge to clench his fists, instead he brought them behind his back. "I am aware of what has been said and written about me. Too long that has been a stain on my name. But, my Lady, I am trying to repair that reputation. If I can recall, I believe you yourself even said that was admirable?"

Lady Hemmingway began to fan herself as she remained silent. Bram caught Lord Hemmingway glancing to his wife with a curious expression, but that still did not give much as to what the man was thinking.

He continued, but this time, Bram decided it was time to speak from somewhere else within him. "When I first ever saw Anita, a piece of my soul shifted. It was like a puzzle had fallen into place, and I needed her to complete me. She was a dream I never thought would exist. I was afraid, for the first time in my life. I feared that for once, my questionable character was going to take away the one wish I have longed for. You must believe me when I say that my presence here was a difficult decision to make. Because the reality that I dreaded was that I would have that dream denied to me."

The room was silent, and in that moment, Bram thought that was the end. Hanging his head, he was prepared to excuse himself, and walk back into that dark void that was before Anita. Sighing, he nodded, and quietly thanked them for their time. He could not deny the strain in his voice. Bowing, he turned towards the door. *Goodbye, Anita...*

"I give you my blessing."

Lady Hemmingway's shocked gasp escaped her as Bram stopped in his tracks. "Stephan, what are you saying?!"

Bram slowly turned to see Lord Hemmingway rise from his seat. Clearing his throat, the man smiled gently. "It is clear, Eloise, that this Lord Kenwood is in love with our daughter."

"Oh, but they don't even know each other! This is outrageous!" Lady Hemmingway exasperated.

"Did we when I first called on you? Or when we shared our first kiss? Eloise, we were but children compared to Anita."

Blushing harshly, Lady Hemmingway was stunned at her husband's forward words. "That does not change the fact that Anita would be living with constant gossip over her head." She sniffed, "I wanted her to be free of such torment. She had already been through too much of that."

"Our daughter is strong, Eloise. She pays gossip no mind. You taught her that." Sitting beside his wife, Lord Hemmingway grasped her hand. "But wasn't it love that you wanted for Anita above all else? Look at this man, listen to what he had just said. You can't deny that is how he truly feels."

Looking back at Bram, Lord Hemmingway grinned. "Besides, I would rather have this man as Anita's husband, than that pompous arse Cox. He's really the one you ought to hate, considering the recent scandal he is recently a part of."

Nodding, Eloise could not deny the words her husband was saying. Quelling the trembling in her lip, Lady Hemmingway held up her head. Standing, she came toe to toe with Bram. He could see the strong love burning within her gaze for her daughter. How much that reminded him of Anita.

"Do you promise to keep her safe, and happy? That you will change your old ways? Will you bring her honor?"

Bram was in disbelief, closing his mouth, he smiled. Placing his hand over his heart, Bram bowed his head. "With all my heart, your daughter will be loved till the end of my days."

Swiftly turning away from him, Bram could see the tremble over her shoulders. "Very well. I, too, give you my blessing."

In awe, Bram smiled brightly. "Thank you…"

Lord Hemmingway came to stand beside his wife, and lovingly stroked her back before smiling approvingly at Bram. "You must hurry. Anita is at the docks. She wanted to return to our home in America. Her ship leaves at four o'clock."

Stunned, Bram scowled. "She wanted to return to America?"

Lord Hemmingway nodded as he gave his wife a handkerchief. After wiping away the tears, she turned to face him. "Anita felt that she would be better off away from here. She feared that she caused scandal, and no matter how many times I told her that no one knew of that night between the two of you, she still insisted on going."

Lady Hemmingway sniffed back the remainder of her tears. Stepping towards him, she removed something from her hand, then placed it into Bram's. "Please, bring my daughter back. This is her home."

Bram bowed and agreed. As he hurried out of their townhome and entered the carriage, Bram thought of Lady

Hemmingway's words. Though he did not say them aloud, he thought, this place was not her home. No, HE was her home. Bram also guessed the real reason why Anita decided to leave. It was because of him, not scandal. He broke her heart by not coming to her sooner. He left her to doubt their love, and because of that, she ran. Taking a deep breath, he promised himself, and to Anita, that this would be the last time he would ever let her run away from him again. Bram only hoped he got there in time to convince her otherwise. For both their sake.

Anita took a deep breath of ocean air, but this time, the scent of putrid fish also stank the port. Boarded on the ship that will take her back to America, Anita could almost feel the tears that had dried within her soften from the salty breeze. Holding them back, she released her quivering breath. Anita was ready to leave London. She was tired. Her raging emotions exhausted her. Her memories left her sleepless, and her heartache was too painful. A week ago, Anita realized that she would not be able to stand it this time. She could no longer wait for Bram. That night at the Masquerade ball showed her that Bram had given up. And so, Anita had to tell herself to do the same. But when that was too much for her to cope with, Anita knew then she had to leave. She could not stay in a place where Bram was so close to her. The temptation of running back into his arms was too much to bear. Because the truth was, she would start an affair with him again, just to be with him.

Shaking her head, she knew that would only start this crazy play all over. It would only summon more scandal to themselves, and that was the last thing she wanted. Checking the pocket watch her father had given her, she saw that there were still thirty minutes left till they departed. Looking over towards London, she choked on what little time she had left. Within her thoughts, she said goodbye to her family, but it was only when she silently said farewell to Bram a tear fell. Swiftly wiping it away, she turned back towards the ocean horizon.

Despite how she felt, a small ironic smile replaced her frown. Anita always wanted to venture out to new boundaries. She often pictured it. Being the explorer she always dreamt of. She just never realized that the first time she would sail away on her own, would be to return to America. How pitiful, she thought.

"We be set to sail soon, Miss. If you will like, there are refreshments down below," the captain announced beside her. Nodding, she thanked him.

Realizing that her mouth was dry, Anita did feel thirsty. She turned to make her way down below, but as she was halfway down the stairs, Anita felt a presence behind her. Thinking it was perhaps another passenger, she glanced back. Anita lost her footing on the next step.

She let out a shriek, but when she thought she was about to tumble down the stairs, two strong arms caught her. Breathless, Anita looked upon Bram's alarmed eyes. The dark color of midnight, she once thought. Swallowing, she found her footing, and straightened.

"I did not mean to startle you," he said with a frown.

"At this point, I really shouldn't be surprised that you are here. But I suppose it still astonishes me." She swallowed, her mouth still dry.

"Come, let's get you something to drink," he said pointedly. She did not reply, just simply followed him below the deck. Few other passengers were there drinking and plating food. Anita observed an older man, a couple, and another gentleman who could be close to Bram's age. They were greeted by the ship's cook, who offered them libations and slices of cheese with bread. Bram thanked him and filled a cup of water for Anita.

Once she drank away the dryness from her throat, Bram placed her cup down. "Do you have a room that we can talk in?"

Her eyes fluttering, Anita glanced to the other passengers, but it seemed that neither of them paid any mind. Anita nodded and led the way to her room. Once they entered it, Bram closed the door promptly. When he turned to her again, Anita was surprised to find the anguish within his gaze. Her heart skipped, but before she would let it, Anita reminded herself that what was between them was done. There was no other way. Standing a bit straighter, she tried to muster her voice to sound calm.

"Bram, the ship is about to set sail at any moment. You cannot stay here for long."

He laughed under his breath and nodded. "This is true," was all he said.

For the first time, Anita felt frustration towards him. "This is no time to dally. You really must go now, Bram."

Shaking his head, Bram stood firm. "Not until I say what I need to say."

Nearly throwing up her hands, Anita released a sigh. "After all this time, you come now? Where were you in the last two weeks?"

"I was like you, mournful, and angry. So heartbroken that I ended up feeling dead inside. I was so lost, that I tried desperately to hide deep into a bottle," Bram declared honestly. His eyes were piercing into hers again, that Anita nearly felt hypnotized.

Forcing her gaze away, she wrapped her arms around herself. "You don't look lost. You look perfectly well."

Bram stepped forward. "That is because I was reminded of what it means to fight for what you love."

Anita frowned, still unwilling to look at him. "Then why did you not fight the night of your Masquerade? Why did you leave me alone for two weeks after you made me think that you would court me? Why do any of that?!"

Anita's sharp tone surprised even herself. But she was furious. Angry for the dream that was torn away from her, having to face the fact she would never have it again with Bram. Her lip trembled, and she turned away from him. She promised herself no more tears.

"I wasn't brave enough, Anita." Her eyes widened at his words, remembering their conversation in front of the

Cleopatra painting. She swallowed her sob. "I was convinced that your mother was right about me. That I did not deserve you. She reminded me of how precious you are, and there I was, ruining you in front of her eyes. I was so ashamed."

"But I realized since then, that I should have confessed my feelings to your mother right then. And to you. I was a fool, Anita. I know this now."

Anita closed her eyes at his words, holding herself even tighter. "But now it's too late," she whispered. "My mother abhors you and is ashamed of me. That is why I am returning home. This is the best for either one of us."

"NO. You leaving will kill us both, and you know that," Bram said sharply.

"But I cannot live anywhere you are, Bram! It will break me!" Anita screamed.

"It won't have to," Bram said softly. He reached for her and took her into her arms. Despite her anguished feelings, Anita fell into them, their warmth only breaking her heart more, but there was no greater comfort in the world for her.

"Anita, will you be brave with me?" Bram whispered into her hair. Pulling far enough away to look at him, she frowned.

"Let us finally make our dream a reality..." he said softly, before taking a knee. Anita was stunned to see him pull out a ring from his pocket. But what shocked her more was how familiar the ring was. It was her grandmother's golden ruby. Her mother had always worn it since Anita was young. Breathless, Anita stared at Bram astonished.

"Bram...? What-?" She was speechless.

Smiling, he rose to meet her gaze. "Your parents send their blessings."

Anita nearly felt faint, as Bram grasped her hand and kissed it. How could this be? Did Bram truly go to her mother and father? Had they really given their blessings? Seeing her grandmother's ring should be proof enough, she thought. But why did it still feel like a dream? Was Anita honestly awake?

"Are you really going to leave me in suspense, Annie?" Bram laughed softly under his breath.

Shaking herself, Anita slowly smiled. Caressing his cheek, she leaned forward and kissed him with all her heart. His breath caught as he pulled her to him. They were smiling brightly into one another's eyes once their passion was sated.

"I'll take that as a yes, then," Bram teased as he raised her hand and placed the beautiful ruby onto her finger. Anita was so overcome with happiness that she drew him back into her arms. This time, she led the kiss. They were laughing against each other's lips when suddenly they felt the ship rock beneath them.

A commotion of noises rose above them as men ran across the deck. A bell rang out, and the first hand announced the ship was departing from the dock. Anita drew back and quickly grabbed her one luggage.

"Oh no, Bram! We must get off the ship now!" Anita was grasping her purse and shawl when Bram stopped her. Frowning, she tried to make sense of his actions. He looked calm and content.

"We are going to stay on board, Anita."

"Why? This ship is going to America," Anita replied, astonished.

Smiling, Bram caressed her cheek. Stroking the fallen curl at her temple, he kissed her once more. "It will be stopping at Portugal first. From there, we will be boarding another vessel."

"Bram, what are you planning?" Anita asked him in awe. She was beside herself, her emotions still whirling from the shock of it all.

Grinning, Bram pressed her down onto the cot beside her. Anita was overcome with chills to feel him against her again. Kissing her lips gently, he stroked them down her cheek to her neck. Taking off his coat and necktie, Bram began to work on the buttons of her dress. Sighing with pleasure of feeling his lips back against her skin, Anita was delirious with the joy she thought she would never have again.

"Your mother asked me to return you, and I promised I would. But not before I marry you and show you the world that you have so yearned for." Kneeling between her thighs, Bram feverishly suckled the place that wept for him the most. Anita was overcome, both by the pleasure Bram was giving her, and the love she felt for him. She knew then, she truly was awake. By the time Bram entered her, they both yelled out in ecstasy, their climax bringing tears of love to them both. Anita held him to her, as her beating heart filled his ears.

"Thank you... thank you... thank you."

Epilogue

London
The Earl of Kenwood's Estate
Two Years Later
1860

Anita sat peacefully in the atrium, after a light rainfall had filled the room with a clean fresh scent. She was reading aloud the King of the Golden River while sipping on mint tea. As she read how the brothers in the book climbed a high mountain to the mythological golden river, Anita was reminded of her and Bram's honeymoon adventures. She smiled warmly as she recalled the moment they arrived in Porto, Portugal.

It was sunrise when they met with a priest, who was still recovering from his Sunday communion and port wine. They were married in a small cobbled chapel that overlooked the sea. By the time the noon day sun reached the center of the sky, Bram and Anita walked through the bright colored merchant markets, hand in hand, stocking up for their travels. Before boarding their next vessel to Italy, Bram pleaded they stop to witness the completion of the Palacio de Bolsa. Anita was in awe of its neoclassical architecture and the history.

That was only the first of many monuments Bram showed her. He had promised her the world, and he began with a tour of the Mediterranean. Anita witnessed the ancient worlds that she had always read in her favorite books. It was more than a dream, and they made love in every ancient ruin they visited. Even in some other public areas that Anita blushed to remember.

They finished their tour in Morocco, and that thrilled her above all else. Bram took her to the first home he had built, and it was a palace. They lived there together for the remainder of the year, and all the while Bram introduced her into his culture.

When they returned to London, it was to excitement and celebration. Anita's family were thankful to have her back and were so welcoming to hear the stories of their adventures. Bram's mother, Magenta was so elated by their marriage that she threw celebratory parties in their honor, with Bram's friends and acquaintances. It was more than anything she and Bram could hope for. The news of their marriage was accepted and congratulated, and hardly noticed, mostly because of the gossip that was primarily focused on the scandalous elopement between Miss Lucinda Kenyon and Mr. Richard Henry Cox.

Anita shook her head, chuckling to herself over the memories. But the sound of splashing and giggles took her focus away from her thoughts. Smiling, she watched her son playing in the shallow pool, and she stood to join him. Lifting the hem of her dress, she stepped into the cool water, her son squealing joyfully when she did. His golden-brown hair glowed against his sun kissed skin, and his jet-black eyes shone with delight. They played with the fallen leaves that flew in from the earlier rainfall.

"Oh my, I guess bath time can be skipped." Magenta laughed. She walked in and kissed her grandson's wet hair. He bounced happily in place, reaching towards her wanting to be picked up.

"I'll take him and get him ready for bed. Come, my little *amyr*. It's time for the prince to sail away to his dreams." She hummed as she took him to the nursery.

Smiling, Anita stepped out of the little pool, and dried her feet. She let her now wet hem fall, but paid it no mind, as she reached up to pull out the pins from her hair. Stroking it over her shoulder, Anita felt the peaceful quiet enter her soul. It was then she knew she was no longer alone though. Anita felt Bram's presence even before he kissed her nape. Closing her eyes, she felt his chest lean into her, and she tucked herself against his warmth.

"Mama took Alexander to bed?" His hot breath whispered into her ear, sending tantalizing chills down her skin. Anita nodded.

Bram reached around her, gently stroking her neck until caressing down her chest. Anita sighed as she reached her hand up to glide it through his silken hair. When he began to tease her breasts, she was panting.

"Perhaps we should *tuck* ourselves into bed as well." He grinned against her hair and grasped her hand.

They were already in each other's arms by the time they reached the door. Bram pressed her against it, savoring her mouth slowly. Pulling off clothing, and quickly unbuttoning her gown, they made it to the bed this time. Bram suckled her tender breasts, sending waves of pleasure down between Anita's thighs. Once his fingers found her wet lips, Anita feared she was to cum right then. Pulling away, she straddled him, knowing how well he enjoyed seeing her at eye level. She kissed him lovingly, as she guided him into her. They moaned in unison. Bram tightened his arms around her as she rode him. When he began to thrust faster, Anita's pleasure climaxed, and she felt herself tighten around him. She focused her gaze onto his as she came, and that drove him to go deeper. He closed his mouth over hers as he came within her, Bram's warm seed driving her to cum once more.

They fell over onto the mattress, panting, and relaxed. Bram pulled her closer to him, laying her across his chest. Anita was so blissfully happy, she felt she could purr, and laughed at the thought.

Bram grinned, "Still wondering where babies come from?"

"Depends. Will there be one down the road?" Anita beamed back with a laugh.

"Quite possibly. Actually, highly likely." Bram winked, and they giggled together.

Anita traced her fingers across his chest and listened to the beating of his heart. Even with all their time spent together, Anita still had to remind herself that it was not a dream. From the beginning of their story, she never thought that this could be real, and that Bram would one day be hers. But the fairytale did happen, and she was now awake. As she peered up at him with all the love in her heart, Bram smiled, and wiped the dust from her eyes.

"I love you, Bram," she whispered, falling asleep within his arms.

"I love you too...Annie."

About The Author

S. M. Harlow

Susana discovered her love of ro-
mantic fiction about two decades
ago with her family in a book-
store. She browsed through the
historical romance section and
picked up her first novel, Let It Be
Love by Victoria Alexander. After completing the
book in three days, Susana was hooked.

After years of reading historical romances, Susana
became inspired to write her own tales of love and
desire. What began as a simple idea in high school,
grew to be a full fledge novel series.

When she is not writing, Susana is studying to
become a Doctor of Traditional Naturopathy. She
lives with her husband, newborn son, and their
adorable fluffy Welsh corgi in Southern California.